JAY TINSIANO & JAY NEWTON

Pale Horse

Acknowledgement

We would like to extend huge thanks to everyone who helped craft this book. Your contribution helped us make Black Horse the best story we possibly could.

A special thanks to Jim Newton for his considerable support.

Also, thanks to the following beta readers:

Diane Velasquez
Dorene A. Johnson USN (Ret)

Join the Jay Tinsiano Reader Group

Free Thriller Starter Library
Books and stories
Previews and Sneak Peeks
Exclusive material

To join the VIP Jay Tinsiano reading group, head to:

www.jaytinsiano.com/newsletter

Revelation

"And I looked, and behold a pale horse: and his name that sat upon him was Death, and Hell followed with him. And power was given unto them over the fourth part of the earth, to kill with the sword, and with hunger, and with death and with the beasts of the earth."

Chapter 1

Colorado Air and Space Port
Zero Day 1

The chopper descended through the cloudless sky onto the airfield at Colorado Air and Space Port, fourteen miles from the main Denver International Airport. A group of twelve grim-faced Ghost 13 Special Forces soldiers jumped from the chopper to the tarmac, ducking under the slowing rotor blades, moving in single file to the back of a waiting nondescript military truck. No one spoke; the only sounds were just the 'whup whup' of the rotors cutting through the air as they were slowing down and the rhythmic pounding of boots on tarmac.

Agents Salazar and Collins headed towards their own transport, an AM General Hummer, and after taking a backseat, the two vehicles were driven across the airfield and onto a private road. Jamall Salazar glimpsed endless blocks of hangar buildings before they sped along a service track for a mile until a vast white hangar, protected by high electric fences with armed guards in towers at each corner, came into view.

In the back of the Hummer was a cloth bag. Jamall dropped his service weapon into a cloth bag to be disposed of at Denver. Sitting opposite him, Agent Collins did the same. Both men remained totally impassive and behaved as if they were disposing of something soiled through the completion of a menial household chore, not the assassination of the most powerful man in the world, the US president.

The vehicles stopped at the entrance in the fence, and their clearances were checked prior to being allowed to proceed. They turned and passed through the expansive doors of the hangar, under the cooling reinforced concrete roof and away from prying eyes. The floor quickly turned into a ramp that descended into the ground, buttressed by massive walls and eventually leading to a substantial 25-tonne blast door that was opened to give them access to Station 12.

As far as Jamall knew, this was just one of several entrances located on the east side of the massive underground base. Through the thin slits of the rear window, Jamall could see the circular metallic walls gleaming with an otherworldly luminance.

As the vehicles continued their journey through the brilliantly illuminated tunnel, the rumbling of their wheels echoed off the smooth, circular walls—with each rotation of the massive tyres reverberating through the metallic confines of their cramped vehicle.

The tunnel wound, twisted and continued ever downwards, each level revealing more of the sprawling, well-lit open expanses that lay hidden beneath the earth. After around ten minutes of driving, they entered a colossal storage chamber lined with military supplies, and the vehicles finally came to a stop.

After a few moments, a soldier opened the rear door and Jamall, followed by Collins, stepped onto a vast concourse as the truck carrying the Special Forces soldiers rolled to a halt behind him.

Jamall stood up straight, stretching his back, and took a few moments to look up at the vast space, the arched ceiling of which must have been higher than an average New York skyscraper. The space above his head was crisscrossed with the various pipes, and the walls sported vents that disappeared into the darkness. At ground level, on one side, an endless row of huge, numbered storage bays interspersed with hundreds of trucks, military vehicles and tanks. Groups of soldiers in dark combat gear milled around as if waiting for something. Above the bays, illuminated rectangular windows protruded from the wall, revealing moving figures within.

From out of one of those bays, a jeep made a beeline for them, pulling alongside where they stood. Jamall recognised the tall, thin, spectacled figure with cropped blonde hair straight away. He wore a black jumpsuit that made him almost indistinguishable from all the other military and security on the base. His glasses glinted from the artificial lights overhead, and he approached Jamall first.

His padre and controller. Doctor Red. The man he once called 'Daddy.'

This was the man who had nurtured him into this stark world back when Jamall had not earned his name and was simply called Delta 459.

The same man who had trained him to become a killing machine and expert hunter. The perfect agent for the cabal.

And the man who had made sure his terrible burns, inflicted by that *puta*, Hugo Reese, were given the best corrective treatment possible. Although the scarred ridges remained on one side of his face as a constant reminder to him.

The doctor did not smile or greet him in a friendly manner.

3

He simply nodded and said, "Agent Salazar, Agent Collins." Then, he gestured for them to both get into the back seats of the jeep.

Doctor Red drove them to the far side of the concourse and along a wall that housed rows of pillars leading to a pedestrian hub of elevators and walkways within. After a few minutes, the doctor pulled into a parking space, switched off the engine and stepped out. He ushered the agents to go with him to an elevator that was different from the others. The door was red, and a sign above it marked it as 'Private: No Access'.

The doctor swiped a card and then held his eye to a transparent panel for a second. There was a bleep before the doors to the elevator parted, and they all stepped inside. The doctor pressed a button for the lowest level, and they descended into the very depths of Station 12.

When the elevator doors parted, they were in a very different world from the vast coldness of the concrete and metal storage bays they had just left. Now, it was almost like stepping into the grand reception area of a luxury house featuring polished marble flooring and a high ornate ceiling with a hanging chandelier. Beyond the reception, arched doorways seemed to lead to other spaces in the elite quarters.

A shapely woman, immaculately dressed in a military-style uniform, was waiting for them. She gave a crisp salute to the doctor, who did not return the gesture. "We need Agent Collins to be immediately re-assigned to the inauguration," he said. "Could you take care of that, Sergeant Major? Agent Salazar will remain with me."

"Yes, sir," she said.

Agent Collins turned to Jamall, and both men shook hands, a silent acknowledgement of the dark operation they had undertaken together. Then, Collins was led off down a hallway by the Sergeant Major, while the doctor turned to Jamall and patted his arm.

"Come."

The two men headed towards one of the archways, past huge oil paintings and gilded mirrors, the sound of their footfall echoing in the air. Passing through the archway, they came to a space like a courtyard, and for a moment, Jamel thought they had stepped outside. The lights in the ceiling cleverly imitated sunlight, and the air conditioning came in waves, giving the feeling of a gentle afternoon breeze. In front of a set of tall mahogany doors stood a guard. The doctor gestured to him, and the guard clasped one of the gold handles and opened it slightly to let out a murmur of voices from within. The doctor encouraged Jamall to walk closer with the gentle pressure of his hand on his back.

Inside, Jamall saw groups of high-ranking military personnel, aged men and women in suits, who were all watching as Natan Helms held up his hand and repeated indistinguishable words.

"Our man, Natan Helms—the new president," the doctor whispered. After a few moments, they continued on through the labyrinth and then into a spacious, stately room, deep underground and decorated in keeping with the rest of this luxurious estate.

The doctor gestured to a chair just inside the doors.

"Please wait."

Jamall slowly took a seat on a velvet-upholstered armchair. The doctor strolled towards a group of figures sitting around a low coffee table in front of huge windows, a scene that disorientated Jamall for a few moments. For through the

5

windows was a vast vista of tree-covered mountain ranges, with rolling clouds above them against a blue sky and the occasional flight of birds traversing the landscape. All an illusion. This was the product of a high-resolution screen that made it feel like they were located in a building high on a mountain ridge.

The figures around the coffee table were talking in low murmurs, looking at a flatscreen attached to the wall in front of them that flickered with images of faces that Jamall couldn't quite make out.

On one adjacent wall was a faux fireplace with its realistic log fire, and on the wall above it was a huge hanging metallic Baphomet, the cabal's emblem.

Doctor Red waved a hand, indicating for him to come over.

The men all turned their heads and looked at Jamall as he came over.

He scanned their faces and recognised some of them: Doctor Black, his slick dark hair as shiny as ever. Laurent Wolf, whose old, freckled skin was stretched over a bony skull, an original member of the Council of 13 who must have survived the purge. And the leader of that council, Jason Runeshield, perfectly preened and wearing a black turtleneck sweater under a pale cashmere jacket. He placed down a silver goblet that he was drinking from and stood up to greet his assassin.

"Mr Salazar, Jamall. My congratulations on a job well done." He shook Jamall's hands and smiled, revealing perfectly capped teeth, his eyes watering with intensity.

"Thank you, Mr Runeshield," Jamall replied, his eyes looking over Jason's shoulders at the screen on the wall. It was a rotation of full-faced mugshots and also of covertly taken images. Jamall immediately recognised Hugo Reese's face as it flashed up, just for a couple of seconds.

Runeshield noticed this and smiled, half turning to the screen. "Oh, that? Assessments of our new enemies." Then, his face hardened as if remembering something. "We will be hunting them all down... soon. If for nothing else, then for my dear friend Henry."

Jamall looked at him blankly for a moment, unsure what he meant. Then, Runeshield touched Jamall's arm to move away from the group, and the doctor followed. The men in armchairs continued talking in low whispers.

"'I'm not a man big on details, Jamall. I prefer to deal in broad strokes. But everyone must do their part, and you have certainly proved that. Now, we must all prepare for the next stage. There will be many necessary sacrifices." Runeshield glanced at the doctor. "See to it our friend gets rewarded before being re-assigned."

Doctor Red nodded, and Runeshield turned away to rejoin their group.

"Padre," Jamall said quietly as they headed to the doors.

"Yes?"

"The targets on the screen. One of the men—he did this to me." Jamall lifted a hand to the scarred side of his face. "And I would like to assist with that operation."

Doctor Red looked momentarily at Jamall, then smiled, revealing small animal-like teeth, his eyes glinting through his glasses as he understood immediately what was being asked.

"Ah, yes. Of course. It is the right of every man to find revenge. Perfectly natural. I'll make the arrangements. Harness that darkness within yourself, Jamall, and happy hunting."

Chapter 2

Station 12, Colorado.
The day before Zero Day.

Zak Bowen headed back along the long circular corridor that led from the G13COMMS zone to the holding cells on the lower levels of Station 12. Above him, long black pipes encasing a myriad of optical and power cables spread across the roof like dark, gnarled, varicose veins.

Despite his frustration with having to participate in the seemingly endless drill scenarios as part of his current assignment, he was grateful that through them, he had chanced across Haleema Sheraz, discovering she was now being held as a working prisoner within the Station.

Operation Hallows was less than seven hours away, and he had a shit load of data backlog to review. However, the need to talk to Haleema gripped him with a sense of urgency.

Although she was in secure confinement in block D12, and getting to see her would create a stir within the security system because of her tenuous connection to him, he knew he had to, and soon.

She was a good friend of his sister, Zoe, who had met her from their university association, and Zak just knew Haleema must be working for Joe and Liberatus in some way.

He had questions. Lots of questions, and all that demanded answers.

He arrived at an intersection where various tunnels spread out in different directions across the base and headed down one that was signposted as the security section. At the end of a relatively short walk, the tunnel ceased, and a low-lit lobby opened up before him. The floors were dark marble, their embedded quartz crystals sparkling in the low light. Ahead of him, he faced a row of transparent plastic barriers fixed between electronic posts blocking the way. As he approached one, it automatically activated, a dim glow emanating from within, and a voice sounded from above.

"Show your identification and state your business," came an emotionless voice that had been automatically triggered by his approach.

Zak held up the pass lanyard that hung around his neck, displaying it in a semi-circular arc, unsure of the direction to display it.

"I'm Intelligence Officer Bowen from G13COMM. I'm here to speak to one of your prisoners urgently. Haleema Sheraz: 089."

"Approach Gate 5 and pass through. Stand in the yellow circle in front of you with your arms raised to your sides while you are scanned," the computer-generated voice said.

Zak stepped forward slowly, and as he did so, the plastic gates parted with a soft swish. He moved through between the two posts, the machine beeping as he passed and stood within the designated circle while a series of lights scanned his body. Ahead, tall black titanium doors slid open, revealing a room with metal lattice mesh just behind. The same emotionless voice intoned the words, 'Scan complete. Proceed,' as two figures in dark grey jumpsuits approached Zak. One of them studied his id card and looked him up and down for a moment before motioning with his head.

"Come with us now, Officer Bowen."

Silently, they guided him through a labyrinth of winding corridors. Passing numerous rooms, each fortified with a state-of-the-art biometric scanner guarding its entrance. Some spaces stood fortified with high-sided cages and fortified barriers, while others hummed with the ominous energy of electric defences. As they navigated through another double set of imposing security doors, Zak couldn't help but feel the oppressive weight of his surroundings. Finally, the guards ushered him into an austere interview room, furnished minimally with only two seats and a steel table complete with a restraining loop in the centre for chained cuffs fixed securely to the floor. The pale pallor of the lighting on the stark furniture cast an unyielding atmosphere of isolation and anticipation.

"Wait here, we'll bring the prisoner," they stated curtly, then left.

After waiting for ten or so minutes, Zak heard the door click and swish open. Haleema, dressed in an orange jumpsuit, stood in the door frame for a moment, her wrists handcuffed in front of her. She looked pale, and dark rings circled her dark eyes that stared at Zak. Then, she was shoved forward by one of the guards and told to sit.

She walked slowly around to the chair.

"Hello, Haleema," he said. Then to the guard, who was about to chain her to the table, "You don't need to do that." Then, gesturing to Haleema's wrists, continued, "Let's get these cuffs off, too, and I need you to bring some refreshments in here. Now, please?"

The guard, a bulky Indian man, stared back at him, a look of incredulity on his face at having been spoken to in such a manner but said nothing.

Zak sighed. "Do you want to answer to Kate Foster from G13COMMS?" When there was no response from the man, Zak asked, "What is your name?"

The guard, obviously taken aback by Zak's authoritative tone, cleared his throat, then moved around to Haleema and slowly unlocked her cuffs. She gratefully rubbed her wrists and nodded at Zak, although still eyeing him suspiciously.

"Are you hungry?" Zak asked. Before she had a chance to answer, he addressed the guard again, "Let's get some coffee in here and something to eat as well. No prisoner crap. Something decent."

"Like what?" the guard asked incredulously.

"Haleema?"

She didn't answer initially, and both men stared at her.

"Stew," she finally managed to say, "and bread."

Zak waved the guard away. "Sounds good to me, too. Let's have it delivered quickly."

The guard turned on his heel and slammed the door behind him.

Zak leaned back in his chair, appraising the young woman in front of him who stared down at the tabletop.

"I'm intelligence officer Bowen for G13COMMS," Zak said, breaking the silence.

There was the faintest spark of recognition in Haleema's demeanour just for a moment, and then she lifted up her face to look at him.

"I'm just curious about a few things," Zak said, steepling

his fingers in front of him, "I read your file. I know you're not here by choice, and I'm sorry about that."

He paused, but Haleema stared back down at the tabletop while he continued. "Your file says you're in here because of a security breach. Apparently, you were trying to communicate or send something beyond 'our walls', right?" Zak held out both his hands. "The question you've failed to answer is, to whom?"

"I answered all these questions under duress," Haleema spoke, her voice low but steady. "I wasn't trying to breach security. In fact, there's no evidence for that or even that I did anything wrong. I should be freed immediately."

"So, you deny it all?" Zak asked,

"Yes," she replied, her voice quiet but adamant.

"You weren't trying to send information to Joe Bowen?"

There was the briefest of pauses.

"No."

"You know him, though. You've worked with him. I know you were friends with Zoe."

At the mention of Zoe, Haleema raised her head to look at him, her eyes narrowed, and then a flicker of realisation crossed her features. "You are Zak. I thought so."

Zak didn't answer and pursued his line of questioning instead.

"You're working with Joe and Liberatus. We've got intel on that. Did that sonofabitch put you in here?"

"What the hell is it to you?" Haleema's face suddenly flashed with anger and frustration.

"Ah, interesting reaction. You're mad, and you should be," Zak said, nodding to himself.

Haleema immediately looked away and crossed her arms.

12

Zak could tell she was cursing herself for her reaction.

"You know, the last time I saw him, and Zoe, for that matter, was, well, interesting. She was getting involved in something, and I know Joe must have gotten involved. And somehow, this all links up, and I intend to find out what you're up to."

The door clicked and opened. A different guard entered with a tray holding two coffee mugs with sachets of creamer and sugar, plus cutlery wrapped in a paper napkin. Another guard entered with their food on a tray in two steaming bowls. They placed the food and beverages on the steel table and left.

Haleema sipped on the stew, fully focused on the food in front of her, and then she looked straight at Zak. "What about Operations Hallows? The biggest interdepartmental drill this decade. You can't see it yet? It's page one in the CIA playbook."

"What do you mean?" he asked.

"Well, it's clearly a set up for some kind of False Flag. Even you should be able to see this coming. Do I need to spell it out for you?" She paused, looking at Zak, but didn't wait for him to respond. "There's a drill that depicts exactly the same scenario as what actually happens! Take the attacks on September 11, 2001. There were three separate drills that simulated hijackings scheduled that same day, drills that emulated planes hitting the Pentagon and the World Trade Center. NORAD, who intercepted sixty-seven planes in the twelve months before the attacks, received a stand-down order because of these 'drills'."

Zak opened his mouth to interrupt, but Haleema continued before he could utter a word.

"When the real attacks came, massive confusion. What flights on those tracking radar screens were real, and which ones were part of the drill? When the real attack came, no one could really know what the hell was actually going on until after the event. And then it happened, for all the world to see and with it the instant guilty party, Osama Bin Laden, once a CIA asset, but now no longer useful to his masters."

She sipped her coffee.

"All these theories usually have an explanation," Zak said with a slight condescension in his voice.

"It was the same thing in London on 7th July 2005," Haleema continued, "A drill for the exact same scenario plays out in reality. The manager of a security firm accidentally let slip on TV and radio that their simulation of crisis drills was taking place at the same tube stations, but no one noticed or cared. Questions should be asked, but the media are controlled, so of course, they'll never investigate, and of course, it's all a 'conspiracy theory'. The usual bullshit term thrown at anything that doesn't follow the narrative."

Haleema continued, "The results of these events? Consolidation of power through the Patriot Act, USA Freedom Act, Section 702 of the Foreign Intelligence Surveillance Act, all through surveillance. Liberties taken away from the general public. The justification to roll out of a decade-long war; to take control of the global oil supply, push national defence budgets to skyrocket, and use the media to rage against opponents of the dollar-based system," she said, looking him straight in the eye.

Zak held up his hand, indicating he had heard enough.

"Don't forget Hong Kong too," Haleema added quickly, ignoring him, "The drill that your father got caught up in."

At that, Zak slammed both of his hands down on the tabletop, causing the mugs to bounce on their bases.

He fired back, "All this is coming from someone who worked for a terrorist state. I heard all this bullshit from Joe already.

That's who I hear talking to me right now."

"I have my own opinions," Haleema countered.

"You worked for the Iranian Government," Zak fired back.

"Yes, I did," Haleema acknowledged. "However, I never supported them. I simply did what I was told I had to do. Look at the work I've been asked to do here. Do you think I personally support your cause?"

"Listen," Zak pointed and wagged his finger, "we're not here to chat about your theories about what happened decades ago. There are explanations and plenty of debunks for all of that crap you're spouting. What I want to know right now is what you're doing sending messages to Liberatus, a known subversive organisation. What are you trying to achieve?"

Haleema shook her head. "Present me with your evidence first."

Zak sighed. "It's a shame. Your skills were a great asset." He stood up and waved a hand at Haleema's half-finished stew. "Finish your meal. I'll tell the guards to give you five."

"Thanks," Haleema said, her voice laced with sarcasm.

***

Station 12
Central Operations Room
Zero Day

The mission control room was buzzing with the anticipation of the impending drill. In the dimmed light, figures moved to get to their stations. Rows of screens flickered with maps and blinking data below a vast projection screen that displayed a map of the entire United States.

Major cities were highlighted with red circles, and a count-down timer on one screen ticked away, less than an hour to the zero that indicated the Operation Hallows exercise had begun.

At the right side of the vast space, looming above the floor, a long observation room protected with dark glass, where the top military brass gathered, surveying the operation below them.

Zak thought he recognised the figure of General Wexhall, talking to several other generals. Zak had never heard of such a huge exercise involving all the top brass and even the president playing a role. Apparently, President Woodside had his journey home from a tour in Utah interrupted and was being diverted to an air base. The vice president was on a flight heading to Colorado.

The initial warning, all part of the drill, had come through forewarning of a wide-scale attack, not just on the US but also on all the allies in the Western Powers: Canada, UK, Australia and Europe. Each country had their response protocols in place and was coordinating a similar response to the one taking place inside Station 12, deep under the International Denver Airport.

There were teams responsible for overseeing the impact of the exercise, including getting high-level government person-nel to safety. High-ranking military staff were descending into various secret underground facilities across the country. Over the previous few weeks, vast, endless trains had been transporting military hardware such as vehicles and tanks to underground protective areas as well as military equipment and supplies.

Then, there was the emergency response plan, which in-volved directing resources in the aftermath of any attack or disaster. As the drill was based on a nuclear attack, this would involve the challenge of dealing with the fallout of radiation.

Zak pulled up his chair and glanced an eye over the relentless drill reports that popped up on his screen while cradling his coffee mug in his hands, waiting for the simulation to begin. His headset hung around his neck. On one screen, he had a bird's eye view of a map that showed G13COMM Special Forces units and their locations. Four separate squads were on site inside Station 12. Another five teams were on the ground, spread out in various locations across the country.

The incoming reports alerted him to a list of other exercise events, such as emergency response units were now on standby.

The clock numbers all gradually switched to zero.

It was time.

The speakers crackled to life, and a voice that was both authoritative and calming spoke through the intercom system, "Emergency broadcast incoming."

Although this was yet another drill, it had been hyped to the point where Zak couldn't help but hold his breath for a moment. The excitement and anticipation were palpable.

"This is a drill. I repeat, this is a drill. This exercise is a simulation of nuclear war scenarios and is conducted for training and preparedness purposes only."

The map on the projection screen that dominated the control room displayed a first hit on Los Angeles, quickly followed by San Francisco, then Portland, indicated by a red light that began to radiate outwards, just like the training scenario that Zak had seen.

Other screens displayed real-time data, such as initial mortality estimates: 150,958. Causalities; 467,925. The numbers rapidly moved upwards. Voices were raised as personnel in the control room communicated with their various teams through headsets.

Zak felt a sickening knot in his stomach. Although he knew none of this was actually happening, the animated radius indicating fall out, the figures on the monitors, and the tension in those around him made it all seem so very real.

Zak's headset crackled with static, and he pulled them up to his ears.

"Alpha Blue, status reports incoming. Stand by." It was the operator for the G13COMM, codenamed 'Alpha Red.'

"Alpha Blue on standby," Zak responded.

On the main monitor, more red dots were appearing over US cities and towns in the West: Las Vegas, Phoenix, San Diego. Then, right up to Seattle and Canada, slowly west, spreading like a pox on the skin of the country.

"Alpha Blue. Actual reports of mass electrical disturbances across the whole of the west coast. Los Angeles, San Francisco, San Diego—" the voice trailed off.

Initially, Zak, looking up at the map, thought he misheard. The drill indicated those cities had been hit, so naturally, the power would be disrupted. But did the voice say, '*actual*'?

"Can you repeat, Alpha Red?"

The voice did so, then added, "This not, I repeat, not a drill. Actual reports on the ground. Wait—one minute."

What the hell was going on?

Other operators sitting ahead of Zak were beginning to look around, at each other, and up to the glass gallery, where the military men had disappeared. The chattering voices and murmur grew louder.

There was a flicker of the overhead lights, and for a second, the power in the control room seemed to cut out. The monitors fizzed, and then the overhead lights turned red for a few seconds before the power seemed to be restored.

"What was that?" Zak asked out loud. A woman sitting nearby turned to him. "That feels like our power source had some kind of interruption. My guess is the backup just kicked in."

"Shit." That wasn't good.

Zak heard the voice return.

"Our sensor network has confirmed an EMP attack at our location. Actual. I repeat, an actual EMP attack confirmed. Refer to your console for further details."

Zak held his breath. The sick feeling came back like a jolt, and Zak felt a cold wave course through his body.

On his screen, a series of messages began to come through, one by one.

Electrical surge events confirmed in the following locations:

A list of cities and states began to appear, confirming not only the locations infected by the red radius areas on the main screen but also their location in Colorado.

Zak turned to the woman and heard himself stating, "We just got hit by an EMP. For real."

"Oh shit," she replied, then turned away to talk urgently to her counterpart through her mic.

"Alpha Red. These targets are the exact same as we have designated for Operation Hallows. Can you confirm this?"

"Communications are down from the east coast. Reports seem to indicate a countrywide attack. This would be similar to the targets for Operations Hallows."

"Jesus," Zak said under his breath. "How can this be?"

The chances must be several million, if not a billion to one, surely.

On the screen, the map was turning red, west to east, at a rapid rate. Zak was dumbfounded as he recalled Haleema's words. Was this the reality of what was happening on the ground, or just the computer simulations of the intended drill?

Zak wasn't sure what to believe.

The conversation with Haleema came back to him in an instant. The False Flags, the covering drills. Is this what was actually happening now? It seemed that which she had laid out so clearly and which he had dismissed was actually happening, just as Haleema had, almost prophetically, predicted. Were they all part of something much bigger and more sinister?

Zak couldn't believe that, indeed wouldn't believe that. It went entirely against his whole belief system.

A light began pulsing on the landline telephone on Zak's desk.

He picked it up.

"Zak Bowen."

"Zak, it's Kate Foster. Get back to G13COMMs immediately."

Chapter 3

Zero Day

Zak jogged along the tunnelways of the facility to get back to the G13COMM section, his mind racing.

What the hell was happening?

When he came through the doors, Foster was at the doorway of her mezzanine office, already gesturing furiously to him, worry lines clearly visible on her taut face.

Shit, this was serious.

He climbed up the external stairwell, two at a time, his shoes clanking on the metal rungs. As he entered the room, tension was practically visible amongst the other high-ranking personnel from Foster's team. They stood there fidgeting, exchanging anxious glances with each other, waiting for someone to break the tension. The Director of Analysis, Samantha Ellis, and Ryan Blackwell, an Intelligence Analyst, both looked up and nodded to Zak as he entered.

"I need to brief you before we go to the War Room," Foster said grimly.

"War Room? Are we at war?" Zak blurted out, staring at her.

"Could be." Foster gestured impassively, directing him to be seated in an empty chair.

Zak felt the blood drain from his face and a cold chill course through his body as he sat down. Some part of him had hoped this was all a big mistake. That somehow, the massive power outages spreading across the US were part of the drill but had somehow not been communicated to their team.

But looking again at Foster, her expression instantly told him he was deluding himself with such false hope.

"I've got bad news and worse news, I'm afraid," Foster began. "Military surveillance and early warning systems have detected serious anomalies that are consistent with an actual EMP event. There are multiple seismometer and electromagnetic sensor signals that display clear signatures of multiple EMP events. This is definitely *not* part of the Hallows drill," she stated emphatically before continuing, "although, just like Hallows, all the main cities have been targeted in a blanket attack across all the US. Therefore, a Presidential Emergency Action Notification (PEAN) is about to be activated to ensure government continuity as well as the appropriate emergency responses are put into effect."

Ryan Blackwell, a Cyber Threat Analyst, looked the most shocked. The rest of them had obviously already heard.

"There are also unconfirmed reports that the commander-in-chief"—she paused and cleared her throat before continuing—"that our president has been killed in a crash at the secret location he was being taken to for his own role in overseeing Operation Hallows."

The collective shock this announcement had on those present was immediate, with looks of incredulity, shaking of heads and cries of, "What!"

"My God," Ellis said aloud, summing up the general sentiment of the room.

Foster, however, was not done and continued, "We also have the vice president missing. She was on board Air Force Two at the time of the attacks, and it has since gone missing."

There were a few more moments of stunned silence.

"This is unbelievable," Ellis added, shaking his head.

"Who leads the country if the VP is also dead?" one of the younger staff asked.

Foster glanced at him, wondering why he had asked such a question. "As you should know, the protocol is that in the event of the deaths of both the president *and* the vice president of the US, then the Secretary of State becomes president. This means that Natan Helms now becomes the president of the USA."

Foster looked down at her watch, and a frown creased her forehead.

"We need to head over there. Then we should have a clear, actionable plan."

As people turned to move, a thin young voice was heard above the scuffing of shoes and the scraping of chairs being pushed back. "Can I ask a question?" It was Blackwell, a younger man sporting a boyish face and an unruly mop of black curly hair.

"Go." Foster looked impatient to leave but nodded to him to continue.

"So, what happens to our own power source? I mean, right here in Station 12. There's a backup, I know, but how long will that last? I mean, if we go dark, we're screwed." The young analyst looked worried.

Foster smiled and shook her head dismissively. "Good question, but don't you worry about any of that. We have our own energy source. That was thought of a long time ago."

***

Personnel from G13COMM gathered in the War Room. This was an egg-shaped metallic pod that stood in the middle of a much larger space. The air gap and special materials coating the huge pod ensured there could be no electronic listening ears, so there could be no loss of sensitive information.

It was the first time Zak had been there. It was similar to the Sensitive Compartmented Information Facility or SCIF that Zak had been to at Langley when he had been ushered into G13COMM from his post at the CIA. This one, however, looked much more modern and sophisticated, not like the throwback to the cold war like the SCIF at Langley. This looked as if it was right out of some sci-fi movie.

Zak took his allotted place at the oval table next to Kate Foster. Alongside them were heads of the NSA, FBI, NOAA and CIA, although their power now came under the direct orders of Major General Dean Wexhall, who also oversaw the military arm of Ghost 13.

Zak wondered how Wexhall had become so powerful. Especially after that scandal thirty or so years ago when he had been hauled up before a Senate Hearing about some messy operation in Colombia when he was a Colonel. It seemed his star would fall after that, but evidently not. Zak knew some of the story because his father, Frank, had been involved. Since then, with Zak in the CIA, he had been involved with Wexhall in the Middle East.

Several large screens at one end of the room displayed the G13COMM seals with the Baphomet icon on blue backgrounds.

Wexhall addressed the room and occasionally glanced down at a printed report as he spoke, his tone even and measured.

"Firstly, I would like to confirm the terrible, devastating

news that our Commander-in-Chief, President Woodside, is indeed dead."

There was a hushed silence at the confirmation of what everyone in the room had just been briefed on.

"I also need to inform you that Air Force Two carrying the vice president was en route here but went offline. We have a team headed to the last known location, but it's most likely that it came down due to one of the EMP attacks. If this is confirmed, then, as per protocol, the Secretary of State, Natan Helms, will be sworn in. He hopes to address us soon and is currently safe in Washington DC."

Wexhall took a sip of water and then calmly refilled his glass from a nearby jug.

"You've all been briefed on where we're at right now," he continued. "A series of EMP events have been triggered and hit 'CONUS', the Continental United States. As of this moment, the entire country is without power."

He looked around at the shocked faces to let that information sink in.

"We also have reports of similar events in Canada and South America. Just a few minutes ago, G13COMM stations in the UK and Europe also reported similar attacks over there." Pausing to let the weight of his announcements sink in, gravely looking around at the assembled faces, he summarised for all. "We're looking at an unprecedented attack against the Western Powers on a massive scale." Then, he proceeded to outline the plan they had gathered to hear.

"Under the PEAN procedures, measures will be taken to secure and coordinate essential operations, including the functioning of the Government, the military, and critical infrastructure, designed to maintain order, ensure the safety and well-being of the population, and enable a structured response to the emergency. Thanks to Operation Hallows and the preparations that preceded it, we are in a very strong position. However, civilian casualties will be huge, but we should be able to get more accurate figures if we adjust our projections from Operation Hallows."

Wexhall cupped his hands on the smooth graphite tabletop, a grave expression fixed on his face.

"I have activated emergency protocol 13 and Emergency Operations Centres. This enables the functioning of our government and military, and we have the infrastructure in place for such an event as this EMP assault, although it's limited.

"This means the military can operate a limited communication network and have equipment, transport and so forth."

"What about the population and the chaos that will inevitably erupt in the coming days and weeks?" This question came from a man in a crisp black suit whom Zak did not recognise.

Wexhall acknowledged the question with a brief nod of his head and responded, "Martial law will need to be brought in. That goes without saying. At least until we can move the majority of citizens into the FEMA encampments already in place."

"Camps?" Zak blurted out.

"All part of the established emergency protocol. I suggest you study it," Wexhall said coldly, staring at Zak for a moment.

"Federal, state, and local government agencies will activate their Emergency Operations Centres (EOCs) to coordinate responses. As you're aware, they will facilitate communication and collaboration between various agencies and jurisdictions."

Wexhall turned his steely gaze to Kate Foster.

"We will need G13COMM to head up the investigation into the crimes committed today. Can you lead, Foster? I would like to be kept in the loop of any major developments."

Foster nodded. "Certainly, sir."

"Let's wrap this up. We have a major crisis to deal with!" Wexhall said without any further comment, turned away from the table, and the meeting abruptly ended.

Zak walked alongside Foster as they headed back to G13COMM, their shoes clanking on the metal lattice walkways.

"Zak, we'll have specialist teams looking into the possibility of involvement by any rogue nations. Can you head up a team to start digging into any potential domestic threats from internal groups who might have also been involved?"

Zak nodded. "Sure. Yes, no problem. Internal groups, terrorists like UIS?" Zak was referring to the United Islamic State spawned from the ISIS of the 2000s, which he had seen rise up in the Middle East and attack whole countries such as Iran and Iraq.

"Yes, pull up our blacklist, dig into the leading figures. Trace where they were last believed to be when we got hit, which will be difficult, I know, but do your best."

"Always," Zak responded with genuine gusto, then went on to say, "but some of these groups, who are on that list, I can't possibly see how they could pull something as complex as this off?" Zak said, genuinely perplexed.

"In the CIA, we never believed that a group of bearded men living in Afghan caves could have pulled off 9/11, especially as the mastermind was once a CIA asset back in the 1980s. But that's the official story," Foster responded.

"Right," Zak replied, nodding his head and realising the folly of dismissing enquiries with assumptions.

They turned into a pedestrian tunnel overhead, and the light tubes dimmed in a red hue, a reflection of their high state of alert.

Zak's mind was still racing. It was too much to take in. He thought of his friends and families, knowing that what would seem like a normal blackout would soon spiral into something a lot worse. But there was nothing he could do, and there was no way to contact them, no way to help. He gritted his teeth, biting back the emotion that built up inside him. The feeling of helplessness to save the ones he cared about began to crush him. He pushed the thought from his mind, burying the worry inside, his mind going back to the task at hand to find those responsible and bring them to justice.

Chapter 4

London.
One hour to Zero Day

Zoe woke in darkness, restless on the thin mattress and shivering under a couple of thin blankets. She groaned as her aches and pains became more apparent, reminders of the ordeal she had just gone through with Villar, the cold-blooded bitch who was behind her fiancé's murder.

Laying in the dark, she relived the moment of Villar's associate, who had actually killed her beloved fiancé, Ed, being impaled on a rack of scrap railings. Closing her eyes, she could instantly see and hear again the sound of Villar's body being crushed by an underground train as she relentlessly pursued her victim. All this had happened a few scant hours ago, so how she got to this apartment, avoiding the detainment of the Law, was close to miraculous. She took a deep breath in and then let it out slowly. The coldness of the room had raised goosebumps on her bare skin, and she realised that was what had awoken her. She rolled over and reached to switch on the side lamp, squinting as the light filled the room. Checking her phone, she saw it was 2:35 a.m., and there were several missed calls from the same number on her phone.

She had been asleep for a mere two hours.

Zoe yawned, her breath forming a mist in front of her, and she sat up in bed and rechecked the phone. The numbers weren't any she recognised, but the beginning '020' indicated a London landline number. Very few people had this number, it having been set up by the Liberatus team. She called back, and it rang for a while without a reply.

She stopped the call, stood up and looked around the apartment. How much longer would she need to stay here? Hopefully, John Rhodes should have arrived in London by now and would see her today.

Was that him calling?

If he didn't show up, though, it was time to go back to her place, she decided. With Eva Villar no longer in the picture, it felt like the main danger had passed, and she just wanted to go home now. If Rhodes insisted on her lying low for the long term, perhaps she could go to Ireland. To stay with her dad?

Hunger pangs rumbled in her stomach, and she thought of that all-night café nearby that she had seen a few days before. She could get a decent bit to eat. No harm in that, surely? An earlier search had found very little to eat in the apartment, apart from packets of dried soups, canned beans and very little else she could get inspired by.

Naturally, the past twenty-four hours had made her wary and on edge, fraying her emotions. She wondered that perhaps she should then go back home and wait for John's call from there? It was an appealing thought, but recalling her training from John, she knew he wouldn't approve of her going back home, but that was his problem.

She put on her coat, gathered the items that she had brought to the apartment into her backpack, slipped the phone into her inside jacket pocket and locked the door behind her.

Outside, the temperature had dropped, and Zoe could see her breath hanging in the night air. The year so far had been full of so much turmoil with her fiancé's murder and the subsequent fallout that she had barely noticed the summer first turning to autumn with its misty dampness, and now winter's icy fingers permeated the air around them. Perhaps she should hide out somewhere warm? Like Spain? Why the hell didn't she think of that before? Of course. That's what she'd do. Head to Spain and hang out with Joe for a few months.

With her spirit lifted, Zoe walked faster along the streets and turned onto the main road dotted with pubs and bars. Smokers milled around outside the bars that were still open, and taxis cruised along the road, looking to whisk off those who either were unfit to drive or whose partying was done for the evening.

As she approached the all-night café, Zoe could hear the muffled garble of a dozen conversations drifting out onto the street, punctured with the occasional shriek of laughter. A line of lit Halloween pumpkins lined the inside of the steamed-up window ledges. A wall of noise and warmth hit her as she entered. She smiled, delighted to be part of real life again. As she walked further in, the smells from the kitchen greeted her, her stomach grumbling in anticipation. When had she last eaten properly, she wondered. Twenty and thirty-somethings all packed into booths lined either side of a large central space, soaking up the booze with whatever food the kitchen presented them. Most of them were dressed up for Halloween, a mixture of ghoulish painted faces, witches' hats and faux scary attire.

Old 1950s movie posters adorned the brick-tiled walls of the café, and on the end, next to the counter and kitchen entrance, hung a London red, white and blue tube station logo with 'The

Old Tube Café Bar' written on it.

Zoe spotted a space on the end of one booth table and edged around the packed tables. She pointed to the empty seat of the two young women already in there, both with makeup that made them look like zombies. They both smiled. "Join us," one said with mock seduction. Zoe borrowed their laminated menu and scanned the offerings. It wasn't long before she decided and joined the queue to put in her order. When she returned to her seat with her order number, having finally paid for her breakfast and coffee, the other women at her booth had left.

As she waited for her food, her eyes drifted to a large flat television screen above the entrance door. The sound was off, but the text information scrolling across at the bottom of the screen made her sit upright and strain for a better look.

She re-read the text with alarm: "...Blackouts reported across the United States, Canada and South America. Communications are down..."

What the hell was going on?

It made her think of John Rhodes again, and she re-dialled the number from the missed call again.

This time, a woman answered almost immediately.

"Charles Pannett ward," a woman's voice, crisp, business-like, said in her ear.

"Er—hello—I had a missed call. Is this a hospital?"

"Yes, it is. St. Mary's Hospital. Queen Elizabeth the Queen Mother Building. How can I help?"

"Oh, right. Well, I'm not sure. I had a missed call from this number," Zoe said, feeling unsure where this conversation may lead.

"What's your name, please?" the same voice, the epitome

of curt politeness, asked.

"Zoe Bowen."

"Just one moment, please."

There was a pause while Zoe's mind raced. It had to be about John. No one else had her number.

Then, she had a thought. Was it some kind of trap set by someone associated with Eva Villar and the whole Bayer and Xael conspiracy? Were more bastards coming out of the shadows to hunt her down?

Just as she was thinking along such lines, she began to look around the café for the nearest exit when there was the sound of heavy breathing on the line, and a deep male voice grunted, "Zoe?"

She knew straight away it was John Rhodes.

"Hello. Yes, it's me. Are you alright?" Zoe answered, trying to hear his voice over the hubbub within the café.

"Actually, I had a bout of appendicitis on the flight. Nasty all round, I was doubled up in pain, and they carted me off when we landed."

"Oh no, that sounds terrible," she replied, concern for him replacing the previous doubts.

"Yes. They say it's a grumbling appendix. Waiting to see how it goes, but they might operate in case it bursts and I get peritonitis."

Knowing that a ruptured appendix could be an excruciating death sentence for anyone, Zoe was relieved to hear that Rhodes was in a place where he could be quickly treated. "I was told the name, but where was it again?"

"St Mary's Hospital, do you know it? I'm in the Charles Pannett ward."

Zoe made a mental note. "Yes, I know. Near Paddington. Do

33

you need anything?"

John's voice lowered. "Well, I lost my mobile in the confusion—if you come across one. And the bloody airline sent my suitcase to my hotel. Look, Zoe. I'm not sure you're out of the woods yet, but I did make some calls for you, and there are no obvious traces that anyone is actively seeking you at the moment."

Zoe paused and digested that information. John Rhodes, despite his stance against the system, still had a few sympathetic friends in the UK's Secret Service, according to her brother, Joe.

"I'll take that as a positive," Zoe said, feeling reassured by the news.

A waitress put down her breakfast and coffee in front of Zoe, picking up the plastic order tab, as she returned the smile Zoe gave her.

"—but I think you should continue to be cautious," John added. "I'll make contact again when I'm out of here. Fingers crossed it'll be soon."

"If you think that's best? I want to go home, though."

"Yes, well, if you must. Just keep your phone close by, and I'll call when I'm on my way. See you soon, Zoe."

"Okay, take care. I'm sure you'll get well soon. Bye."

She stared down at her plate of food and hoped he was right in that no one was seeking her out anymore. It was time to get her life back.

A boisterous group who had dominated the café with loud conversation and shrieking laughter all made moves to leave, much to Zoe's relief. She tucked into the steaming food and hadn't realised just how hungry she was. The fried potatoes, beans, mushrooms and veggie sausage, which she washed down with coffee, all tasted like a dream. She mopped up her plate with a wedge of sourdough toast and then pushed it aside.

As she did so, the lights in the café flickered, and then the whole café was plunged into darkness. A collective jeering cheer went up from the other customers, and then a voice from one of the women behind the counter addressed the café.

"Everyone, stay calm. We'll get some lights going until the power is back up."

There was a murmur of low conversation among the café customers while Zoe assessed her options.

She needed to get home as soon as possible.

A flicker of flame, then a number of candles came to life from behind the counter, radiating small auras of light. Then, a few of the waitresses brought the candles to each table, creating a warming atmosphere.

In the dim light, Zoe checked her phone, but there were no signals or networks of any kind.

She got up and carefully made her way around the tables where people continued chatting and eating by candlelight. Perhaps at any other time, Zoe would have appreciated how romantic the atmosphere had become, but a growing feeling that something was very wrong pushed that thought aside.

Outside, the streets had been plunged into complete darkness. There was a slight hue around the dark, tall buildings from the sky, but apart from that, it was like someone had pulled the plug. As her eyes adjusted, the stars and moon seemed brighter, more clustered, which made sense to Zoe. Light pollution usually dulled the night sky. Now that was gone, the canopy of stars above her appeared particularly radiant.

Some of the crowd who had been outside when the power failed still lingered, judging by the 'woo woo, scary' comments she heard, and the back light from the candles inside offered enough light to make out shapes. Zoe bumped shoulders with someone, and they both apologised. Voices, unseen, continued around her.

Overhead, what sounded like a distant sonic boom quickly faded before shouts and whistles from other late-night revellers cut through the darkness. There was revelry in the confusion. A sense that this power outage was all a bit of fun. Zoe felt the opposite. Fear and panic rose in her stomach. Her bad feeling wasn't going away.

Without thinking, Zoe cautiously walked down the street away from the café and the gathered crowd. She kept close to the shop fronts to keep her bearings. Ahead, a small orange light moved around in the middle of the road, and she realised it was someone smoking, drawing on a cigarette. It was the driver of a taxi standing next to his vehicle, which was stationary on the road as if the engine had suddenly stopped. As she got closer, she could make out that the driver was attempting to connect his mobile phone without success.

She thought about heading back to her apartment in Surrey Quays. But it was at least five miles, and she had the distinct feeling there wouldn't be any transport options. Attempting to get across London in pitch blackness seemed like insanity. The place she had just left was a lot nearer, and she still had the key. She could leave it at first light.

Zoe cautiously made her way back and entered the dark building. It was quiet, and there were no signs any of the other residents had been alerted to the blackout, but then it was 4 a.m., and most would have still been asleep. She entered the apartment and immediately began rummaging around the cupboards and drawers for a flashlight or candles, just something to use as a light source, but got nowhere. Frustrated and suddenly feeling completely exhausted, she made her way to the bed and lay down again.

After a moment, she knew that she should just rest until daylight. Then, maybe she could think straight.

If power wasn't restored the next day, that would mean a wider problem. Perhaps something long-term? That, in turn, might mean serious problems, widespread chaos, even.

Her anxiety meds! Her sudden recall that she didn't have any passed through her like a cold wave.

She knew she had a stash at home, maybe a month's supply. Should she head there first, then go and find John at St Mary's? Could she keep her anxiety under control until, hopefully, things got back to normal?

Stop overthinking it all. One hour, one day at a time. She remembered a line from one of her self-help books. 'Don't stress out over things you cannot control and focus only on what you can'.

From where she was, near Battersea Park, her own apartment was east, and St Mary's Hospital was north of her location in Paddington. As she couldn't access the map on her phone, she would have to rely on memory and road signs. Luckily, she had grown up in London and returned to the city after finishing university, so she knew it well.

She lay, desperately trying to sleep. While her body felt washed out and drained of energy, her mind was too active, processing all that she had experienced. What stuck in her mind was the television bulletin about massive energy and communications blackouts being apparent across the United States just before the power went out in the UK. That would mean this wasn't just a local power cut.

This was bigger. Much, much bigger.

Or was it just a huge coincidence? Zoe turned onto her side, squeezing her eyes shut and waiting to drift off.

Chapter 5

London
Day 1

Dawn light slowly crept into the room from a cloud-covered sky. It was still bright enough that Zoe squinted, her blurred vision slowly adjusting as she listened to the window frame shaking from the wind. Zoe sighed before stretching to the bedside table and reaching for her phone. Still no network. She checked the light switch by the bed. Still nothing after the early morning power cut that had blackened London.

She decided to head to her apartment in Surrey Quays, grab her meds and a few other things, then hopefully go to see John and take it from there. There was no telling what state of recovery he was in, though. The hospitals should have backup power generators to keep incubators and ventilators active.

At least, she hoped they had.

Zoe shuddered at the thought of the damage that could have been done. No heat. No electricity for essential equipment in the hospitals. In the modern world, almost everything relies on electrical power.

Zoe lifted herself from the bed and headed to the bathroom. There was still cold water, at least, so she washed her face, then packed her bag, this time including packet soups, crackers and biscuits. In one of the cupboards was a water bottle, which she filled up and slipped into a side pocket on her bag.

She took one last glance around the apartment, and with a deep breath, she left. Outside, the air was harsh. The cold wind seemed to drain any remaining warmth right out of her body, and dark clouds swirled overhead, promising a day with more rain and wintery weather. Zoe pulled her collar up and headed out into the elements.

What a time for power to go down, right in the middle of a bloody cold snap, she thought. The streets were quiet, apart from the howling wind. Debris lay strewn across the road. Cars had been abandoned where they had lost power. Most were electric or hybrid, but Zoe wasn't entirely sure why so many vehicles had stopped working. A few early risers tried to start their cars but were struggling. A woman held up her mobile phone in the air, waving it around, trying to get a signal, swearing out loud.

Distant emergency vehicle alarms cut through the noise of the wind.

On her left loomed the vast concrete chimneys of Battersea Station, where just 24 hours or so earlier, she had stupidly met Matt Fulford, and her nightmare encounter with that evil bitch Eva Villar had begun.

On the other hand, that was at least now behind her. Eva was dead, her body dismembered by a train.

Zoe reflected that had she not gone to that meeting, Villar would still be hunting for her even now. Although, she wondered, if this blackout continued, any surveillance operation would be dead in the water. Were all the agencies and police out of action due to this power outage? The thought of the possible lawlessness that would ensue if all authority was gone sent a shudder down her spine.

And what was the authorities' plan to deal with this crisis? There surely must be an emergency plan for this kind of thing? But, so far, at least, Zoe hadn't seen any sign of it.

In the distance, north of the river, a column of black smoke could be seen rising high over the city.

What the hell was that from? Must be some buildings on fire. Was it connected to the blackout, perhaps? If there was a fire, how could someone call the fire department? And even if you got through, what if the fire engines weren't working? What could they do? No phone lines, no vehicles, no emergency service. The whole city was a tinderbox waiting to go up. The thought of the chaos that could erupt around her made Zoe shudder.

On the main road leading to Vauxhall, more vehicles lay abandoned by the side and sometimes in the middle of the roads. A couple walked towards her direction, arm in arm, seemingly oblivious to the blackout and the disruption it caused.

As the morning matured, more people were on the roads, and there were even some older vehicles being driven. People still stoically heading to their workplaces, many on foot, but most must have opted to stay home and wait for the power to return.

As she passed through Vauxhall towards Bermondsey, along endless roads, interspersing the mix of residential and industrial sprawl, Zoe wondered if she had made the right choice going home. She thought again of John being in the hospital, and what if they moved him somewhere else because of the lack of power? Could she lose touch with him?

It was too late now. She was probably an hour away from reaching home.

The road ahead passed under a railway bridge, and a shout caught her attention. It was from a group of youths, all hoodies and tracksuits, who had congregated around the underpass, milling around while one circled around on a BMX bike.

Zoe continued her quick pace down the path towards them, conscious not to stare over or draw attention to herself. She knew the game of not drawing too much attention when approaching a potential threat but, at the same time, not becoming a shrinking violet and playing the role of a potential victim. Besides, with all the events over the previous weeks, being shot at and fighting with Eva Villar, Zoe had dispelled a lot of fear.

She felt their glances as she passed by and couldn't help holding her breath as the inevitable, "Yo!" came across the street from where they stood. Zoe looked over the road without breaking her stride and realised they were just kids. Everyone grew up so fast these days.

She turned away, ignoring them and continued walking. Another, "Yo! I is talkin' to you, bitch."

That touched a nerve, but she just glared back at them while tightening the straps of her backpack. The one on a bike peddled around and began to circle around her, giving her a menacing leer while the others moved towards her.

There were other people, including grown men, around as this was happening, all of them walking past, keeping their heads down. Zoe's heart quickened; the situation could deteriorate quickly, and not one of these people would lift a finger, such was the degeneration of society over the past years. Power outage or not.

The biker kid stopped in her way, blocking her from moving forward as the others began to swagger ever closer.

"What do you want?" she said, her voice low and focused.

"Whatever's in the bag," grunted the tall one who seemed to be the leader.

Zoe could sense what was coming next. She really didn't want to fight them, but young as they were, they were still a substantial threat. Without any obvious warning, she suddenly pushed past the biker, shoving him against the tunnel wall, and just ran as fast as she could.

One thing she could do was run fast and for a long time, thanks to her daily runs in her previous life.

She heard the shouts of abuse from behind as she headed down the long road and looped down a side street.

Fortunately, Zoe knew these roads well from her previous jogging circuits. The backpack strapped to her didn't help, but she just focused on the path ahead as she felt the pounding muscles in her thighs ache.

Ducking down the side alleys of the housing estate, she glanced back. Most of the gang has given up chasing already. Clearly, exercise wasn't at the top of their priority list, but the kid on the bike was gaining on her.

After sprinting a few metres, she sidestepped into a brick alcove that led to another group of council houses deep in the estate.

She heard the wheels of the bike come close, her heart pounding in her chest as she sucked deep, long breaths of cold air. Then she stepped out from the alcove, reaching out and grabbing for the arm of the rider as he passed by.

A look of shock danced across his face. As Zoe held on, the handlebars of the bike turned sharply, tucking the front wheel under the frame.

He came down hard over the handlebars, his head hitting the concrete pavement as he skidded and crashed into the opposite wall, yelping in pain.

Zoe stamped her foot down onto the rear wheel of the BMX, caving it in. Not that the youth looked like he was in any state to keep following her. He sat up, a vacant look on his face as he tried to process what had happened. She bent down to where he was sitting, grabbed the boy's throat, and squeezed his windpipe, digging her finger in behind it.

His eyes bulged in terror, his breath rasping harshly as he tried in vain to pull her hands off.

"Do yourself a favour, go home to Mummy. And stop being a dick towards women." His eyes widened as she finally cut off his air. She had to suppress the urge to *really* hurt him, but the fear and anguish in his face stopped her.

He was just a fuckin' kid, after all.

She released him, pushing him so he sprawled backwards over his fallen bike.

"You hear me?" she growled.

The boy nodded frantically, too much in shock to do anything else.

Then, she took off at a steady jog, heading out of the estate and onto Southwark Park until she knew she was well clear. The rest of his mates would be angry when they found out what she'd done and start looking for her, but she was practically home now.

As she approached her building on Surrey Quays, a couple whom Zoe recognised as one of the other apartment tenants stood outside, smoking as they often did.

A brunette woman caught her eye and said hello for the first time ever.

"Hi, have you heard anything about what's going on?" she asked as Zoe stepped up to the front door and took out her keys. She shrugged in response.

"Well, one major power cut is all I can guess," Zoe replied.

The woman looked confused. "Yeah, but hardly any cars work, and no mobile phones work either."

"I know, it's weird," Zoe responded as she stepped inside the entrance to the apartment block.

"Yeah," the brunette agreed, turning back to draw on her cigarette.

She went inside and headed up the stairwell to her apartment. It was hard to know what to say to people. She had her theories and was in no doubt this was some deliberate attack of some sort, but this wasn't the time to get into theoretical conversations.

Inside, she threw down the bag and slumped down on the sofa with a rush of relief. It felt so good to be her own home. Of course, there was no Goya to greet her, and without power and no electrical heating, her home felt cold, gloomy, and neglected.

There was a twinge of sadness, too, and suddenly she felt vulnerable. She wished Ed were around. They would have dealt with this shit together. No matter what came at them, at least they would—

Zoe tutted out loud to stop her train of thought.

He's gone now. He's not here. You're on your own, girl, she reprimanded herself.

She found her Buspirone pills and took two, then headed to the bedroom and opened her bedside table. Rummaging around, she found a small passport photo of Ed. She smiled, remembering when they had taken it and the holiday that followed. She slipped the photo into her pocket.

In the bathroom, she found more of her meds, quickly swallowing a few. The bitter taste was a welcoming relief. Returning to the kitchen, she began rummaging around for something to eat. There was very little of anything fresh. In the fridge, the salad was more like a soup, swimming around in plastic bags, but the fruit bowl items were still good. She bit into an apple, made up a bowl of cereal with oat milk, and took a seat by the window, looking out on Greenland Dock and the distant buildings on the Isle of Dogs beyond.

Enjoy the calm, Zoe told herself, because tomorrow she would have to go back out there.

Chapter 6

Cache 5
Parque Nacional Sierra de las Nieves, Andalucia, Spain
Day 1

It was the incessant sound of early morning birdsong close to where he was sleeping that pulled Joe Bowen from his troubled dream.

That and the unfamiliar smell from the canvas tent that surrounded him in an almost claustrophobic cocoon. He rolled onto his back and sat upright on the cot bed before taking a long pull from his water bottle, the coldness of the water in his mouth sending a sharp pain through his jaw even as he swallowed.

He had set up the single-man tent when the previous evening had drawn in, just a few hundred metres from the supplies cache hidden in the woods near Iznájar.

He checked his phone: 6:25 a.m. No signal.

Within fifteen minutes, he had taken down the small tent and packed everything away so there was no sign of him being there and walked through the surrounding dry woods to where the hidden cache was located. It was unusually cold for the time of year, and Joe remembered Javier talking about some extreme cold front coming across Europe in the coming weeks. Perhaps this was the start of it?

The fresh morning air was almost sweet as Joe set off, and at a circle of trees that formed a natural clearing in the woods, Joe paused and knelt down on one knee by a clump of rocks. There, he brushed a hand over an area of dry bracken and loose stones, revealing a rough wooden hatch with a thick combination-styled padlock looped through a locking clasp. When the hatch was clear of debris, he held the padlock, forcing the little numbered wheels to correct the combination, and when it clicked open, removed it. Pausing for a moment, he looked around the still woods, straining his ears for any unusual sounds.

Satisfied he was alone, Joe pulled up the hatch door. A step ladder descended into the dark hole, and Joe took a flashlight from his backpack before climbing down. The space was just a bit higher than Joe, standing at six feet, but he still stooped a little as he moved along the recess, pointing his beam of light towards a larger space ahead that was around seven metres long and just as wide. Along the walls, metal shelves stacked with crates and tubs of supplies filled the underground room. Joe focused his light on one of the sealed tubs, marked as containing packets of freeze-dried meals. The dates, written in marker pen, told him the dry food bags inside only had a few months left before they needed to be replaced. He intended to take these back to base camp. He walked around the shelves, inspecting each one, then began moving the tubs containing outdated supplies to the bottom of the ladder, ready to take out. He regretted not bringing someone to help at the thought of hauling it all out of the hole by himself, but he'd manage.

This cache was one of many 'holes' in the ground that

Liberatus groups on the ground had prepared in the previous years to provide supplies in whatever scenario they would be needed for. The location of such hidden stashes with food supplies, tools and basic survival packs was known only to those who needed to know.

Time to bring the truck nearer, Joe thought.

Joe climbed back out, closed the hatch and began heading through the trees, his boots crunching once more the dry bracken. The air had assumed a metallic edge, tainted now with a hint of chemicals, as if there were a distant fire.

Joe checked his phone again and frowned. Still no signal. He stopped and rummaged around in his backpack and pulled out an older Nokia 'burner' phone he always kept on him that had a better internal aerial. No signal on this one either, which he thought was quite unusual. He'd never had connection problems in all the previous times he had been in this area before. He continued walking until he reached the truck. It was parked in a clearing just off the narrow road that ran through the woodlands, again hidden from any passing vehicles.

Joe's plan was to drive it a mile down the road and turn off into a track that led nearer to the cache. They had used it many times when supplying the hole, and the relative seclusion kept any supply runs away from prying eyes.

That plan wilted on the vine as Joe turned the ignition key and was met with a distant spooling of the starter motor but no spark of life from the engine. After a few more failed attempts, Joe leaned his tattooed arms on the steering wheel and considered his options. If the battery became dead by fruitless cranking of the engine, he would certainly need to commandeer another vehicle and use his jump leads to get the vehicle going. Assuming it was the battery. He checked his phones again. Both still without signal. He was going to have to take a walk and see if anyone in the nearest town could help.

This was going to take a while.

Joe took out a flask of black coffee and poured himself a mug, gulping the now cold beverage down between bites of a wrapped pastry he had bought the previous day en route.

He began to feel unsettled, as if something was wrong. It was more than the phones not working or the vehicle not starting, but he realised it stemmed from an odd quietness which had settled around him. Even at this far distance, in this relatively remote location, he could normally hear the traffic from the highway, but as he strained his ears, he could hear nothing apart from that which was coming from the wildlife. He scanned the clear blue skies and saw no contrails of any passenger aircraft anywhere, although he knew this area was under the flight path of several major airlines.

Then there was Operation Hallows. Zoe had suggested the date might be significant, alluding to October 31st. The files retrieved from Faber and Xael mentioned implementing the worldwide drill involving the military, political and intelligence apparatus of the Western Powers.

Joe knew these drills were often used as a cover for some nefarious event. Usually, the details were the same as the drill to cause maximum confusion for those involved. His own father, Frank, had once been caught up in one such event in Hong Kong where a supposed anti-terrorist exercise became an actual 'live' event, and his father had been caught like the proverbial fly in some web of lies and deceit. It had changed his father's life forever and had led him into a life of deception with MI6 and Ghost 13 before he had seen the light and then used his skills to help Liberatus.

Frank, and to a lesser extent, Joe had learned valuable lessons from that, mainly that the governments and their military and intelligence agencies would do absolutely anything to keep the power structures and influence they exerted in place for their real masters.

Joe grabbed his bag, jumped down from the truck and locked it before walking back to his former campsite. He packed up his rucksack, which he had packed with dry food supplies, water, and MREs.

He was now unsure what was happening and wanted to be prepared. If there were bigger issues than just his truck not starting, he needed to get back to the hive.

Joe left the truck hidden and walked along the winding, narrow road that snaked through the woodland where some morning mist still lingered. It was a good twenty minutes before the nearest town, Tolox, came into view. This was a town Joe had only driven through a handful of times when he had visited the supplies cache. Normally, there would be little sign of any life in this sleepy town of only a couple of thousand souls, but this morning, small groups of people were gathered out on the main road and around one of the food stores in deep discussion.

Joe approached them, and a tall man on the outskirts of a group turned towards him as he approached and nodded a greeting.

"*Hola. Buenos dias.*"

"*Buenos,*" a few muttered in return before the group continued their discussion. There had been a complete loss of power by the sound of it.

Joe caught the eye of the tall man again and asked him in Spanish.

"What is happening? My truck's broken down, and there's no phone signal."

The man nodded his head vigorously. "*Si senor*, there seems to be some kind of power outage. None of our phones work, and most of our vehicles will not start. My friend has just arrived from Madrid and said there was a rumour of a passenger plane crashing into the sea up the coast. We don't know what is happening!"

At these words, Joe felt a lurch in his stomach. A feeling of dread. Along the street, he saw, for the first time, a handful of stationary vehicles in the middle of the road. A group of people were helping push a Subaru station wagon onto the side of the road. He drifted away from the group and walked down the street, looking into a dark café where a few customers were also in animated discussion, gesticulating at their mobile phones. A young woman behind the counter gestured to him.

"There's no electrical power here, but our cooker runs on a gas bottle, so we can give you something."

"Thank you. Do you have a phone? A landline, I mean," Joe asked as he went to find a seat in the café.

The girl jabbed a thumb over her shoulder towards the back room.

"There is a dial tone, but it doesn't work," she said with a shrug.

"Do you mind if I look?"

The girl waved her hand. "Go ahead."

Joe walked into the café, nodding at a few of the elderly men who simply regarded him suspiciously. Guided by the girl, he went around the back, where he saw an older man leaning over a large cooking pot sitting on a gas ring connected to a propane bottle, stirring the pot's contents and mumbling to himself.

"Just here." The girl pointed to the phone in the hallway. "Do you want a tortilla? No coffee until the power's back, though," she said, pointing to a Keurig coffee maker.

Joe smiled at her. "A tortilla would be great. And I guess just some water then."

He picked up the phone, but if there had indeed been a dial tone, it was gone now. He drummed down the connectors a few times. Still nothing.

This was a major outage, but something gnarled inside him. The loss of power to the electrical grid and phone lines seemed to follow exactly what he had read about Electromagnetic Pulses.

Joe returned to the café, shrugged at the girl and sat down, placing his backpack under the table. He rummaged around, brought out his laptop, and fired it up. There was still battery charge. He clicked on the Internet Access icon to check if there were any Wi-Fi networks available at all, but his settings were blank.

Of course, without power, there wouldn't be, but Joe felt compelled to make sure. With no phone signals, connecting to a hotspot wasn't an option either.

Joe put away his laptop as the girl brought him the omelette and water, and he focused on eating his food, but his dark thoughts soon returned. He needed to get back to the base and fast.

Despite telling himself that it might just be a power outage, one maybe on a national level, and that things would still get back to normal for the country, deep down, he felt this was it. They had flicked the off switch to cause chaos, hunger and death. That would be the next phase. Now, it seemed obvious. All the signs had been there.

The massive drill that was Operation Hallows was in effect as the mask for the more sinister and real event: Pale Horse.

Chapter 7

Joe hurried back to the cache and, following previous precautions, opened it up again. This time, he retrieved a Walther P99 semi-automatic pistol along with half a dozen magazines and a box of 9mm shells, a folded map of South Spain that had been tucked into one of the crates and an orienteering compass. He then went through his backpack, discarding anything that wasn't deemed essential, then repacked with as many MRE dry meals and snacks as possible.

He locked the trapdoor, kicking leaf litter and debris fallen from the trees until it was well-hidden, and then headed back to the truck.

He spread out the map on the hood of the truck, orientating it to the compass points, and then studied it. To get home on foot would be an awkward route if he wanted to avoid Granada. It would take at least a few days, and that was assuming he had few stops or distractions. He checked his watch. It was near mid-morning. Time to get going.

As he trekked back down the hill, he noticed how cold it felt, especially for this part of the world. If there was going to be some freak weather or storms ahead, Joe was ill-prepared for that. He had a light combat jacket over a zip-up hoodie.

He wondered if this power outage event was local or if the problem had reached other parts of Europe. If it had taken down the grid en masse, how would Zoe do in London?

If this dragged on, large cities would be the worst place to be. He knew full well that people turn on each other, even during the best of times. So, with the threat of food becoming scarce, it would be a lot worse. England's inhabitants weren't exactly prepped to survive without takeout delivery on hand. Nowhere in the industrialised world was for that matter. If this carried on, Joe thought grimly, people would die in droves.

He walked back through the town where he had been earlier. The locals were still milling around the square in deep discussion. A couple of older men were sitting at a table outside the café, having taken to playing checkers. Others glanced at Joe curiously as he passed them by, but it didn't take long, and the town buildings soon thinned out, and Joe was on the open road. In the distance, the patch quilt of wheat fields and olive groves of Andalusia. Their usual vibrant colours now muted in the grip of an uncommonly cold winter.

Joe kept to the road, mostly seeing very few people or anything of interest until a cluster of abandoned cars, their drivers nowhere to be seen.

He approached the first car, a Ford Focus, and peered through the windows and tried the doors, which were locked. There was nothing to see inside, and examination of the other cars yielded the same result. Joe moved on and came to a path that led up the grassy hill that bordered the road but headed generally in the same direction.

Joe made good progress over the dry terrain, covering 7-8

miles before he stopped for a break and something to eat. He settled on a mound of smooth rock and chewed on a piece of bread as he stared across the landscape around him. Ahead lay a valley with clusters of trees and, in the distance, a couple of houses set deep in the lines of the terrain.

A distant yet distinct sound of a gunshot echoed through the air, and it shook Joe back into the present. He stopped chewing and looked around. It was hard to tell where it had come from, but probably over the hills somewhere.

Joe packed up and headed on, checking the pistol inside his jacket for reassurance. The coastal road was still visible from his vantage point, and Joe spotted numerous abandoned cars. Then, the first signs of life, a small group of people. Men, women, and a few kids spread out and walked along the road in silence. Joe crouched down and watched them pass. The adults looked tired and worried; however, the kids seemed oblivious to the situation, revelling in a day not at school. A few of them carried plastic bags or pulled little carts laden with supplies. None of them seemed prepared for a long hike. Joe sat still. There was no need to engage with them. What help could he offer them? *Keep moving, Joe*, he told himself. *You're on a mission here, and you cannot fail.*

Joe continued walking, following the path that snaked further inland until he eventually came to a junction with another, larger road with what looked like a few homesteads and industrial sites scattered in the distance. He headed towards the nearest building, a tall hay shed on what appeared to be a farm. As he approached, he strained his ears for any sounds of life. Nothing that he could hear. There was a driveway into a large yard just before the house. A couple of cars were parked in front of it.

Joe wondered if he should go in and see if anyone was around, or pick up extra supplies, but decided against it. He should be good until he got back home. Again, he reminded himself to just stop wasting time. Joe continued along the empty road, past an abandoned industrial metal building, then found a spot to rest for five minutes.

He was crouched on one knee, rummaging through his backpack for that protein bar he knew he had placed there when the slightest of noises spiked his senses.

Before he could act, he heard a threatening voice behind him.

"*No se mueva.*"

Joe froze as he felt the threat of the barrel of a rifle pressing hard against his back.

Chapter 8

Hugo Reese swung open the door to the large meeting room and was met with the babble of a dozen or more conversations from concerned voices. Gianna followed him in, clutching a notepad as they both waded through the crowd, some sitting around a large central table while others stood leaning against the walls. A few of the gathered people stopped talking and stepped aside to let them through, eyes following them every step of the way to the front of the room. Here, there was a small desk and projector facing a large whiteboard, and Hugo and Gianna stopped, turning to face the assembled throng.

As the babbling conversations ran on unabated despite his obvious waiting to address them all, Hugo placed two fingers in his mouth and let loose an ear-piercingly loud whistle. The talking instantly stopped, and every eye turned to face him.

For a moment, he didn't speak as he scanned the worried faces staring at him.

The power had been down in their location for the whole day. Not only that, but some of their vehicles also stopped working, along with a total loss of mobile phone and internet services.

"Alright, amigos. So, this is what we know: we got a major disruption to our power grid and comms. But there's plenty we don't know, so no point jumping to any conclusions." His authoritative tone drew a few nods from the crowd.

"The reason we're all here, in this hive, is because we have been preparing for something like this. As you already know, all our own power is down, but we have our backups set to go?" Hugo looked at Gianna, who nodded.

"Yep. However, not all of our generators are working properly. We have people on it," she said curtly. The expression etched on her features suggested it had been a stressful day.

"There's no power in any of the neighbouring areas from what we can see," a voice from the audience volunteered."

"What about those reports of blackouts out west as well?" Someone said, "Less than an hour later, everything went to shit here."

"Yeah, there were reports of total blackouts. All electric, internet, comms, all gone," another woman said with alarm. "Could be an EMP."

"I heard those reports," Hugo replied, holding up a hand, "If that's the case and if the whole of the country is down, then we need to make our next few moves carefully," he said.

"Damn right!" Marty Faulkner's tall frame bristled among the faces. "We need to arm up and start consolidating because shit is gonna go south real quick. We need to take control of some of those farms down towards Mount Crest and Cold Springs."

"We ain't doin' nothing until our own situation here is crystal clear, okay!" Hugo said evenly, cutting off Marty. "Let me go through what we need to do, alright?" Hugo scanned the eyes in the crowd before resting them back at Marty with a glare.

"We been preparing for something like this for some time, whatever the fuck 'this' is," he added. "As a community, we're self-sufficient, we've got food growing, we've got some weapons. So, we've got nothing to fear. Once we've assessed the whole situ, to do that, we'll get some more scout teams further out."

"What about comms?" someone else asked.

Hugo turned to Gianna, who cleared her throat before speaking.

"I've been getting some of the HF radios out of the Faraday cages. The circuits in the one we had left out and set up were fried, which does indicate we were hit with an EMP, as someone has already said. One seems to be working, but even then, anyone else in the area would also need working equipment for us to communicate with, obviously."

"I haven't even got round to looking at the Quantum tech equipment yet," Hugo said, referring to what Rhodes had sent over for longer-range comms. "I'm kind of busy, but Hodge is going to help. Right, Hodge?"

Hodge Balfour nodded, and a grin spread across his craggy features.

"Of course. I'll do what I can." His grin faded. "If Billy was still with us, well, we'd be golden, but yeah—no problem, let's take a look."

There was a moment's hush at the mention of their comrade who had been killed in the operation in Alaska.

"What about vehicles?" Marty asked.

"Well, nothing much worked so far with our newer ones," Hugo replied, then turning his head to one side, he called, "Derek, can you take another look. See if there's anything

61

working? See what you can do?" Hugo gestured to a small, skinny Black guy leaning against one of the walls.

"Already on it," Derek replied. "Some start, some don't. The older ones seem okay."

"So, it *is* an EMP then," Marty said emphatically, nodding his head. "Gotta be!"

Hugo focused back on the main crowd. "Alright, Derek. Keep doin' what you're doin', and I'll swing by."

"Okay, back to work. We meet again at 0800 hours tomorrow and see where we're at," Hugo said, raising his voice to the assembly.

The murmur of voices began, and the crowd began to disperse. Hugo turned to Gianna.

"Let's go check the perimeter and see where we're at with the power and transport."

They began to leave, along with the rest of the community, when Marty beelined for Hugo.

"I gotta speak to you," Marty said, his voice low and demanding.

Hugo didn't hide his look of disdain at the forthcoming conversation, then turned to Gianna.

"I'll be out in a minute, G," he said before turning back to Marty.

Gianna glanced at both two men, then nodded and headed out with the others.

When the large space had emptied. Hugo put his hands on his hips and tilted his head slightly.

"What is it, Marty?"

"This crap that's goin' down around us. It's an EMP, there's no doubt. So, either it's a prelude to some bigger attack, or something else, eh? Either way, it is what it is. And things are gonna go south pretty quick."

"I know that, Marty. Ya think it's gonna help if I panic everyone? We need to establish an accurate Sitrep, assess what we got, what we haven't."

"We need to grab some other farms, supplies, by force if necessary and lay a bigger perimeter around," Marty said insistently.

"Hey, Marty. Last time I looked, I was in charge." Hugo tapped a forefinger on his own chest, staring up at the looming older ex-military man with his dark eyes. "I agree we need to act, but there is no need to rush and make piss-poor decisions. We have enough resources here to last and remain self-sufficient. We don't need the extra space or equipment right now. Once we've figured out the extent of the damage from the EMP, we can make our move."

"Yeah, well." Marty seemed to scowl at the statement of the obvious as if it were a reprimand. He turned away, his eyes focusing on the windows and one of the courtyards beyond. "I think we need to get out there and find out what's going on at least."

Hugo's eyes narrowed slightly.

"Yeah, we will. But we'll do it when I give the order and not before," he said low and sternly.

"Now, I got shit to do, as do you. Dismissed."

***

Hugo and Gianna didn't talk as they left the main sprawl of houses that made up the communities' main island of living quarters and headed to the gate. The bush road that led out through the woods from the seclusion of their hideaway was deathly quiet, apart from the long 'peeee-uur' sound of a buzzard call. A steady wind blew, bringing with it the sweet smell of late autumn.

They continued strolling around the perimeter fencing that bordered some of their property.

"Marty's getting antsy," Hugo said, breaking their silence. "He wants to break out and grab some territory."

Gianna couldn't help but snort with derision. "Yeah, I got that impression. But even so, good freaking grief!"

"We gotta keep an eye on him. He's a potential loose cannon."

"Everyone's spooked, I guess." Gianna responded, "But yeah, we'll keep an eye on him. Maybe he's better out of the way. Send him on a recon mission. We probably could do with some intel on what's going on out there."

Hugo thought for a moment, saying, "Yeah, I was gonna do that. Just need to see where we're at. Let's go and see what Derek's saying about the transport, then we can check out the power and water situation."

The garage was more like a shack, an old hay barn that could house at least six vehicles. Derek pretty much lived there, tinkering around with engines and getting covered in oil. It was his favourite thing. Ever since he was a kid, Derek would spend his time taking apart bicycles and their gears and getting to know how they worked. His mom would constantly give him an earful about all the bike parts lying around the yard outside their kitchen.

His father was an auto mechanic, and Derek would spend every single Saturday hanging out at his garage, eagerly learning from his dad. The smell of motor oil lingered in the air as he was patiently guided through the intricate workings of various motor engines. Piece by piece, they disassembled and examined the mechanical marvel, each component revealing its purpose and importance. As they worked side by side, Derek absorbed every lesson, not only about the nuts and bolts but also about the need for patience and developing problem-solving strategies.

When his feet reached the gas pedals, Derek was cranking through the gears of his old man's Datsun around the streets of Louisville and took to it as naturally as a duck to water. He inherited the ageing automobile when his dad passed away, and by that time, he knew it inside out.

Technology moved forward, of course. The newer electric cars slowly took over as government mandates shoehorned the public to give up their gas guzzlers. It was a never-ending learning curve into the world of vehicle computers and the power electric. But for Derek, that was a challenge well worth rising to.

Now, Derek looked around at the Ford Econoline minibus and the old Audi 5000 station wagon. Those gas guzzlers were the only cars that still worked, from what Derek could see. All the newer ones were kaput.

"Hey, how's it going?" Hugo said as he and Gianna entered the shed.

Derek pulled his gaze away from the vehicles.

"Hey, guys. It's like I said. The older ones, those two"—Derek gestured at the two vehicles—"they crank up, no problem. The newer mothers, they're dead—electronics all fried."

Both Hugo and Gianna nodded as they all looked over the cars. "Alright, what gas do we have?"

Derek sucked in a wisp of air between his teeth. "Well, the

65

Ford is half full, and we have about ten jerry cans of fuel. Twenty litres each, that's just over five gallons each, so do the math."

Hugo squinted at Derek. "Five gallons per can, so—"

"Fifty gallons all told," Gianna cut in. Derek smiled. "Plus, what's in the cars," she added.

"And at an average twenty-five miles per gallon, that gives us 'bout a 1200-mile radius of ride time," Derek responded.

Hugo let out a short laugh. "Glad someone's good with the numbers. So, will they run?"

"Yep. Well, they started up, but I need to give 'em a full check over. We got plenty of spare parts for 'em, anyway," Derek said, looking at the two older vehicles with unashamed affection.

"Do we know the state of the rotator and emergency pump for the well?" Hugo asked.

Derek cleaned his hands with an old rag. "Not yet, next on the list."

"Okay, we'll need a list of anything broken and what parts we need. We better check the solar panels."

"We need to check everything. Our lives might depend on it," Gianna said.

Just then, she noticed Marty standing in the garage doorway with a slight smirk on his face.

"Hello, Marty," she said slowly.

Chapter 9

Tennessee, US
One hour earlier

Marty drained the last gulp of coffee and, still feeling vexed at his conversation with Hugo, slammed the tin mug onto the trestle table. Josh was sitting opposite him, still fixated on searching for a signal on his mobile phone, as if doing so would magically re-activate the network.

"Ain't gonna work," Marty grunted. "Whole system will be fried. Like I said in that meeting."

Josh tossed his phone onto the table with a clunk.

"Yeah, I know. Just..." his voice trailed off.

"So, as soon as we get a look at the map, we're gonna load up and go recon. I don't give a damn what Hugo says," Marty said, growling resentment in his voice.

Marty leaned forward towards his compatriot, resting his elbows on his knees. "You know something, Josh? I could never understand why the hell Joe chose Hugo over me to lead the hive. A dago hood, for fuck's sake. Over me, us, with the military experience, our time together in the fuckin' Ranger Battalion?"

Josh nodded in agreement. "Yeah, it never made sense to me

either. Maybe he just don't trust you."

"Who, Joe? He ain't here. He's on the other side of the Atlantic in sunny freakin' Spain. Won't be seeing him for a while, if ever, I'm guessing. After we went into Iran to save his sister's friend, that Haleema, her brothers..." His voice trailed off before he spat out, with concealed bitterness, "And what fucking thanks did we get for that, eh? Jack shit, buddy!"

Marty leaned back and glanced around the hut that served as a temporary barracks. There were fold-up beds arranged in rows and a few shuttered windows. Backpacks lay scattered between them.

Dwayne King, another one of Marty's cliques, walked into the hut waving a paper map in his hand. "Got it!"

Josh stood up and moved their mugs and his phone out of the way as Dwayne spread out the map on the table. Marty leaned over it, exhaling slowly through his nostrils as he studied the inked splattering of roads, highways and terrain of their immediate area.

"Well, let's have a look here. The way I see it, we either check out McMinnville or head north to Crossville. Anything in between is just a few farms and houses, which, if I had my way, we'd be—well, 'liberating stuff'." Marty waved a hand across the map.

"We should also be expanding our field of operation so we can guarantee the hive's got solid supply lines. Then, recruit, swell our numbers and expand again. Things ain't going back to the way it was before. Law and order is gonna disappear in no time, and shit's going to hit the fan big time... and real fast."

Marty stopped short of voicing how he would run things. Having a simplistic view of what should be happening and when using brute force was his preferred option in almost every situation. He'd rule through fear because that shit worked. Any other groups or communities he would force to join or get severely punished. It was the only way he knew how to work it.

"What about Pikeville? It's closer." Dwayne tapped his finger on the lines of the small town.

"Hmm, Crossville's bigger. It'll better reflect what's happening on a wider scale. We should dress in civvies, carry side arms only. Get your bug-out bags ready, and I'll see if we can grab a vehicle."

***

When Marty approached the garage, he heard the voices of Hugo and Gianna talking with Derek.

Bad timing.

He stopped and stood in the doorway without announcing his presence for a few moments. Gianna spotted him. Their eyes met, and they stood there, locked in the moment. The conversation between Derek and Hugo halted as they followed her gaze.

"Hello, Marty?" Hugo said in an emotionless tone.

"How's the motors' looking?" Marty asked, trying to sound casual. "Are any working?" he said, looking them over. "I wanna get outside on this recce."

"You might have to hoof it, *vato*," Hugo said. "As Derek said before, only two work, and we're still testing. We got limited gas to go around." Trying to give his subordinate some acknowledgement for his initiative, he went on, "You go on this one, Marty, if that's what you want. I'll go next if needed."

"Well, how limited is the gas? How much have we got?"

Marty said with a scowl at being denied a vehicle.

Hugo sucked in air between his teeth. "I said it's limited. We don't want to waste it."

"It's a good fifty miles to Crossville!" Marty protested, "You want us away for days on this?"

"Who the hell said anything about Crossville? Pikeville is only four or five hours on foot. You can handle that, can't you, Marty?" Hugo retorted. "I need you to just see what's goin' on over there. Get a feel for the local situ, and see if we can secure some more gas. Then we can plan a bigger trip to Crossville. Should have a shopping list of things we need by then to keep this place running."

Marty stared back at Hugo for a few moments, feeling a flush of anger rise within him. He didn't like the dago's tone.

"Crossville's tiny. Ain't gonna tell us squat. It'll probably be no different than before. D for dead. What's the point."

Hugo let out a long sigh, as if he were trying his best to be patient, which irritated Marty even more.

"Listen, Marty. We don't have a clear idea of what's going on anywhere right now. If you take one of our two working cars out of here to a large city, where most people's vehicles aren't working, you might as well paint a target on your back. I know you want to do your 'divide and conquer' thing, and it may well come to that. But don't you get it? Information is power. We gotta take our time and make better choices, not run headlong into the unknown and cause more problems. Okay, vato?"

Marty just stared back at him.

Hugo continued, "Our set-up here is running fine right now; we can support ourselves comfortably for the foreseeable future. Now I need you to pack light, head to Pikeville and report back. If you can speak to any law types, see what information they have, that would be a bonus. Any questions?"

Marty opened his mouth but then thought better of it. There was no point in arguing with this little prick. Now was the time to act, take advantage of the confusion and make some gains for the hive. There was a major crisis, and here they were, taking baby steps. He could feel his confidence in Hugo as a leader crumble even further. Instead, Marty just clenched his fists and breathed slowly through his nostrils.

"No, sir," he replied flatly.

Then, he cast each of them a steady, deliberate glare, turned on his heels and left the garage.

Back at the barracks, he walked inside and slammed the door behind him. Dwyane and Josh were by their bunks, packing bug-out bags, and both looked up at him.

"No wheels, we're on foot, so we'll check out Pikeville first as it's nearer," Marty said gruffly. "Then we'll circle back via Mount Crest."

"No wheels? It's getting damned cold out there," Dwyane muttered.

"We could do that in a day, leave at dawn. Be back by nightfall for whisky and steaks," Josh said hopefully, adjusting his worn baseball cap.

"No, we're going right now," Marty said firmly. "Need to see what's going on out there. Just pack for the cold."

Less than thirty minutes later, the three figures headed out of the gates and followed the entrance track out and through the dense woods surrounding their location.

As they trekked through the woods, the three men didn't speak, their breath forming misty clouds in front of their faces, their boots crunching on the frosty ground. Their movements were purposeful and disciplined. Each step they took revealed their military precision and training. Each wore medium-sized backpacks and kept handguns hidden inside chest holsters. They navigated the wintry terrain with an instinctive awareness, each covering the blind spots of their patrol, their movements displaying an unspoken bond of trust between them as they traversed the landscape.

After twenty minutes of walking, they finally emerged from the woods and headed along the long road across the endless flat plains of Tennessee, under a cold, harsh sky, towards the small town of Pikeville. After a few miles on the road, they came across an abandoned pickup truck. They examined it briefly before moving on and coming across a few other abandoned vehicles left by their owners in the middle of the road as if they had suddenly stopped running.

"Guess folks are having the same problem we are," Josh said.

No one responded to the obvious statement.

At the first house they came across, a middle-aged couple were outside wheeling an electrical generator from one of their outdoor sheds.

"Hey, good luck with that. Need a hand?" Marty shouted out.

"We're good, thanks," the bulky man responded. "Know how long this blackout's gonna last?"

The three men stopped at the fence that lined the property.

"Could be awhile," Josh offered. "Save ya food if you can."

"Freezer stuff has already started to spoil," the woman said and shrugged.

"Damn, shame."

"Yep."

"Any of you heard any news from the towns?" Marty asked, waving a thumb towards Pikeville.

"Not much. No news, of course. Our truck's stone dead, so can't get anywhere, anyhow." The man stooped down again to lift his generator, indicating he wanted to get on with it.

"Stay lucky," Dwayne said.

"You too."

The group continued walking.

"Keep a note of any properties we pass that might have food storage or other supplies," Marty said when they were out of earshot, his tone low.

"Sure. We're gonna be robbin' 'em or something?" Josh asked, his voice etched with concern.

Marty half snorted through his nose with derision.

"That's not a term I would use, Josh. Let's just say we might get to a stage when we need to carry out 'requisitions' for the good of the hive. I mean, if this shit carries on, as we know it's gonna, we get to that point where our people need supplies to survive. Then what choice will we have?"

Marty looked over at both his accomplices.

"Right, boys?"

They both looked back, both with mild apprehension at this overt suggestion to steal from the local community.

"Yeah, course, Marty," Josh replied.

"Yeah, sure," Dwayne added, pulling his woollen hat down over his ears.

Marty stopped, turning to face both men, his breath visible in the cold air as he spoke.

"Look, guys, the way things are gonna play out, we need to act fast, or we'll die. We know what has just happened is some shady part of the Government has initiated this shitstorm. What we need is an army to fight back, or we'll just get mopped up with the rest of the common folk. I know we have enough

73

supplies on our base to survive and keep the hive going, but where's that going to get us?" He looked each man in the eyes, half waiting for a reply he knew wasn't coming.

"We need a fucking *army,* boys," he said with emphasis, "so we need to start recruiting now. We ain't going to do anything significant with the small militia we got at the moment. People now are going to be looking for answers and help, and we need to step up and start showing them that we are the answer." He paused for a moment before elaborating on his rationale. "If we can get another, say, fifty people from the local area to join us, they are only gonna hang around if our promise of food and providing personal security is backed up. I don't want to just 'survive'. I want us to thrive."

Marty looked from Dwayne to Josh before continuing his stream of thought.

"So yes, if we have to steal supplies or 'commandeer' more farmland so we can build up an army, then we should do it. Fuck Hugo and his pussy ass approach. Now, are you with me in this? Are you ready to step up?"

Both men nodded.

"Will do. Whatever it takes to thrive," Josh said, offering his hand. "Fuck that 'just surviving' crap."

"We've got your back," offered Dwayne also. "Always have done, brother."

The men continued in silence, passing mainly quiet or deserted properties that were set back from the road. After a few hours, the first buildings of Pikeville appeared, with more abandoned cars but very few people in sight.

"Alright," Marty said, low, one hand rising to indicate caution as they began to approach a cluster of buildings. Dwayne and Josh slowed their pace and increased their vigilance.

"Keep the peepers peeled. We need to know what the food and supplies situation is around here."

Dwayne headed to the opposite side, and they continued down past the first building, which was a gas station. A closed sign was strung over a heavy metal chain that blocked the driveway. Along a further ten metres stood a local bank, outside of which a group of people stood arguing with one lone clerk, who was also outside the doors.

Marty glanced over at Dwayne and pointed his finger forward, and the group kept moving. He knew what that was all about without having to go over. All the systems would be down, and no one would be doing any business there today.

On the corner of a crossroads, a small queue of five people was steadily shuffling into a 7-11 store. As Marty approached, he saw a sign reading: 'Cash Only'. Marty joined the back of the queue and jerked a finger at Dwayne and Josh to keep going up the street. A brunette woman in front of Marty turned and looked him up and down.

"From around here?" she asked, her tone filled with suspicion.

Marty wasn't about to give away any details and just nodded. "Sure am." She turned back and folded her arms. As the queue moved forward, those in front came out with bags of shopping, and Marty came inside. A tall man in his fifties leaned his burley arms on the store counter.

"Locals only, fella. Can't have Travellers comin' by hoovering up our last supplies."

Marty held up the palm of his hand. "I'm good. Not here to buy anything. Just want to ask some questions."

"What kind of questions?"

Marty looked around the small store. The shelves had mostly

been emptied, with any fresh food long gone. The vegetable section had a few sorry-looking carrots and potatoes strewn on the bottom of the crates. Only tins and jars remained.

"Gonna get some more deliveries, you think?"

"Listen, fella, as you're not local," the store owner began to say until Marty cut him off.

"I am local. Up the road at Cold Springs," Marty lied.

"Well, never saw you before."

Marty shrugged. "Just want to know if I can feed my kids in the next few weeks, that's all."

The old man's scowl softened slightly at the mention of children.

"Well, there was a delivery due yesterday, but it never turned up, which is no surprise as hardly any vehicles seem to work anymore. Apart from military ones, it seems. Their wheels are fine."

"Oh yeah?"

"Yeah, we saw a small convoy of them pass through here yesterday. Hopefully, they're trying to restore some sort of order. Not that they stopped or nothing."

"Yeah. It's a damned mystery," Marty offered.

"I got backup supplies in storage, just more cans and jars of stuff," the owner volunteered, continuing with, "We'll restock in a few days. Swing by then if you like."

Marty made a mental note of that. Storage supplies were the places to target, not small high street stores.

"Okay. I thank you, sir," he replied.

Marty left and rejoined the other two.

"Food is scarce here. They'll be cleaned out soon enough," he announced to them.

Looking around, he took in a row of various types of stores, including a hardware store; all were shuttered. "We could come back and look at those," he thought out loud, "although I'm not sure if there's anything inside those places."

Further up the road, they came across a tall, wiry-looking man in a cowboy hat leaning against his car that faced out from a mall parking lot, smoking a cigarette. He blew smoke in a wide arc in front of his face before turning his attention to the three men approaching and eyeing them warily.

"Afternoon, folks. Nothing's open today, I'm afraid," he said.

Marty strolled over to him and glanced a look at the shuttered mall behind him.

"Yeah, figured. Don't suppose you know how widespread this power outage thing is?"

"Well, I jus' been in from my place outta town. All power gone from there. My own wheels are fine, but as you can see, it's an old girl." He patted the side of the car as if it was an actual animal. "So, what does that mean—electrical power outage? Only explanation is some kind of—whatta they called?"

Marty shifted his weight but didn't offer any help.

"—electromagnetic pulse thing. You heard of them?" the man volunteered

Marty cast a glance at Josh, then smiled at the guy.

"No, not heard of those. Probably just a big electrical outage that took down all the power lines or something. They'll get it all up and running pretty soon, I'm sure." Marty moved a few steps to his right and gestured to the vehicle the man was still leaning against.

"Say, how much for a ride to Crossville?"

The wiry man sucked in air through his teeth.

"Crossville? Well, I don't wanna waste my gas, seeing as the gas stations are all closed. Well, all the ones here, anyhow."

"Ah, I'll make it worth your while, fella." Marty pulled out his wallet and flipped out a couple of hundred-dollar bills. He held it up to the man with a raised eyebrow. "You can get yourself a lot of gas when they're open again. Get a lot of other supplies, too, while stocks last."

The man stared at the money and nodded.

"Well, that's a compelling proposal you're giving me there, but I—"

"Tell you what, maybe I can sweeten the deal." With that comment, Marty swung his backpack off his shoulder and unzipped the top flap. Marty, just for a few moments, considered pulling out his pistol and just taking the damned car. Maybe it would come to that soon enough, but not yet, he decided. Not yet.

He fished out a can of Coors Lite and held it up before him with a grin.

"Your lucky day. I was savin' this."

The man chortled deep in his chest. "Thought you were gonna offer me a nice hunk of gold. But the beer's just fine right now. Alright, you win. Let's get going, though. I'm freezing my balls off."

He flicked his cigarette butt onto the ground and headed for the driver's door.

"I'm Ethan, Ethan Wells."

"Glad to meet ya, Ethan."

Ten minutes later, they were headed along Highway 127, and Ethan kept his speed well under the speed limit. He had to slow down frequently to negotiate around numerous stalled modern vehicles scattered all over the road; their drivers and passengers long gone.

From the back seat, Josh pointed ahead to the skyline.

"What's that? Smoke?"

"Yeah, looks like it," Ethan agreed. "Over in that field."

As their car got closer, it became apparent this was a helicopter that had crashed. It was a black husk; the fire had mainly burned out, but the smouldering smoke that they had seen still lingered. A few cows loitered close by, curious by the spectacle that had obviously crashed on their turf. Ethan pulled the vehicle over to the fencing that bordered the field and switched off the engine.

"Let's check it out."

They all exited the vehicle and climbed the fence before walking in a line towards the helicopter. As they got closer, the distinct smell of burning plastic, an acrid sharp smell, assailed their senses with its harsh, chemical odour. The main cockpit of what looked like the remains of a standard military Bell 407 was on its side, surrounded by an arc of blackened ground. One side of the propeller was bent in half and buried into the ground. Debrie lay scattered across the field.

The cows gathered together and watched the four figures approach.

"Someone forgot their cattle anyways," Josh said, looking at the animals.

They got up as close as they could and walked around the twisted and charred metal skeleton.

"There!" Ethan pointed at the charred corpse, still strapped into the pilot seat. The front window had been blown out, and they were able to get within a few feet of the body.

Marty narrowed his eyes and studied the dead body. "Impossible to identify by sight. But long gone, anyways."

79

"Yeah, there's nothing much we can do here."

Marty circled the helicopter just to check if there was anything to salvage but concluded it was just one big crash site with little to offer.

"Come on, we're wasting time," he said, and they headed back to the car.

Chapter 10

Tennessee, US
Day 2

Just a mile before Crossville, Ethan pulled over again, this time next to a small gas station that looked closed and locked up.

Ethan looked over at Marty in the front seat. "I know these folks, and they might have a jerry can or two of gas. I'm gonna need 'em. Wait here." Ethan took the keys and walked over to the small store, took a look inside, and then headed around the rear of the building.

"Take note, boys," Marty said, turning his head.

"Say, are we gonna let this fella just drop us in Crossville. Don't fancy the hike back much," Josh said.

"Let's see if he comes back with gas first. If he does, then I'd say we're obliged to 'borrow' his wheels."

Ten minutes later, Ethan headed back towards the car with a smile on his face, carrying a large jerry can and plastic pipe.

As the vehicle entered Crossville, there were familiar scenes of queues outside stores, 'cash only' signs, and a general air of desperation that was tangible. They drove past the lines of people queuing up outside the few stores that were open and continued up the main street.

"Okay, fellas, I'll drop you here," said Ethan, then suddenly blurted out, "Hey, that's the first time I've seen cops." Just ahead, a group of police officers were milling around by the side of the road.

Marty cast a quick glance back to Josh and Dwayne. He ran through the options in his head. Chances were they were going to ask some questions, name, address, IDs. So, was he going to lie? They did have a cover story, and legends for their IDs that had been ready-made for this kind of situation.

On seeing the car, two officers came onto the road and began to flag them down.

Ethan stopped, and one of the police officers bent down to take a good look at the driver and Marty. And the four men in his car. Didn't look great.

"Good day, sir," the officer said to Ethan and then to them all. "Would you all mind stepping out of the vehicle?"

"Something wrong, Officer?" Marty asked.

The cop ignored him and took a step back, resting a hand on his belt close to his sidearm and repeated, "Just exit the vehicle, please." This time, there was steel behind his words.

The other cops had stopped talking and spread out, walking around the car, checking it out. All four men slowly opened the doors and got out.

"What are you doing in Crossville?" the officer asked anyone who may answer.

"Just dropping these folks off," Ethan offered quickly. "I'm from outside Pikeville," he added.

"And you?" The cop looked at Marty, who kept his expression unreadable.

"We're simply looking for food. Pikeville was cleaned out, and we were hoping Crossville had more to offer."

"Not really. There'll be shortages everywhere," the cop said.

As they spoke, another police officer walked over towards them from one of the stores where the queues were and was holding a plastic bag containing what looked like food.

Clearly keeping himself ahead of the game? Marty thought.

This one was staring at Ethan as he walked towards them, then looked around at the faces.

"Well, well. Hello folks. Ethan. How ya doing?"

"Hi, Sheriff," Ethan responded with a nod. "I'm good."

At the sound of this pleasant exchange, the tension in the other officers relaxed their body language.

The sheriff turned his attention to Marty and his accomplices.

"Friends of yours?" he asked, gesturing at Marty, Josh and Dwayne

"We were lucky to get a ride," Marty responded. "We're from outside Pikesville. Just looking for some extra food for our kids."

The sheriff nodded, apparently satisfied, then cast his eyes over the vehicle. "Your old car's still going, then, Ethan?"

"Yeah, seems to be at the moment. I'm hoping it'll stay that way, too," Ethan replied.

The other cops seemingly now lost all interest in them and began to talk amongst themselves. The sheriff moved closer to Marty and Ethan.

"So, you boys might be able to help me out?" he said in a lowered tone.

"Sure, Sheriff. What do you want to know?"

He pulled out a flat leather pouch from the rear of the nearest police car and fished around inside before pulling out a paper report and taking a look at it.

83

"This lot got faxed through from the powers on high before the power went," he muttered. "He was reported to be near Pikesville or Crossville."

Then, he took out a photo and held it up for each man in turn.

"Seen this fella?" he asked them all.

A mugshot of Hugo Reese stared back at them.

Ethan shook his head. "No, don't think so, Sheriff."

Marty managed to keep his expression impassive.

"Nope," he said without hesitation, resisting the urge to side-glance at the others.

Dwayne and Josh followed his lead, shaking their heads.

"Local criminal?" Marty asked.

"Can't discuss it. But he's dangerous and should not be approached. I doubt you fellas have any kind of radio comms still working? Lotta CERTs are having problems."

Marty nodded. The sheriff was referring to Community Emergency Response Teams, who kept in communication via radio.

"A lotta radios are fried, of course, unless you happen to be super organised and tucked 'em into a Faraday, huh fellas?" the sheriff said as he eyed Marty, Josh and Dwayne each in turn.

Marty shrugged. "I have friends who may have some comms up but haven't seen them since this shit storm started."

The sheriff gave this response some thought and seemed to accept it at face value.

"Okay, then. Well, I'd much appreciate the word if you see this guy."

"Sure, Sheriff," Marty replied. "We can bear that in mind."

The sheriff took out his notepad, leaned it on the low wall they were congregated by, and began writing. He tore off the sheet and handed copies to Marty and another to Ethan.

"If you can get your hands on a working radio, you can use the Sheriff Channel, Channel 7 on VHF. I'm Sheriff O'Leary, just so you know who you're talking to, but just holler for the Sheriff's Office. Do you have an assigned call sign so I know who's calling?"

Marty hesitated for a moment. "Well, I don't get on the radio much nowadays, but long ago, when I did, I used M7ART."

The sheriff took a note of that in his pad. "Great. Spread the word, if you will," he said.

***

Tennessee, US
Day 4

"So, the local food stores we saw were already running empty, but cash is still good. Not for much longer, I'd imagine," Marty confirmed, crossing his arms. He sat opposite Hugo, who was behind a desk in one of the old portacabins that had become a makeshift office, writing down the occasional word on a notepad.

Because of the cops, Ethan had taken off back to Pikeville, and Marty's brief thoughts of taking those wheels for himself had to be shelved. He and the others had actually ended up having to hoof it back.

"What else?" Hugo asked.

"We saw a downed chopper. Looked like it had just dropped

out of the sky, all burned up. Dead pilot, toasted. That was outside Crossville, so I guess there's an airfield somewhere."

"And did you see any cops or army guys?" Hugo pressed.

"Nope," Marty lied.

"So, it kind of confirms what we already know," Hugo said with a sigh. He tossed down his pencil onto the desk, and it rolled gently up against Marty's mug.

"Yep. We're in for the long haul," Marty affirmed.

Then Marty leaned forward onto the desk, his tone more urgent. "We need to be ready, Hugo. We have an opportunity while everyone is still trying to figure out what the fuck is going on and expand our defence lines."

Hugo winced, then shook his head.

"Don't wanna go over this again, Marty. We need to consolidate, prepare to take the fight to the enemy in Colorado. That's the strategic plan agreed with Joe outlined before this all went down.

"Colorado? That plan's still on the table? How're we all going get over there with no transport? Fucking horses?" Marty felt his eyes bulging, his blood rising again.

"Yeah, maybe we'll get some fucking horses. Listen, we ain't going next week"—Hugo waved a hand dismissively—"we got time to prepare. Yeah, it's a long journey—twenty days on foot, if it comes to that, but we got wheels, which is why we need to keep the working vehicles and all the fuel."

Marty shook his head. He wasn't gonna follow this prick to save that Iranian bitch, or whatever the hell he was planning. Because that's what this was all about. Joe had sent Haleema to rot in some underground military base, and they were all supposed to ride in like the cavalry. Probably all get killed doing it.

Well, not on his watch, he thought.

"Alright, *vato*," Marty said, slapping his hands on his thighs and standing up. He left the portacabin and headed back to the barracks. Now, all he had to do was bide his time until Hugo left. It was just a case of making sure the bastard actually went out there, not before finding out exactly where he was going to go.

It was time to make his move.

Chapter 11

Something woke Zoe up, but she was unsure what it was at first. Then, she heard a distant shout echoing from a few streets away. Through the window, Zoe peeked out but could see very little. Dark clouds shaded the even blacker city. Only a glimpse of moonlight that edged through the clouds, glittering off the Quay water, was clearly visible. In one of the nearby buildings, a solitary dim light flickered in one of the windows.

The city was dead.

From somewhere across the river came a series of sharp cracks, like pistol shots.

Not quite dead.

More shouts, but these were different voices, but again, from a few streets away. Zoe returned to her bed, glad of the warm duvet around her, snuggling deep within it.

Whatever was going on out there was happening, and there was not much she could do about it. The noise faded, and sleep overtook her.

When morning finally came, Zoe dressed in fresh clothes, a zip-up sweater, combat trousers, and then went through her chest of drawers for underwear, t-shirts and thick socks. She had an ominous feeling that when she left, she might not be home for a while. She found a money belt with a hidden zip compartment that she had used on a travel trip with Ed once. It would be useful to hide cash. She had always kept a few hundred pounds in cash for emergencies and fished that out from the hiding place at the back of her wardrobe. Zoe then filled the belt while keeping some cash out in her trouser pockets for easier access.

She laid out on the table all the items she had gathered so far. A few warm clothes, packets of dried soups, crackers and biscuits she had brought from the previous apartment. Then she turned her attention to what she had here at her own place and added cereal bars from the cupboard, her water bottle. She found an old camping flashlight with extra batteries and a multi-function pocket knife.

Recalling her need for medication, she stacked up all her meds, taking the foil packs out of the boxes and stored them in a ziplock baggie. Then, she retrieved an old London A-Z map book from the bookshelf, just in case she found herself in an unfamiliar part of town.

Finding a larger rucksack, she started packing the items away. It wasn't exactly a great 'bug-out bag' as Joe had called it, just a very basic version of one, but it would have to do.

As she studied a route to the hospital, she heard a distant breaking of glass. She felt her heart jump and went to the windows, but she couldn't see anything. It sounded like it was a few streets away, but she wasn't sure.

Panic started to well up inside her. The walls felt like they were closing in, and Zoe felt her throat tighten. She rested one hand on the wall, steadying herself and took short gasps of air. She unpacked her anti-anxiety meds and took one before pacing the living room.

The outside world was becoming a more and more scary place for her. She pushed back the idea of leaving straight away. Perhaps she should wait? Maybe in a day, the police or army would have some sort of control over the city. Or maybe things would have deteriorated further? Indecision gnawed at her.

No, she'd stay a while. Perhaps the power would come back.

For the rest of the day, Zoe obsessed over what to take, going back over the items in her bag. To calm herself down, she did some simple exercises to get the blood flowing and keep warm.

Then, the day drew to an end, and darkness enclosed the city once again. But still, the power did not return.

***

London
Day 3

As the morning light appeared afresh, Zoe awoke with a new determination to leave her apartment. The uncertainty of the previous day washed away. She got dressed, tied her blonde hair back into a ponytail, tucked it through a baseball cap, pulled on her old trekking boots, lacing them up tightly and finally pulled on a jacket. Ready to face the world, she looked around the gloomy apartment one last time and the memories that it held. This was one chapter of her life; she could remember when she had first bought it along with the housewarming party that week and the killer hangover that followed. Her first night with Ed here, their first fight. Was this the last time she would see this? Was this the beginning of a new era? Taking a deep breath, she then shut the door behind her and said a final goodbye to that part of her life.

Zoe's plan was to see John and go most of the way on the south side of the city, then cross at Westminster. She headed to Southwark Park, skirting the use of the main roads for a few miles. A few of the shops she passed had been damaged. Debris lay scattered across the pavements and roads. On every street, stationary and mostly looted cars lay abandoned, sometimes completely blocking up the roads, their drivers long since gone.

On Druid Street, she passed the endless brick railway arches that housed garages, studios and workshops. A few figures stood around, talking amongst themselves. They looked to be just people who worked in the area, business owners who were just trying to make the most of an unprecedented situation.

As she walked by them, she overheard snippets of conversation, mainly about how to protect their business property from widespread vandalism and theft.

Zoe now stuck to the main roads as much as possible and continued parallel to the river, passing Tower Bridge and London Bridge but not crossing them. Looking down towards them, Zoe could see the odd person moving amongst dead cars and other vehicles, but overall, it was eerily quiet.

She decided to continue on towards Waterloo, and she was partly intrigued about what was happening around the Westminster area. This, after all, was the seat of government. What were they doing to deal with the crisis?

She came across a food shop with a 'cash only' sign outside. She was glad she had brought cash, correctly guessing that some might be accepting it and trying to keep the wheels of commerce rolling. Zoe bought a couple of bottles of water, a few packs of sandwiches and some energy bars, all at an exorbitant cost.

At the end of a narrow street, she came to the historic borough market with its old ornate buildings that bustled with people. Entrepreneurial vendors had opened up as usual, but all were now taking cash only. Zoe walked under the skeletal green roof covering the market and used some more of her cash to buy fresh fruit.

Heading back onto the main road, Zoe continued east towards Waterloo. To her right, at Blackfriars Bridge, a crowd of ten or so people crossed, walking away from her. In the distance, she heard a loudspeaker coming from somewhere on the northern side but couldn't make out their words.

Zoe drifted towards the embankment where a harsh wind whipped down from the Thames, seemingly cutting right through her.

Further along, groups of people were drifting around aimlessly. A group of people gathered around, warming themselves with a flaming oil drum. One of the guys picked up a guitar and began strumming a tune and singing in a clear effort to lift up everyone's spirits.

A few people asked her for money or food, but she shook her head and continued on.

As she approached the bridge on the embankment, she could hear a distant hum like a crowd shouting, but then the wind took it away. As she crossed the bridge, Big Ben and the Houses of Parliament loomed in front of her. She took a left on the main Embankment Road and headed towards Parliament, walked around the side of the building and was confronted with the sight of armed police and some army personnel guarding the doors and the entrances of the building on Parliament

Square. A large crowd had gathered, Zoe estimated at least a few hundred, and they were chanting and shouting.

On the far side of the square, opposite the chanting crowd, Zoe spied a line of riot police on horses. She approached one of the police officers who was on the perimeter of the square.

"Excuse me, Officer, do you have any information about the power cut and when it might be back on?" The policeman barely looked at her and simply said, "We're advising everybody to stay indoors for the moment, miss. There will be help coming. Please just return to your home, which is what we're going to be telling this crowd shortly. The power will be restored at some point. I've no doubt about that." With that, the officer simply looked away from her, concentrating instead on the crowd in front of him.

The tone and delivery of this response gave Zoe no doubt that it was just a bullshit answer, a generic phrase to tell pissed-off people. Across the square, the police on horseback edged towards the crowd in a line with shields raised. Someone in the crowd threw a bottle, which ricocheted off one of the shields.

"Please return to your homes immediately!" demanded a loud shout from behind the police line.

More people were seeping into Parliament Square from different directions, swelling the crowd almost tenfold and growing all the time. It was a typical unorganised, impromptu, angry protest that looked very much like it was going to take an ugly turn.

The crowd ignored the orders and began to surge as one towards the police. Zoe could predict what was coming next and moved away as fast as she could. There was no time to get embroiled in this shit!

Striding quickly away from the intensifying shouts, cries,

and mounting fury in the air, she hastened her pace, distancing herself from the escalating chaos. The sound of shattering of glass echoed behind her, and then the clamour of the furious crowd gradually faded into a distant hum.

Chapter 12

London

Day 3

Zoe walked around the labyrinth of buildings that made up the hospital grounds. She recycled through her memory the directions she had been given as to where John Rhodes would be located. She recalled that he should be in the Charles Pannett ward within a specific building block named the 'Queen Elizabeth the Queen Mother Building'. Using the signs, she found herself outside the reception to the ward's emergency room, where a group of five people were milling around. Then Zoe spotted they were surrounding a hospital security guard standing in front of the entrance doors.

Not good.

As she drew closer, she heard raised voices. Angry emotions. It seemed that no visitors were being admitted.

Zoe came to a stop in front of the guard, a middle-aged Asian man looking stressed, and caught his eye.

"What's the situation in there?" Zoe asked.

"We're only on generator power at the moment, but not good," he answered, obviously glad to respond to a reasonably asked enquiry.

"I need to know someone is alright. I know that they were brought here, but that's all I know," Zoe said, keeping her tone of voice respectful.

The guard shook his head.

"I'm sorry, no visitors at this time," he said firmly.

"I just need to know my friend is—"

The guard shook his head again, his eyes apologising.

Zoe turned to leave, walking a few steps away as another group arrived. Two of the men began asking the same guard questions. Again, he refused them admittance, too. However, they raised their voices, clearly intending to get in to check on someone. Calmly facing these two men, the security guard stood his ground, clearly used to dealing with the demands of irate loved ones.

As he became distracted, Zoe slipped past, behind his back, through the sliding doors and entered the dimly lit hospital reception. She moved quickly across the foyer, walking purposefully as if she belonged there despite her backpack looking out of place. She saw a nurse with her back towards her, speaking urgently to someone unseen through a side door, complaining about the lack of staff and the power cut in general.

Passing the reception area, Zoe caught sight of a sign for the Charles Pannett ward and turned right towards the elevators, where a yellow and red striped barrier blocked access and a sign reading 'Out of Order'' pinned to it. Not that she would have used them anyway. She ascended the adjacent stairwell to the eighth floor, noticing that some floors lay in unlit darkness. A group of doctors passed her by, giving her no more than curious glances. On reaching the eighth floor, Zoe slowly opened the double doors and peered both ways. Seeing only the sight of a nurse walking away, Zoe then crept in the opposite direction, past a row of private rooms, some located in alcoves off the main thoroughfare. She glanced through the door windows of each one, looking for any sign of John Rhodes. Looking in a larger area with six beds, she scanned the occupants where there was one frail-looking man with white hair, but it wasn't Rhodes. He turned his head and looked at her, a face ashen pale with worry, then he managed a faint smile, which Zoe returned, then moved on.

She shuddered and, for the first time, realised how cold it was inside the building.

The emergency overhead lighting flickered for a moment, then died completely as she reached the far end of the corridor. At the last room she looked in, Zoe immediately recognised John, lying with his eyes closed, hands resting across his stomach. An IV line led to a vein in his arm. He looked so much older than the time she had seen him on a video link only just a few weeks ago.

Zoe quietly opened the door and slipped inside, closing the door behind her.

"John. It's me. Zoe," she whispered as loudly as she could

He didn't move.

"John?" she said again, this time in her normal voice.

Slowly, his eyes flickered to life, opened, and he tilted his head towards her. He broke out into a smile, then suddenly flinched, moving his hand over his stomach.

"Damn it," he blurted. Then, he managed to smile again. "Am I happy to see a friendly face."

Zoe turned around to draw the curtain back along its track so as not to be seen from the hallway and sat down in a visitor's chair next to him. She looked him over, concern etched on her face.

"How're you doing? Tell me what happened," she asked anxiously.

"Ah, it's fine. I'm bearing up." he rasped back. "The pain? It all comes in waves, and, believe it or not, that was the first I have felt for ages." He sat up on the bed, reached for a bottle of water on the side cabinet, and took a hard pull from the plastic bottle.

"Grumbling appendix, nothing to worry about. I think they were considering operating, but then the power went," he said. "I've been in and out of sleep through the pain meds they gave me and lost track of what's been going on. How long has it been down?"

"This is day three. But it's worse than a blackout. Most of the vehicles stopped working. Lots of fires and smoke. No comms, no power," Zoe told him, shocked by what he had said.

John's face dropped. He clearly hadn't realised the extent of the mayhem.

"—and another thing," she continued, "just before it happened, I was in a night café. The TV said there were reports of there being rolling blackouts across the US, then bang, everything went black here."

"That doesn't sound good, so not just local, sounds like—" Rhodes mumbled, his face looking grim.

"What?"

"Well, it's probably an EMP, an Electromagnetic Pulse, wipes out all electrical power, which, considering how much our society relies on it, is not good at all. Nuclear power stations will fail, running water will stop, if not already. It could mean that we're back in the proverbial Stone Age." Pausing to reflect a little more on what Zoe had told him, he concluded, "We thought it was always a possibility they would pull this one out of the box."

"They?" Zoe asked. "Do you mean the cabal is responsible for all this?"

Although Zoe had learned a few things in recent months, it still came as a shock.

"I can't know anything for sure," John began coughing and took another sip of water.

"So what do we do now?" Zoe asked.

"We can't stay here, that's for sure. Things are going to deteriorate very quickly as people seek food, heat, basically just try to survive." John pushed his legs over the side of the bed and sat up.

"Wait, you have appendicitis. You can't just leave," Zoe said, her voice again full of concern.

"It's just a grumbling appendix and has really calmed down a lot. Besides, I overheard that all the operations were cancelled. The backup power won't last much longer, then this place will be the last place we want to be."

"But out there, it will be—is, getting worse too. What is our plan exactly?" Zoe asked.

John stood up and started gathering his clothes. "We planned for events like this for decades. We knew there was always going to be an event like this or similar events that would cause the world to pivot into a worse place. People naively thought that because it hadn't happened before, it could never happen. Well, here we are."

John turned to her and smiled. "We've got communities, or 'hives' here in the UK as well as abroad. There's a place near Addington. We'll head there. Good people, a safe place with food and shelter. It's the best place for us to be at the moment, trust me."

"What about the local authorities? Won't they have an emergency plan to help people?"

John laughed without humour. "Yes, you could say that. As far as I remember, they did stress tests a few years ago in the UK, and it all failed. As a consequence of that, demands were made for an overhaul of both the energy security and backup systems. But even if these had been made, I've a feeling they'd be totally unprepared for such a global event like this." John unfolded his jumper and pulled it over his head.

"The Government's protocol will be to save themselves first, then just maybe herd people into so-called 'humanitarian camps'. But it won't be pretty. They can't possibly save and feed everybody. Not a chance. Without a solid food chain supply and unlimited access to clean water or energy, we're going to be looking at population deaths probably on a massive scale."

Just then, the corridor light came on and ominously flickered briefly before going out, almost in agreement with his words.

"John. I'm not sure about going back through London. It's a long trek. Are you sure you can make it?" Zoe assessed the route to Croydon from memory. The direct way was back through Central London, then back across the river through Battersea, Clapham, Streatham.

"Have to—no other choice," John said, with a hint of despondency. "How long do you think it'll take?"

"Well, assuming we won't be running," Zoe said with a wry smile. "Best part of the day. We should be there by late afternoon, but we'll need to get going right now."

John touched Zoe's arm.

"Zoe, in case anything happens to me, I need you to know

about some things. Now's a good time to tell you. The Singh family: The main contact is Raj Singh, his wife, Binita and his brother, Harish. They're part of our group. Mention my name and the term '*Shadowfox*', and they'll open their doors to you, no problem."

Zoe nodded. "Okay, but nothing is going to happen—"

"I know, just in case. And you have the contact details for Danny and Bel Thorpe in Suffolk?"

"Yeah, Joe gave me that. It's all up here." She tapped the side of her head. Zoe smiled weakly. The feeling of trepidation and fear now had crept back.

Zoe helped John gingerly descend the fire exit stairs. Progress was slow as John couldn't move too quickly, and he winced occasionally, pausing for a breath before waving Zoe on.

"Maybe this wasn't a great idea," Zoe said quietly.

"I'll be fine," John insisted determinedly.

Zoe wasn't so sure. With John's obvious mobility problem, they would be extremely vulnerable to any opportunistic assaults. She wouldn't be able to just run at the first sign of trouble and leave John stranded. As if to confirm her fears, there was a distinct sound of angry shouting from the ground floor.

Just below them, on the next floor, the doors burst open. Two nurses appeared with an elderly male patient in a wheelchair and through the windows, Zoe saw them carrying him down the stairs.

Zoe moved suddenly, as if she was about to offer her help, but John grabbed her arm. She turned to him, annoyed.

"I don't know if they'd let me leave," he whispered.

She nodded, understanding.

They waited until the nurses had gone through a set of doors below.

"Come on," she said.

As they slowly descended the stairs, they were met with an increasing uproar of voices coming from the reception area.

The familiar sounds of angry people clamouring to be heard amidst the chaos. There was the sound of shattering glass, as if a window had been smashed, followed by a scream and then the swell of agitated voices rose again.

Chapter 13

Andalucía, Spain
Day 1

Joe felt the barrel of a rifle press hard against his back. Footsteps. Then, noiselessly, a second assailant appeared in front of him.

"*¿Hablas Español?*" the man in front of him demanded.

"A little," Joe replied in English. He was fluent in Spanish, but why let on?

"Stand up!" the man commanded.

Joe did so, raising his hands, and he felt the gun barrel lift from his back. He assessed the man in front of him.

He was stocky, in his forties, with cropped black hair and a haggard face with tattoos creeping up his neckline. He wore a long coat with simple olive fatigues underneath. Joe's inner senses guessed he was possibly ex-military, but from a long time ago. He could always tell.

Another man appeared and stood alongside. Scandinavian or Nordic-looking, with long blond dreadlocks and a contemptuous sneer on his face, the kind that Joe wanted to punch immediately.

The gunman or woman was still behind him, and he knew he

couldn't move that quickly, so Joe decided to comply for now and watch.

Crop head ordered the Nord to frisk him in Spanish, and he did so, immediately finding Joe's Walther P99 in his chest holster. He tossed it back to whom Joe assumed to be the boss of this trio, who looked over the gun with a wolfish smile.

"Very nice," he said, then looked at Joe from under hooded eyes.

"You a cop?" he suddenly demanded.

Joe snorted with derision but didn't answer.

The Nord grabbed Joe's backpack, took a step back and began to rummage through.

"Just basic food supplies," he pulled out a couple of MRE packs and held them up.

"MRE packs. Where did you get these? Are you ex-military?"

"Found 'em," came Joe's terse reply.

Nord tossed one over to his boss, who scanned the label and then shrugged as if suddenly deciding he couldn't care less.

"Alright, we'll take it all. I'll keep the gun, of course."

"You're leaving me with no food?" Joe asked in exasperation, turning his head to try and gauge who was behind him.

"You look like someone who can figure it out—when you wake up," the boss said, looking over Joe's shoulder and nodding.

Before Joe could react, there was a flicker of movement on his right side, then an explosion of pain hit the side of his head, and the ensuing blackness funnelled him into a vortex of stars.

He stumbled onto his hands and knees, head swirling and felt a hard kick into his torso. He slumped onto the ground, trying to force himself into a foetal position, bracing himself for more attacks, more kicks to the stomach.

A moment passed, but there were no more violent kicks raining into him, just the fading voices of his assailants, carried by a gust of wind as they got further away.

Dazed and groggy, Joe lay still for a few moments, then tried to push himself upright, but his head swam so badly he gave up and just lay still.

By the time he recovered, the daylight had faded, and darkness was drawing in fast. The cold, harsh air seemed to penetrate through his clothes and reach his bones.

Joe reached his hand up to the side of his head. It was tender and wet. He drew his hand back and rubbed the blood between his thumb and forefinger. He felt around the tender bump and winched.

"Bastards could've killed me," he said out loud.

A few minutes later, Joe tried again to rise himself, this time with more success and got to his feet. He looked around and found his bag, emptied apart from one protein bar and a small bottle of water that was mostly empty.

"Fuck you very much," he muttered.

He finished off the water with one long gulp and slung the empty bag onto his back. He needed to find more, otherwise he wouldn't be going anywhere fast.

He decided to go back to the farm he had seen earlier. No other choice now. Joe decided to approach the building straight into the front, walked into the front yard, and briefly checked out the vehicles.

"*Hola?*" he shouted, but only his echo returned from the whitewashed Moroccan-style house.

Cautiously, Joe approached the front door and immediately noticed it was ajar. The wood around the door handle had been smashed as if by a heavy object. Then, as he pushed the door wider, he spotted broken glass shards scattered across the terracotta tiled floor.

Step by careful step, Joe navigated the shards of glass and moved further into the house. The main living area had obviously been ransacked; bookshelves had been overturned, and cabinets with their doors opened wide had been emptied. Through a double doorway, Joe could see the back dining area and caught movement outside the rear window, then the low murmur of voices.

There was the sound of a door opening, then voices speaking in Spanish.

"They took everything," the male voice said to someone unseen. A man in his fifties with grey swept-back hair then appeared in the doorway and froze when he saw Joe.

Joe held up his hands, palms out.

"I mean no harm," he said in Spanish.

The man turned his head and shouted back.

"Anja, go back outside."

The woman, who Joe presumed was his wife or partner, ignored him and came up to the doorway, glaring at Joe.

"What do you want?" he asked Joe firmly. "You want to take our stuff too. Well, we have nothing left to give you."

"You were robbed?" Joe responded as he slowly lowered his hands.

The man ignored his question and asked again, "What do you want?"

"I'm just passing. I was robbed too; I just need some water, but if there's none to spare?"

The man's posture seemed to relax slightly as he assessed Joe.

"Maybe. Go back outside. I'll bring it."

Joe did as he was asked and waited outside the front door. When the man returned, he handed Joe a plastic one-litre bottle.

"That's all I can spare. The running water has stopped."

"Thank you, as long as you can spare it?"

The man nodded, frowning.

"Just take it and be on your way," he said with some finality in his voice

Joe took it, nodding his head appreciatively.

"Tell me about who robbed you. When was it, and could you tell me what they looked like?" he asked.

"It happened about an hour ago. Two men, one with cropped dark hair and a big coat. The other man had blond hair, all matted. And a woman with a rifle. They did this," he said, gesturing at the damage and debris.

Joe studied the man's cracked, weathered skin, his eyes staring back at him like black coals and thought for a moment. Definitely sounded like the same people who had taken his stuff. The gun held at this back must have been the woman.

Joe nodded sympathetically.

"*Muchas gracias*. Keep safe."

Joe headed off down the road, trying to ignore his rumbling stomach. It was getting dark now, and he needed to rest. The assault had disrupted his plans and drained his energy.

Further down the road, a large dark-shaped cattle shed loomed into view, and Joe approached cautiously. It was impossible to make out any details or see what he was walking into, but once inside the shed, he could discern there was a concrete floor covered with straw bordered by empty stalls, along with the distinct smell of cattle, no longer there.

He found a corner of one stall, gathered up as much straw as he could and crawled underneath before drifting into a restless sleep.

Chapter 14

Andalucía, Spain
Day 2

Joe thought he might have grabbed just a few hours' sleep, but he wasn't sure. Through the gaps in the metal, Joe could see the dawn breaking and the countryside around him becoming more defined silhouettes.

He wondered how everyone was getting by at home. How was Javier coping running things? He had trained all of them for situations like this, so there shouldn't be too many problems. They also had the resources to survive, although the infrastructure wasn't perfect. If this outage continued for months, then clearly, the long-term food supply would eventually become a problem, but right now, those inside the hive could bunker down and stay alive. That was the main thing.

They had enough land and tools to grow their food to support themselves, although up until now, growing food had just been a supplement to what could be bought at the local markets. Now, it could well be an absolute necessity to 'grow your own' or go hungry.

His partner, Hanna, was probably worried sick about him.

Just as long as they didn't send out search parties for him.

Joe crawled out of his makeshift bed and, in the increasing light, gathered his things and headed out to the road, continuing towards home.

He came to a crest on the road and looked across an expansive area of waste ground. He could see the top of the circular greenhouses that frequented the Andalusian landscape. Surrounding them were what looked like the tops of trees in an orchard.

Perhaps there were some winter vegetables or fruit, like pomegranates or oranges.

He headed over, crept into the orchard, and smiled at the sight of orange and Membrillo trees. Most of the trees had already been harvested, and their fruit had probably been made into quince paste. He searched around and finally found a few oranges hidden amongst the branches of one tree. He plucked the juicy orange, tearing off the skin so he could take a bite. The taste of the sweet juice was an instant relief to his dry mouth. He savoured it as he scanned the orchard. It overlooked a valley of farmland, with houses and buildings scattered throughout.

Joe walked through the trees to the greenhouses. Perhaps he could get a good batch of tomatoes.

As he approached, the sound of distant banging came from somewhere unseen from the valley side but, nonetheless, close. Joe cautiously moved towards the sound, pausing momentarily to check his surroundings, eventually coming to the edge of the gardens. These were lined by trees and bushes that bordered a drop into a steep valley. The banging sound grew louder as he approached, but also came another sound, the murmur of voices. Then, suddenly, the distinct sound of a child's scream or startled shout.

Keeping himself well-hidden inside the treeline, Joe crept closer and saw a sprawling camp of caravans in an area of wasteland below. There were a couple of large dark green trucks that looked like they had been converted into homes. They also had four horses tied up behind one of the vehicles, their backs covered with blankets.

The banging noise had come from a man working underneath an old army truck, but it had been painted a splatter of blues, greens and whites.

A small group of men and women were sitting around an open wood fire. Some were eating from metal bowls, while a trio of kids ran around the waste ground, laughing and shouting. Another group to the far right of the camp appeared to be sorting through bags of clothes that had been hauled out from the back of another van.

On the far left was another caravan, the longest, with a group of tables and chairs arranged outside covered by a tarpaulin.

Joe lay prone to the ground and watched for a while, taking in the scene. It looked like a Traveller's camp, *one to pass on by*, he thought.

In fact, he had first met Hanna at one of these camps all those years ago.

Where had that been? Somewhere near Seville.

He couldn't quite remember how he had ended up there. He recalled that music had blasted from speakers and beers handed out from ice bins, accompanied by the distinct waft of weed. Then, as the evening had cooled down, a guitar was brought out while the group huddled closer to the fire. One of the Travellers had strummed songs as Joe caught the eye of Hanna more than once across the dancing flames of the bonfire.

And, almost on cue, as the memory of that night crystallised, Joe saw a face he immediately recognised as the door to the longest caravan opened, and a tall, slim figure stepped out along with a large German Shepherd. The man sported a drooping moustache and a long olive coat and boots. A distinctive character who had been the guitar player at that previous party with Hanna. Yeah, that was it.

Joe didn't know his name, but he recognised the face; there was no doubt about that.

Hanna knew this guy or had known him once; he was sure of it. As far as he knew, she'd not been back to the Traveller camps since they had begun their relationship.

Then, as he was considering approaching them, another thought crossed his mind.

Had Hanna been in a relationship with this guy before she and Joe had met? The faint embers of jealousy stoked inside him. She always told him she had only been staying at the camp just a few weeks before meeting Joe. It was after they had both taken a road trip around the coasts of Spain that she moved in with him.

Joe watched the man, with his dog, talk to a woman under the tarpaulin for a moment before he walked over to the group huddled around the fire.

Maybe he should go introduce himself, get some of whatever they were eating and solicit some information. He needed more water, for sure.

Joe got to his feet and began navigating a route down towards the camp.

***

Joe approached them with a confident stride suggestive that he had every right to be where these Travellers had settled. He held his hands aloft as a few of the men stood up and approached him, one young one armed with some kind of bat in his hand.

"*Hola!*" Joe offered, "I'm not looking for any trouble. Just passing by, looking for any spare provisions."

"Can't help you there," one of the men replied.

"Just some food, water, then I'll be gone." Joe scanned the camp. He counted five men and three women, all looking at him. The kids had since disappeared.

The man with the bat, not much more than a skinny teenager, took another step towards Joe.

"Nothing for you here, sorry," he said in a hard tone, his eyes wary and defensive.

Joe assessed the kid. He most certainly could take that bat off him and snap his arm inside a few seconds.

The tall figure with the moustache approached, appraising Joe from under his woollen hat and held his hand up in a restraining manner to the young man with the bat.

"Maybe we can spare something," he said. Joe detected an East Coast American accent.

Joe nodded over to him. "I think I came to one of your parties once. A few years ago."

The man with the moustache looked Joe over, clearly trying to remember, but if he did, he wasn't letting on. He shook his head.

"I don't remember," he said.

"We'll give you some bread, water, and you can be on your way," the man said.

"That's all I ask, thanks," Joe responded gratefully.

The group that had gathered at his approach had now dispersed, although the teenager, while keeping his distance, tracked Joe as he walked further into the camp.

"I'm Carlos," the moustached man said, his tone now more amicable. "So this party, was it here?" he asked.

"I'm Joe. No, it was near Seville."

"Ah, right. Yeah, we were based there a few years ago." He looked at Joe with renewed trust.

"I met a woman called Hanna there," he said. "German woman," Joe added in a nonchalant tone.

Carlos's eyes remained fixed on Joe's for a split second, then he pulled a face that suggested he had no idea.

"What did she look like?"

"Blonde, dreadlocks, thirties?"

The moustached guy only returned a blank expression at that description.

"Lots of women would fit that description, and we partied often. Good place that, shame we had to move on," was the only reply he offered.

"Where's home, Joe?" Carlos asked, gesturing with his hand to an upturned crate set away from the fire.

Joe looked around. The kid still stared at him but then finally looked down at Joe's return gaze.

Carlos shouted over towards one of the caravans that seemed to be the cookhouse.

"Any of that oatmeal left, Leb?" he called.

There was an indistinguishable grunt as a reply, and a few minutes later, a kid walked over with two bowls with plastic spoons in them.

Carlos took them both off him and handed Joe one. Joe thanked him but didn't eat anything until Carlos started eating.

Then he tucked into the warmed oats with large scoops.

"Leb, get us some coffees, will ya'?" Carlos ordered.

The teenager hesitated, then walked back to the kitchen area and came back five minutes later with two metal mugs filled with black liquid.

"Thanks. Joe, black okay with you?"

"No problem."

"So, you're far from home?" Carlos asked.

"A few miles, yeah. My truck broke down. Yours all working?"

"Well, the engine on that one turns—" Carlos waved a hand towards the vehicle Joe had seen someone working on earlier. "But everything else has gone kaput, no power, vehicles, except the old ones—know what happened?"

"Hope it's just a power outage, though I've the feeling it's worse and could be really serious."

"Sure, I understand a power cut, but how come none of the cars work—even my radio?" Carlos asked with genuine concern.

"An explanation might be what they call an 'EMP'—an electromagnetic pulse. They can come from the sun as solar flares, but with the wide scale of what's happened, it's far more likely to be an attack."

"Attack?" Carlos' face showed surprise at hearing that option.

"Yeah." Joe shared earnestly, "Could be by a foreign, or even by our own government." He paused to let the information sink in before continuing. "Could even be a prelude to some kind of nuclear attack. It's just impossible to know right now."

Carlos shot him a concerned look.

"Nuclear?"

"It's a common enough military tactic. Cause chaos on the enemy infrastructure, then hit hard."

"But we're in fucking Spain?" Carlos protested.

"Well, the whole of Europe would be a target." Joe took a couple of big spoons of oatmeal. "I don't think that's gonna happen now, though, so you can relax. It's been a few days. It would have happened by now."

"You think so? How do you know?"

"I studied a lot of military planning stuff. It was kind of a hobby."

Carlos began a low guttural laugh that increased in tempo. He shook his head and pulled off his beanie hat, revealing an afro mop of curly hair, and ran his hand through it.

"Well, that's just great, man." He shook his head in bewilderment at the prospect of what he'd just heard.

"I'm just guessing, really. I don't know shit," Joe conceded as he finished off the last of the oats and put the empty bowl down by his feet.

"And if it continues," Carlos asked, "what 'say' ye' happens next, Joe?"

"Whatever is going on, if it continues, it's gonna cause mass starvation. Lots of people scrapping over the last of the resources. Probably lead to some kind of authoritarian clampdown and martial law being established. Internment 'camps' will be set up that would appear to help, but in fact, all they'd be doing is just rounding up civilians. After a few months, and it doesn't matter if the power comes back or not, we'll all be in a new reality, and not a good one."

Joe paused, then took a gulp of coffee to wash down the oatmeal. It felt good, and he was ready to move on.

Carlos finished his food, too, then raised his hand to greet someone behind Joe.

"My scouts return," Carlos said with a grin.

Joe turned and instantly recognised the two men who had robbed and assaulted him just the day before.

Chapter 15

Zak gathered the small group of personnel assigned to his team into a cramped meeting room along the corridor from the main operations area.

He connected his laptop to the network without any issues. All government, military and intelligence agencies had what was known as 'hardened communication facilities and networks' as part of the Continuity of Government (COG) plans. If these failed for some reason, they had the alternative option of satellite communication, high-frequency (HF) radio, or very high-frequency (VHF) radio.

Zak knew that the 'EMP hardened' systems had all been upgraded and tested earlier in the year. That was very convenient, or was it more than just damned lucky, he thought as he projected his screen onto the wallboard. He then logged into the G13COMM system to access any relevant files before turning to his hastily gathered team sitting around the oval table, laptops open at the ready. The faces looking back at Zak were filled with a mix of trepidation and anticipation. Young faces, twenty-somethings.

Out of them all, Zak only recognised Ryan Blackwell from the earlier meeting. *Was this 'it'?* he wondered. Was this the team he was going to use to dig into the biggest attack since 9/11? He hoped they knew what they were doing.

"I don't know all your names, but I'll pick them up as we go into our mission, considering the urgency of our situation. Our job is to establish what exactly has happened, how widespread it is, and above all else, find out who's responsible for it and where they are located."

Zak clicked his laptop, displaying a long list of national militia organisations and groups on the big screen: The Oath Keepers, the Redneck Revolt, NFAC and others. Zak immediately spotted Liberatus on the list and made a mental note to take that one himself.

He had the feeling this was a colossal waste of time as the same questions he had asked Foster still lingered. Could any of these relatively small and obscure groups truly trigger a series of EMP attacks, and not just across the US, but apparently Canada, the UK, and Europe? It didn't make any sense to him at all.

Nonetheless, Zak swallowed down his reservations and focused on the list displayed on the screen.

"We have prime suspects and secondary suspects. Protocol dictates that nation-states such as Russia, China, North Korea, and Iran will be at the top of the list. Throw in the United Islamic State group, and you have a list of enemies who would happily strike a blow against our country and the West, just as we've seen happen. Right now, though, other intelligence and military teams are looking at those state suspects.

"Our focus will be on other organisations and groups of interest listed here at home. Mainly national anti-government

119

militias. There is a longer list of other state-based groups, but due to our lack of resources, we'll assume they don't have the capability for these types of attacks." Zak didn't voice his own concerns about the national groups, and, anxious to get his team active, he waved in the direction of one young Indian woman standing at the side of the room, dressed smartly with tied-back hair.

"Could you introduce yourself, please?" he asked.

"Miss Paswan, sir. Myra Paswan," she answered.

"Miss Paswan, and is it Ryan?" he said again, this time gesturing at the young man from the earlier meeting.

"Yep, er, yes, sir. Ryan Blackwell."

"And presumably, you know most of the others assembled here and their functional expertise?" Zak asked them both; they nodded in affirmation

"Right. Miss Paswan, you are to form a team from half of those in this room and Mr Blackwell the other half. We will split the list of groups of interest in two, and you will both take half. Pull up everything we have on them; look particularly at any new affiliations they may have made and any significant influx of cash that they may have. I want regular updates as to how we are progressing." Then, as the two team leaders began to address their colleagues, he announced again, "Leave Liberatus to me. I'll focus on that particular group. Just remember, we want to find where the leaders were last known to be. Any cross-communication between groups is an immediate red flag and should be brought directly to my attention. You know the score, any and all chatter or trails that remotely points to a link to today's attack, I want to know about it. Any questions?"

Zak looked around the room from face to face. "No? Then

off we go, guys."

The teams began to form and leave the meeting room to their own enclaves, and Zak waited until they were all gone and switched off the wall screen.

He tried to assess whether Liberatus and his own brother, Joe, would really have the resources to pull something like this off.

They had orchestrated that attack in Alaska, however, the resources they had used were far below the level needed for what had just happened on a global level. They may have the motivation; however, as far as Zak knew, they believed they were fighting against a secretive cabal entrenched at the highest levels of the power pyramid. Joe had always argued this, but Zak had always dismissed it as a conspiracy.

But now, with what Haleema had claimed and with 'Operation Hallows' turning into a real-life shitshow, Zak began to wonder if there was indeed something in these claims.

Chapter 16

Some exhausting hours later, Zak closed the front door to his apartment. "Rhonda?" he called out, slipping his shoes off.

As an employee of Ghost 13, Zak had a larger condo than most. The round central living area was decorated to Rhonda's specifications. Light and airy, with tasteful art on the walls, plenty of plants and Nordic-style furniture and an open-plan kitchen area, along with two other rooms and a bathroom located off the main space.

Since they had been relocated to Station 12, Zak's wife, Rhonda, had taken a job with the station's administration office to keep the boredom at bay. Moving down into the vast depths of the underground facility, cutting ties with all their friends and 'disappearing' from their previous social network by order of their employer was a bitter pill for both of them.

"In here," Rhonda said from the main bedroom.

She wore a dressing gown, half-dressed and sitting on an armchair in the corner, one leg up as she painted her toenails. Her dark hair was tied back into a bun.

"What's going on, honey? There's been a lot of lights dimming and momentary power outages. All seems okay now, though."

Zak slumped down onto the bed and leaned both arms on his thighs.

"It's bad news. Very bad. There's been an attack across the country. An EMP or a series of EMPs have destroyed the power grid. Not just here, but also across the whole of Europe."

"Oh my god." Rhonda's position froze, her varnish brush held just above a nail, as she stared at her husband, dumbfounded.

"Yeah, it's almost certainly a deliberate attack. Terrorists, the Russians, or China. Who knows? Of course, the higher levels of government and the military have a resource plan, and some equipment has been protected, and we're pretty much okay down here. Those glitches in the power were the backup systems rebooting."

"So, no one has any power out there, that's—bad, that means—" Rhonda's voice trailed off into a stunned silence.

"Total chaos. The supply chain is collapsing as we speak, along with the community infrastructure. Everything relies on power. Water, power stations, communications, the list is endless," Zak added, his voice flat and dejected. "With their systems disabled, you can imagine what's happened to all the flights and air transport."

"Oh my god," she said again.

Rhonda stood up suddenly.

"I need to contact my parents!" she blurted out.

Zak shook his head. "Apart from the protected government lines of communications, everything else is down. You can't just ring them. There'll be a protocol they'll follow. But I'll

123

make enquiries. I'm sure there will be a lot of rescue teams picking up any stranded VIPs."

Her father was a former high-ranking CIA man who had pulled the right strings for Zak to get into the agency early on in his career.

Rhonda nodded, seeming a little reassured by his words.

"What about your—parents, Zak? Will they be okay? You said this event also happened in Britain and Ireland?"

"My old man, well, he can take care of himself, I'm sure. Now my mum, well, I don't know? She may have been over in Ireland with him. But honestly, I just don't know what their relationship status is right now. I just hope she's not in London," his voice faded as he recalled Zoe. "My sister's there, of course." Zak stood up.

"Listen, all we can do right now is carry on as normal. That's all any of us can do. We'll get through this," Rhonda said, trying to be reassuring in turn.

Zak nodded and slapped his hands on his knees. "I'm gonna grab a bite, haven't eaten for a while, and then I'm going to head back. Are you feeling hungry?"

They both ate a microwaved meal in silence under the realisation that both of their future plans were now very much on hold.

***

Karim Sheraz opened his apartment door, looking ashen, craggy-faced and drained of all life. He had draped on a dressing gown and wore an old T-shirt underneath. From inside, Zak could smell the faint aroma of unwashed laundry.

"Mr Sheraz?" Zak said tentatively.

The old man looked up at Zak with a mixture of trepidation and fear across his face.

"Yes?" he replied weakly.

"I'm Zak Bowen, Chief Intelligence Officer from one of the intelligence agencies here. I just want to tell you about Haleema. Just to say that she's perfectly well and healthy."

Karim continued staring up at him, waiting for more information, then eventually said, "Did you see her? She's okay?"

"Yes, I saw her. Can I come in?"

"Yes, of course." Karim stood aside, and Zak walked inside. He stood, looking around the open-plan living area, while Karim cleared a pile of books from one of the dining chairs and gestured for him to sit down. His work clothes, a long lab coat, lay draped over an ironing board.

"I won't stay long. Just to let you know, Haleema is currently being questioned by internal security," Zak said.

Karim opened his hands in a gesture of disbelief.

"No one has told me anything. She just disappeared."

"I know, and I'm sorry about that. It was Security who handled all that, and I have just realised no one had told you. Anyway, she's fine."

"Can I see her, please?"

"I'm afraid it's—" Zak stopped himself. "Yes, I'll see what I can do for you, Mr Sheraz."

Karim nodded. "Thank you."

Zak stood up to leave. He pointed at the lab coat on the ironing board. "You work in one of the labs?"

"They wanted me to start at the nuclear facility in..." he stopped talking. "It is classified, sorry."

Zak smiled. "Of course, no problem. I understand."

Zak had tried to access his files, but they were protected by several levels of security above Zak's clearance. But he knew Karim was a high-ranking engineer who had worked for the Iranian Government.

"I remember you," Karim said suddenly.

Zak looked at the old man blankly.

Karim went on, "At the airbase in Iraq, you were there. We had just celebrated our release from the United Islamic State, and we thought we were free. But here we are," he said, gesturing at his surroundings.

"I'm so..." Zak began, but Karim held up the palm of his hand.

"I've not seen my wife or sons. When you spoke to us, you promised our families would join us, but they did not come. Haleema is all I have left."

Zak stared back at Karim, his haggard face devoid of hope, an old and broken man. Zak felt waves of unsolicited guilt course through him. Had he actually said those words, those promises? Probably. He couldn't really recall. So much had happened since his operation postings in the Middle East, but he did remember some details of the case.

"Mr Sheraz, as I said, I'll need to look into it, but currently, we have a global emergency. I do remember one of your sons joined the UIS, which complicated the situation."

Karim nodded solemnly. "Amir, unfortunately, was led astray."

"Let's focus on what we can control. Haleema *is* here, and I'll look into the family situation, but I can't prom..." Zak hesitated. "...can't guarantee anything, especially now."

Karim again held his head in his hands, an image of despondency.

"I'm sorry," Zak added before leaving and closing the door

quietly behind him.

Chapter 17

Zak checked in with his team investigating the other groups of interest. They gathered in the small meeting room and, one by one, went over their reports. They shared that a number of small incidents these groups had apparently occurred in the proceeding weeks and months before the EMP attacks. Details showed that there were a few shootings and a couple of arrests, but no smoking guns to anything remotely as big as what had just taken place.

As Zak already knew, that would probably be their finding. It was, as he surmised, a complete waste of time.

He dismissed the team and headed back to his own desk, logged into the internal G13COMM network, and pulled up all the available intelligence reports on the Liberatus organisation, scanning through the various reports all the way back to the 1990s.

He briefly read through the history of the organisation. It was founded by John Rhodes, a former MI6 operative who had become disillusioned with the establishment. It then became at first merely an alternative media outlet, beginning with a newspaper back in the 1990s, but rapidly grew its readership via the public internet.

That was one facet of Liberatus. Its other was a growing secret aspect of the organisation. They had formed small groups of militias using ex-military personnel as recruited agents, and they established 'hives' or secret communities in different countries for the preparation for what they claimed to be any possible number of apocalyptic scenarios.

Zak thought for a moment. This was the exact description of the cult he always believed them to be, just 'doomsday preppers'. But then, a global apocalyptic scenario had just happened.

He read on.

While he regarded them as having the same characteristics of a religious cult, he knew Liberatus claimed to be fighting and exposing a different type of cult, a politically secret yet extremely powerful cabal that had expanded its influence within the higher echelons of many governments, military making up the ruling establishment of the Western Powers.

This was what Zak had heard from his brother, Joe and, more recently, Haleema.

He looked through the persons of interest who had been connected with the organisation listed by country.

It was believed Libertatus was funded by the billionaire brother of John Rhodes, Michael, who had made his fortune with the tech corporation Goya Tech. They had created various consumer communication systems such as Goya AI, the 'knowledgeable friend in your home'.

Goya Tech also sold software, in particular an encrypted communication or chat app system called Icarus, which Liberatus undoubtedly used to conceal their own internal communications. Their big contracts, and therefore their funding, came with the US military for satellite communications software.

Zak gulped down the last of his coffee.

The latest update he read stated that Michael Rhodes had been ousted by his own board.

John Rhode's son Troy was part of Goya and, therefore, probably secretly helped Liberatus. He had headed up the technology department but left the company soon after his uncle was removed. However, it came to light that Troy had possibly put a backdoor trojan into the software of a Quantum communication satellite previously sold to the military.

"So," he mused, "Liberatus potentially had access to this technology, which in theory meant they could communicate over long distances, even after this EMP attack? Did they know it was coming?"

Zak leaned back in his chair and tried to make sense of it all. A man, Michael Rhodes, who had created Goya Tech, had contracts with the US military, also funded Liberatus? A group that was recently labelled as a terrorist organisation. He could only shake his head and keep reading.

Other names on the persons of interest:

Hugo Reese. Location unknown: Believed to be located somewhere in Tennessee, US.

Zak scanned other names: Marty Faulkner, Gianna Madaki, Hanna Friedmann, Raj and Harish Singh, and Marcus Brady.

Hanna Friedmann?

He was sure that was Joe's partner, although he'd never actually met her.

And then he saw names that caused the most inner anguish to Zak: Frank and Joe Bowen, his father and brother.

Frank Bowen, his own father, once as an MI6 agent, then as a Ghost 13 field agent. He also had worked with John Rhodes and Liberatus.

Could Liberatus be responsible for the current EMP attacks?

Further questions surfaced in Zak's mind, but despite exhaustive searching, he still could not find any solid evidence of Liberatus' involvement in operations using EMP weapons. True, they had infiltrated and recently attacked the Geo Weather Project facility in Alaska and got away from the Ghost 13 team who waited for them.

Of course, all he had to go on was a database of reports and files. Perhaps the teams on the ground would find something from HUMINT sources?

Zak summarised his report over the next hour and, after a few moments of hesitation, removed the names of his brother and father before sending it over to his boss, Kate Foster.

He sipped on a glass of water and leaned back in his chair.

He remembered Haleema and decided to go see Foster in person. He stood up. Perhaps she had more news about what was happening out there as well.

He found her in her office reading the report he had just sent.

"Please sit down, Zak," she said, still reading. Then she took off her glasses and looked up at him as he took a seat.

"Anything on the other groups?" she asked without looking up.

"Nothing has come up. Again, I don't think they have the capability. This has to be Russia, China, or some other nation-state. Has there been anything more about that?" he asked.

Foster sighed.

"All evidence points to the fact that their countries have been affected too. The problem is we don't yet have any data on the ground. There's no response or any hard intel from our contacts there."

After a momentary pause, Zak volunteered, "I know someone who might be able to help with this kind of thing. Internal security has her locked up for attempting to communicate on the external internet before the EMP, but she has considerable hacking expertise that might help us find out more. Good systems infiltration."

Foster cast a suspicious eye at him. "Name?"

"Haleema Sheraz," Zak replied. An ex-hacker for the Iranian Government. Her father is also here, in the base. He was part of a group of nuclear scientists we saved from the United Islamic State in Iran."

Foster thought for a moment, then nodded. "Okay. But there's considerable interest in Liberatus. A lot of pressure is coming from above. You're right about the smaller groups being incapable of this. However, Liberatus needs looking at a lot more closely."

"There's nothing linking—"

Foster held up her hand.

"You're not dismissing any Liberatus involvement because of your father and brother's involvement in the group, are you?" Foster said, looking at him quizzically. "I noticed their names were left off that report I just read."

Zak flushed.

She looked back at her screen and narrowed her eyes. "No, definitely can't see them on there, yet I do remember they are persons of interest in our database."

Zak shrugged. "I've never agreed with their views. Besides, Liberatus couldn't possibly be behind this," Zak said, his voice now tinged with defiance.

"Look, I know we've already cleared you of any involvement with this group, but is there anything else you're not telling me, Zak?" Foster retorted.

"No! I always thought they were on the wrong path, and I made that clear," Zak replied, softening his voice a little,

"I'm sure you're not naive, Zak. But you know we need a narrative behind this. A story. The state needs a bad guy and needs it quickly. And we, rather, you need to deliver one."

"I'd like to know the actual truth," Zak countered.

Foster smiled with her mouth, but for the first time, he saw pure malevolence in her eyes.

Chapter 18

Andalucía, Spain
Day 2

Joe stood up suddenly, turning to face the group, his metal bowl ringing out as it fell onto the hard ground.

The Nord saw him first, and immediately, his thin features broke into a sneer of contempt. The stocky crop-haired guy in the big coat held his hand out in a calming gesture to the woman with them. She had the rifle that must have been pointed at his back during the robbery and now raised the barrel towards Joe.

The three walked closer.

"Well, well. Hello friend," the Nord said.

Carlos looked between Joe and his three adventurers, fixing his gaze on them. These are your people?" he said, turning to Carlos. "They took all my shit and nearly knocked me out." Joe spat the words out with pure venom.

"So, you're all just a den of thieves then?" he continued, looking around at all of them.

Crop-haired man.

"Is that true, Greg?" Carlos asked.

Greg simply shrugged and spat on the ground.

"He was ripe for the picking. Besides, it's gone to shit out there, and we need to hunt and gather," the man replied with disdain lacing his voice.

"Fuck you—I'll hunt and gather you, assholes!" Joe growled with venom.

Carlos held his hands up in an appeasing gesture and then, with authority, said. "Alright, why don't we all calm the fuck down?" his voice booming through the camp. Then, in a calmer voice directed towards the man in the big coat, "What did you take from our friend Joe here, Greg?"

"Our friend?" Greg snorted with continued derision.

"Well, he's a guest, so that changes things, wouldn't you think?" Carlos countered.

Joe scanned his eyes from Carlos to the gang of three. A few others from the camp came closer, drawn in by the raised voices.

He realised he wasn't going to get out of this situation easily and that he needed to remain calm, but his anger, as always, was simmering just under the surface. He tried turning over and assessing the relationship between Carlos and the other three. Carlos was definitely the leader, but this Greg guy wasn't completely toeing the line. What exactly were the dynamics of what was going on here?

Greg held up his hands and then turned to look at his two comrades.

"You can have your MRE packs back—but we're keeping the pistol."

"The fuck you are—" snarled Joe.

A moment of silence. Hesitation. Turning back towards Carlos, he continued.

"Your scouts, Carlos? Seems they don't care too much for

135

your opinion. Be wary of snakes like these, only ever out for themselves." Joe said.

"Alright. I'm going to sort this out." Carlos said, his voice, in turn, tinged with anger, and turning to the skinny kid, said, "Go get that rifle you use and a full box of ammo."

"But Dad—"

"Go get it," Carlos snapped.

The kid sprinted off towards one of the caravans.

Carlos turned to Joe. "I'm giving you one of my rifles. It's a nice gun, a Springfield M1903 bolt action, and it's accurate. Will you take it for the pistol?"

Joe shook his head. "I'll have my pistol back. It's easier to hide."

Greg, the Nord and the woman, still holding her rifle up towards Joe, all remained staring at Joe, unwilling to flex.

"Listen, Joe," Carlos began in a low whisper. "It's either the rifle or nothing. I'd take it. It's a generous offer. Greg's not gonna give your pistol back to you, and someone might end up hurt."

Joe clenched his fists. The guy was right. If these pricks weren't going to stand down, he really didn't have any choice. He needed to get home. That was the important thing to do right now.

He breathed out slowly. "Alright. But you're all thieves," Joe spoke louder for all to hear. "Bunch of scum, and I'm going to get my pistol back."

"Don't be a hero, dickhead," the Nord snorted.

Carlo's son returned and handed over the rifle and a box of .30-06 ammo to Joe.

"It's unloaded, so no funny business. See you around," Carlos warned

"Hopefully not," Joe replied, glaring at the three scouts.

Greg tossed over a couple of MRE packs that landed near Joe's feet.

Joe stashed the ammo and the packs into his empty backpack and then slung the weapon over his shoulder. He turned slowly and began walking, shooting each of the three a deadly stare. Then, when he had walked past them, he said, loud enough for Carlos to hear, "Thanks for the breakfast."

He headed out of the camp and up onto the footpath. When he glanced back, the eyes of the Travellers were all watching him go.

Chapter 19

Joe had found a disused barn and actually got a good night's sleep for the first time since the supply dump. But in the early dawn haze, the breath from his mouth was a visible reminder of how cold it was. He had never known it to be this cold in Spain. Must be a record—and what a time to set a record.

When there's no bloody power to be found anywhere.

His thoughts went back to the Geo Weather Project, which had been responsible for weather manipulation and had caused massive droughts across Asia. Had the cabal, somehow, caused this cold front, too, as a way of turning the proverbial screws in the middle of an unprecedented catastrophe of their own creation? It seemed a bit of a stretch to any normal mind, but Joe knew too well what lengths such people would go to for their agenda and vision. And heaping misery upon populations while killing off the weak was certainly in these bastards' DNA.

Joe rummaged around in his backpack and picked out a pasta with tuna MRE pack that he managed to get back off the thieving Travellers. However, they didn't give him back the flameless heater. The chemical reaction the device provided would have heated the food, so instead, he had to consume it cold.

As he ate, Joe stared at the Springfield rifle that Carlos had given him, propped up against an old rusty piece of farm machinery.

It was a good weapon and handy to have, but Joe wasn't sure how good an idea it was to be walking around openly and so obviously armed. There were pros and cons. The most obvious 'pro' would be dissuading any wannabe thief or mugger. He would still have to be careful and avoid main routes, although there was little sign of any police or military so far. However, if he did stumble across them, they might use the sight of his rifle as an excuse to detain him, lock him in a hole and toss away the key.

He unfolded the map he still managed to hold onto and studied the route he needed to continue on while washing down his food with measured swallows of icy cold water. It was still a fair way to walk; a direct route on the main roads would, of course, be easier, but perhaps staying off the main routes away from anyone would be better? With the onset of a third day with no power, people started to panic as their realisation of the desperate nature of their situation slowly dawned on them.

After his respite, Joe reluctantly left the relative security of the barn and went out into a harsh grey morning as sleet began to rain down, carried by the wind in a diagonal slant that whipped into Joe's face. It cut through to Joe's core, reminding him of his days out training on the Brecon Beacons with the army.

Winter gripped the landscape with the dark, leafless trees; their jagged branches spread like strewn ink against the sombre sky. A harsh wind gathered in strength, and Joe hunched into himself as he headed along a seemingly endless road scattered with more abandoned vehicles.

Through a clump of swaying trees, bending to the will of the wind, Joe spotted a large old house set well back from the road. It had the typical terracotta roof and whitewashed walls, alongside which he could see a small garden and vineyard. As he watched the building, he heard a shout carried in the wind. Joe stopped and turned, looking around, but couldn't see anyone in sight. He continued walking, then heard the shout again. This time, it was clearer and was coming from ahead of him.

As he continued past the driveway that led down to the house, he saw movement from the garden of another whitewashed single-storey house further up the road.

Someone was running. Fast. It was a man, either chasing someone or being chased himself.

Joe jogged along the road, up to the driveway of the second house, and slowly walked in. Straining his ears, his senses on high alert. He unslung the rifle and levered the bolt, cocking it.

More shouts from the rear of the building.

He skirted around the house to a tree-lined garden to see a youth wrestling on the ground with another man, going at each other with vicious punches. The youth had a knife in one hand that the other guy was struggling to keep at bay but, in the process of defending himself, was taking a rain of punches to his head.

Joe dropped his bag and ran across the lawn while flipping his rifle around to use as a club. Just as the youth was close to bringing his blade down on his assailant, Joe brought back his rifle and struck the youth on the back of his head.

He rolled to his side, dropping the blade and slumping over

before somehow scrambling to his feet. His eyes locked on the fallen knife, and he dived for it with surprising speed. However, Joe stepped forward, covering it with his large boot. He raised the rifle as if to bring the butt down again, and the youth cowered back, watching Joe with half-feral eyes.

"Ah, ah!" he said, waving a finger to and fro like a parent would to a misbehaving toddler.

The youth jumped to his feet and ran, heading alongside the house and out of sight. Joe thought for a moment about flipping his rifle back up and taking aim, perhaps winging him with a shot in the arm. But he was already gone. Besides, the dude on the ground was a higher priority.

Joe looked at the man's face. It was badly bruised, and he was semi-conscious. His eyes fluttered open and seemed to take an age to focus on Joe's face.

"You took quite some punishment there, mate," Joe said, sitting down in the shelter of a small eucalyptus tree. He stretched his legs out, leaning back on a nearby old pickup truck, its wheels flat, having long lost air.

The man reached a hand to his face, feeling the bruises and small cuts, and then he began frantically looking around for his attacker. This sudden movement clearly hurt him.

"He took off a while ago after I took his knife and refused to let him kill you," Joe said. "I don't think we should hang around too long, though; he seemed hell-bent on getting you. What did you do?"

"I hurt his father," the man replied in a North American accent.

Joe stared at the man, unsure of what to make of his answer. Should he have saved this man? Was he the real monster?

"I was looking for food, and that prick and his father jumped me and then tied me up," the man continued, reading the questioning look on Joe's face. "As they had me tied up, and I didn't reckon it was a great idea to hang around and find out what their plans were gonna be."

Joe stood up and walked over.

"I'm Joe," he said and offered his hand. The man shook it.

"Ed," he mumbled. "Thanks for saving my ass."

Joe offered him a water bottle, and Ed took it eagerly, gulping down long swallows, before wiping his mouth and handing it back to Joe.

"Come on, we best be leaving before your friend comes back," Joe said, helping him to his feet.

Ed took Joe's hand, wobbling as he stood up. He reached a hand out to rest on Joe's shoulder to steady himself further.

"You sure you're all right to walk?" Joe asked.

Ed smiled and nodded.

"I'm fine. Come on, let's move. I'd rather not see that bastard again," he grunted.

They headed out past the house and back to the road. Joe took a look around, scouting to make sure the way was clear before heading off.

"So, what's your story, mate? Have you been living here long?"

Ed nodded.

"My family and I have been living here for a few years now. It's a long way from my original home, but we love the way of life here. When the power went down a few days ago, and our car didn't start, I started to panic. Moved the family into the garage and came out trying to find help. I don't have much to show for my efforts now. Lost my shotgun when I ran into the Spanish army and then the few things I found when those freaks captured me."

"Why did the army take your gun?" Joe asked.

"To be honest, I'm not sure what they had planned for me. When I saw them, they seemed to offer salvation, but there was a small language problem. I tried to explain to them about my wife and kid, how I couldn't leave them alone. They didn't seem to understand, though, and started hauling me off further away from them."

"I'd guess they have started to make a camp to help look after people," Joe said with a chuckle. "I'm not sure what the conditions are like there, but better than starving to death out here. So how did you end up at the Manson residence?"

"Well, when I realised what was happening, I panicked. I jumped from the back of the truck and took off, ran from those army guys and then came across that—house." Ed spat on the ground. "Big mistake."

Joe led them off the main road and onto a dirt track between two fields.

Ed sighed and rubbed the back of his neck, glancing at Joe. "They were lucky. I woulda killed them both if I could." The words hung in the air before Joe continued, "Sounds like a pretty bad day, mate. Still, you're free now to get home to your family, and here take this." Joe reached into his bag and handed Ed an MRA pack, saying, "It's not much, I know, but it'll help out."

Ed stopped in his tracks and looked at Joe, frowning before he began to weep. He embraced Joe with a firm hug, the action taking Joe by surprise.

"Tha—thank you," Ed said, composing himself. "It might not seem much to you, but with the way things are, it means the world."

143

"No problemo, *mi amigo*," Joe gave him a friendly slap on the shoulder, and they carried on walking.

"So, do you know your way home from here?"

Ed looked around, getting his bearings.

"I think so. I'll have a better idea when we clear this ridge. Do you think that guy will catch up?"

Joe looked back down the track they were on. "He didn't seem like much of a tracker, and we're on hard terrain too. So, unless he gets eyes on us, we should be okay." He turned forward and gestured at the tree line. "The trees should offer us good cover so he can only see us from the road down there."

"But don't worry, I'm heading this way, and I'll see you back to your family," said Joe.

"You're too kind, really. Thank you so much, buddy. So, where are you heading, anyway?" Ed asked.

"I have some land up by the foothills of the Sierra Nevada. A few of us have set up a little community there. Sod's law, I was eight hundred kilometres away when all this happened. No working vehicle has meant I've been walking for quite a few days now."

They came to the top of the ridge and started to descend down the slope. Joe looked over his shoulder and checked the road behind them one last time for any signs of movement before it was out of view.

Joe ran a calloused hand through his beard. The beautiful Spanish landscape lay before them. It was hard to think the world had changed so much, well, at least for humanity. Ed was probably the first of a long line of people who were in need of help. Could their little community open its doors to everyone that they met? Probably not, but what kind of humanitarian would he be if he didn't at least offer?

"You and your family would be more than welcome to join us if you like. If you're prepared to help out and be part of the community."

The man's eyes lit up at Joe's invite.

"Now there is an offer we can't refuse."

Ed stopped and pointed across the valley.

"See that road? The one curving behind that small hill?"

"Yep," replied Joe.

"My house is along there," he said excitedly.

"Great," said Joe. He took the water bottle from his bag and offered it to Ed. They both drank, and Joe put the bottle back in his pack.

They continued down the hill; the only sound was of birds singing in the distance.

***

It was early evening by the time they approached Ed's house. The dark clouds of the still brooding overhead promised more wintering weather. It could easily be the beginning of a storm coming in. Joe could tell the man was eager to get home because as soon as they had reached the end of his road, he had quickened his pace.

Joe thought about how it would be a relief to get on with his journey. So much had gone wrong, and he needed to be with his people. It had been pure bad luck he had been at one of their caches when it happened. He wondered what was happening back at the hive. Were they all okay? How was Hanna bearing up?

Joe decided he would get this guy safely back to his family and then move on quickly. Or if they were going to join them, should they travel together? That would seriously slow him down, but then would they make it on their own? Joe looked over at Ed; there was a little bounce in his step, and a small smile played across his face.

They walked around the house. A typical Spanish casa, with whitewashed walls and a terracotta roof. Joe glanced through one of the windows and noticed it had been trashed. This was becoming a common sight in these dark days.

Ed walked ahead through the olive trees, and Joe spotted a garage that couldn't be seen from the garden. Nice and hidden. Now he understood Ed's plan to move in there. As the garage door came into view, he could see it was ajar.

Joe hissed at Ed, stopping him in his tracks before slowly unslinging his rifle and moving past Ed. He walked cautiously up to the door and nudged it open with his rifle.

A cloud of flies rushed out at him from inside, making him step back in alarm for a moment.

Inside, it was dark. The setting sun offered little in the way of illumination. A dark stench of death came at his throat, almost making him gag. It caught him unaware, and he held his breath.

Jesus.

He reached into his bag, pulled out a flashlight and shone it around the garage, exposing the makeshift home stacked with boxes, a chair, and a laundry rack to one side.

He stepped in to get a better look. There were no signs of a struggle. Then, Joe saw the source of the smell on the makeshift bed.

Shit!

Two bodies on the double bed. A woman and a child, both on their backs, their waxy skin clinging to their bones, flies buzzing around them. Scattered around them were plates of uneaten food riddled with maggots.

As the light shined on them, Ed walked past Joe.

"Hey, it's so good to see you both." He crouched down to an oil lamp and lit it and then walked over, kissed his dead wife, and ruffled his dead son's hair.

"This is Joe," he said, gesturing behind him. "He saved my ass and kindly gave us some food."

"—Ed," Joe said, stunned by the man's reactions to the corpses.

"Are you hungry? What would you like?" Ed asked of his deceased family.

Ed seemed to listen to the silence for a moment and then nodded.

"Yep, okay. Beans it is."

"Ed," Joe repeated, louder now.

Ed grabbed the cans, stood up and headed to the rear of the garage, where there was a makeshift kitchen.

"You'll join us for dinner, won't you, Joe?" Ed said like a convivial dinner host.

Joe looked down at the corpses again, rubbing his beard. He looked back at the door and then back at Ed.

"Can you not see they are dead?"

Ed simply continued to bustle around in the kitchen, opening the tins and ignoring Joe's question. Then, he looked up at Joe, staring at him hard.

"Did you say you're joining us?" Ed asked with now a questioning look playing across his face.

Joe glanced around and nodded, more to himself than Ed. He considered staying, trying to talk to the guy to see the same reality as himself, but he could already see it was a lost cause.

What kind of trauma had caused this?

Joe couldn't imagine.

"I'm gonna move on. I have people waiting," he said quietly. He shouldered his rifle.

Ed moved towards him and smiled, holding out his arms. He embraced Joe, who cautiously patted his back.

"Thank you so much for getting me back to my family," he said with genuine gratitude. Joe could see in his eyes he believed every word he was saying. And worse, he believed his family was alive.

"Ed—" Joe began.

"Safe Journey, Joe!" said Ed, with finality. He turned and then walked to the little kitchen.

Joe exhaled and stepped outside, grateful for the fresh air.

He shook his head to himself as he walked back through the olive trees, past the house and back onto the road. These were unusual times.

What the hell had Ed been through to screw him up so badly?

Hopefully, things at the hive hadn't gone so sideways as they had here.

Chapter 20

Andalucía, Spain
Day 4

From his position on the far side of the valley, Joe lifted his binoculars and scanned the Liberatus buildings tucked into the hill. It was hard to see much, with a group of trees obscuring his vision. His shaking hands didn't help. He had spent the previous night in an old shepherd's hut, but as the temperature was way below what he was used to in this country, he was chilled.

Great timing for such freak weather.

But then he could see home. His *home,* he thought excitedly. Almost within touching distance.

A feeling of relief washed over him. All the bad luck of being away when the power went down and the recall of all the frustrations he had experienced just melted at the thought of being home and seeing Hanna again, wrapping his arms around her.

He hurriedly put away his field glasses and continued walking down the hillside road, daydreaming of a hot meal and a coffee laced with brandy.

It took another hour to get to the far side of the valley, and from there, he trekked slowly up the winding, narrow road that skirted the base. Then, he followed a track that split off from the road and walked through the surrounding scrubland that acted like a buffer to the outside world.

As the sight of the gates and wall to the base came into view, Joe saw his comrades had been busy shoring up the walls with welded metal sections of what looked like old rusty farm machinery.

As he got closer, Joe confirmed it was indeed made up of parts that had been lying around the lower fields for years. Javier or Hanna must have moved them up here.

He stopped and listened, but it was almost silent—no distant voices or signs of life from inside the walls.

He crouched down onto his haunches as a flood of thoughts came to him. He had seen what was happening out there. More and more disorder, people getting desperate.

Has something happened here? he wondered. Something bad, like a home invasion? Did some gang get inside and were now waiting? Maybe just strolling up to the front gate wasn't such a great idea. Best just to check things out.

He backtracked to the road and followed it up the hill, where it snaked around the buildings of his home before disappearing up into the mountains. High white walls surrounded the buildings that made it a natural fortress, and beyond the wall tops were the red-tiled roofs of the rear buildings of the stores and living quarters. Beyond the mountains and caves that stood defiantly on the far side of the riverbed that snaked through the valley below.

Still, there was very little sign of life.

Joe left the road and headed down a slope to the base of the wall, fighting through bramble and scrub bushes before circling around in the opposite direction of the front gate.

He reached a section of the wall, well out of sight from the road that sloped down, and he could see the rails from a terrace jutting out. Joe jumped up, grabbing onto the bottom of the metal railing and was able to pull up his body and haul himself over. He slipped down silently onto the terracotta floored terrace on the far side that served several of the rooms, including his own.

There was barking from one of the dogs inside the building somewhere, and then Joe sensed a presence and saw a figure appear from the far corner of the terrace.

Javier had his rifle aimed straight at him, and Joe slowly raised his hands.

"*Hola Javier*," he said, loud and clear.

"Joe? That you?" a voice called back as Javier moved closer to get a clearer look.

"Just dropping in by the back way. There's a weak spot in the defences back here," Joe replied with a wry smile.

A grin appeared on Javier's face, and he lowered the weapon.

"Ah, *mi amigo*! The wanderer returns, huh?"

Javier shouldered the rifle and moved toward Joe with open arms. They embraced, slapping each other on their backs.

"Thank god you're back," Javier said.

"Great to see you again, too, Javier."

"You didn't knock on the door," Javier queried.

"Well, I wasn't sure what the situation was inside. It's sure going to shit out there, and it's getting worse by the day."

Javier nodded, his smile fading. "*Si, si.* Chaos. *Mucho caos.* We've been okay, but we've got some problems. It's the backup generator; it's too loud, and it will make us stick out."

"Good point. Let's take a look at all that. But it's getting colder. We need to do something to keep the heating going," Joe replied.

He turned and gestured to the way he had got into their compound. "We need to get something done about that weak spot on the perimeter, too."

"*Si*. I'll talk to Pablo straight away."

They began walking along the terrace to a set of doors to go back inside.

"Where's Hanna?" asked Joe.

Javier's head dropped slightly, and he winced. "She wanted to check the local situation. Scout out and see what was happening in Órgiva and other nearby towns. I tried to stop her, said it's too dangerous and said I'd go with her, but she insisted on going alone."

Joe stopped walking and simply gaped at his friend.

"What? Ah, for Christ's sake!" He threw up his arms in exasperation. "What the hell is she playing at?" Joe said, shaking his head.

"I know, Joe. I'm sorry," Javier said sorrowfully,

"When was this?" said Joe anxiously.

"She went a day or two after the blackout."

"So, she's been gone awhile?" Joe said, musing to himself as he looked across towards the mountains. "Alright. Look, let's get this place organised first, and then I'm gonna have to go and find her."

"Also, Diego. He left around the same time," Javier added.

"What! He disappeared without a goodbye, too?" Joe retorted.

Javier simply shrugged.

"*Si*. he left too, and I don't know why."

"I hope he isn't going back to his old ways. The lawlessness that's developing out there could be a real trigger for someone like Diego," Joe replied.

Javier shook his head vigorously.

"*Qué va.* He's worked so hard. After we build so much, I cannot believe he would—"

Javier stopped speaking, aware that Joe was staring at him.

"I know you've worked really hard to pull your brother out of his bad place. That prison time for assault and then everything you did to pull him back."

"Like helping rebuild this place," Javier added, looking around at the building in front of them.

"Yeah," Joe said. "But it's not outside the realms of possibility he might be tempted to return to his old life, now law and order is crumbling."

Javier sighed. "Come on, amigo, let's get you some food and a drink. I'll update you on everything."

***

A few of the families gathered to eat together, as had always been their routine. Usually, this would have taken place outside, under the tarpaulin canopy that stretched over one of the outside courtyards, but that had been in normal times. Each day seemed to grow colder, an unprecedented thing in Southern Spain at this time of the year. It would no doubt have been headlining news had there been any media broadcasting.

Joe's command structure was informal, but he relied on Javier, Pablo, Diego and Andreas, one of his old army comrades whom Joe had served with in Iraq, to keep day-to-day things running as they should. Andreas had helped him out back when they had been assisting Hugo Reese while running into Jamall

Salazar and his accomplice. Just a few months previously, Andreas had joined the hive, moving his family over from Seville.

Joe could smell the welcome aroma of food and felt his stomach rumble in anticipation. It somehow reminded him of when he was a kid back home with his mother in London.

Javier's partner Amy, and Andreas, brought over bowls of stew heated via the gas canisters. They had dry crackers to go with it.

The children were ushered to their places, blankets around their tiny shoulders to keep out the cold, while Andreas took a seat next to Joe with their bowls and gestured to him to tuck in.

"So, I'll get the bad news out of the way. A bearing or something has gone in our backup gas generator, so when it runs, you can hear that thing from clear across the valley. Our other backup was, unfortunately, not in the Faraday cage when this thing hit. It's gone beyond repair. Just incredibly bad timing."

Joe breathed out slowly, holding a spoon of stew near his mouth.

"You can say that again. Why the hell did we leave them out?"

Joe took a mouthful of stewed beef, potatoes and carrots. It tasted so good after living on rations or whatever scraps he had hunted around for.

Andreas cast a glance over at Javier, then back to Joe.

"We had it out to test if all our electrical stuff was working. We were moving a lot of stuff around down there, and unfortunately, it was just left outside. It was just the worst—"

"Timing. Yeah," Joe said, finishing his sentence.

"So, all the freezer stores would be gone then?"

"We've had to use what we could," Javier said. He gestured to his bowl. "This is the last of the beef."

Joe shook his head. This was bad. A good portion of emergency supplies had been in those freezers. Of course, they still had freeze-dried crap, MRE packs and emergency tinned foods.

"So, we've no power and the solar panels won't be working either."

"No," Andreas agreed.

"We have the gas generators. Nice and loud, though. We may have to risk it if we need the power in short bursts. But it's risky," Joe said.

Javier brushed imaginary dust off the wooden table top and cleared his throat. "We also took on some more people while you were gone, Joe."

"Great," Joe said flatly. He had stopped eating and held his hands together over his bowl.

"The Ortiz family from up the mountain. They were struggling, and, well, they've helped us out on so many occasions. Some others."

"So, more mouths to feed," Joe said evenly.

"They will all work for their food and shelter, and some are weapons trained and very practical, too. Hard workers."

Joe sighed and began to spoon down on his stew.

There was a palpable tension around the table. Joe could feel his dark mood emanating from himself, but he couldn't snap out of it. Even the kids fell silent, and for a few minutes, only the sound of clinking spoons filled the room. Joe wanted to help the hive prosper, but if they took on too many others and stretched their resources too thin, then the whole enterprise

155

could sink. They just had to survive the winter on what supplies they had and hope that next spring, they could plant and grow enough to sustain themselves. *They should be okay*, Joe thought to himself. *We've been preparing for this for long enough now.* Was it the fact that too much had happened in his absence or that Hanna wasn't here that was darkening his mood? Seeing the problems and not the solutions.

Joe finished up his stew, gulped down a glass of water and stood up.

"I'm gonna walk around, see where we're at. Then, I hit the sack for a few hours of sleep. I'm knackered. But if Hanna comes back or there's an emergency, wake me. Then, we'll look at the power and comms situ later."

There was a murmur of acknowledgement, and Joe slipped through the doors onto the terrace. He walked under an archway that connected the old part of the building to the new sections that had been built on in previous years that Javier's younger brother, Diego, had been focused on. During those months, everyone who lived in the hive had helped out with the building work in some way.

He walked into the adjoining courtyard, where a large cotton tarpaulin was strung across overhead, acting as shelter from the sun. A starling dipped into the courtyard, then flew in an upward trajectory and disappeared over the stone wall.

He reminisced for a few moments on those days, toiling in the heat to expand the place. Now, the sun was long gone, replaced by a bleak, washed-out sky that promised nothing but a continuing drop in temperature. In the distance, beyond the mountain ranges of the Sierra Nevada, dark clouds gathered.

Joe walked along the inside of the exterior wall. It was around ten metres high and part of the original building, although he had ordered for it to be further strengthened and upgraded. It was already high enough to keep out any ambitious stragglers. Although the place was not a fortress, the steel gates that would open out onto the track were securely chained shut on the inside and were a formidable barrier.

Satisfied with the security status, Joe headed back to his rooms, which he shared with Hanna. He walked in and looked around. They had a living room, sparsely furnished with a dining table, a couch and a music system. On the whitewashed stone walls hung framed oil painting prints of locations around Spain, which Hanna had sourced from a market in Granada.

He walked into their bedroom. The bed was made, and the place was immaculate, but it felt cold and empty. He opened the wardrobe, flicked through the hanging clothes, and then rummaged around at the bottom of the unit. Her main backpack and a good supply of clothes were gone. He opened all the drawers at the bottom and began pulling everything out onto the floor. T-shirts, tops, and underwear all began to pile up. Then, he went to a cupboard door that housed various storage items and found a campus bag that belonged to Hanna. He opened it up without hesitation and pulled out a digital camera, some notebooks and other personal items.

That was all the meagre possessions that she had. She liked to travel light, she had said. Which only in that moment seemed odd to Joe. This was all she had in the world? He had never thought about it before now. Why would he?

Joe put everything back as it had been and scanned the room again. Where the hell had she gone? And, more importantly, why had she gone? A fleeting thought came that made him shudder. Had she actually left him? All these thoughts swirled around his brain as he began to feel more concerned. Even anxious, which was most unusual for Joe.

Then Joe whipped open the curtains in front of the balcony doors and looked out across the river at the bottom of the valley. To the left of his view, a section of the Sierra Nevada mountains, where a series of dark caves lay at the foot of them. Caves that they had used other caches for their supplies. At least they had that nearby, but he began to fixate on how Andreas and Javier had been so stupid to leave the generator out. Okay, that an EMP could happen was such a long shot it was hard to place blame, but Joe felt his irritation rise nevertheless.

They'd just have to use the older gas generators. There was absolutely no alternative. Not if they were to power the solar panels and assess the situation with all the comms equipment, not to mention heating and cooking. Those gas canisters were only going to last so long.

Joe went back into the main room, checked the door to the hallway, which was locked, and headed for one of the small shelves tucked into the corner stacked with books. He pulled out the paperback copy of 1984 by George Orwell and then lifted and moved the bookshelf back at a right angle. It was easy enough to move back, as he had done dozens of times. He crouched down on his haunches and rolled back a section of rug that covered the floorboards underneath. He put his hand out to lift up the loose section of floorboard there, then noticed something. The thread he always carefully stuck across the joint with clear plastic tape at the end had been disturbed.

He racked his memory. When had he last accessed this? It had been a while. A few weeks? Could it have come loose by itself? He was sure that was not possible. Someone had lifted the board. Or had he just forgotten to do it last time? He looked closely. No, the thread was there, but it was broken.

Joe lifted up the board, put his arm down, and reached in, feeling around. Then, he got hold of the notebook and pulled it out. He studied it for a few moments to see if there were any signs hands other than his own had held it. Impossible without all the gear needed to find fingerprints, which Joe did not have.

He opened up the book and flicked through the pages: endless pages of numbers. These were encoded lists and records, from cache and hive locations to the number of supplies in each cache that he needed to track. Now that technology was pretty much useless, he was glad he had kept with this simple system.

Everything was coded using the simple book cypher method. A method of encryption that involved encoding messages by using specific words or phrases from an agreed-upon book as a key to represent each word or letter in the plaintext message.

He flipped through to the end and updated the supply figures he had noted from cache 5: food packs, weapons, ammo, medical kit and so on. Despite all that had gone on with the EMP, it was important to know what they had available and where.

He carefully went through the pages of George Orwell's book, gathering the individual letters from the written words and translating them into numbers that he wrote down.

The information or location about the caves over the valley had not even been entered into the book yet, and Joe thought he'd need to go over there and do an inventory check at some point.

After he'd found Hanna.

When he had finished updating the book, he replaced it and the bookshelves and left his room to find Javier. He found him just leaving the kitchen where they had been eating. Joe assessed him carefully, looking straight into his eyes.

"Javier. Did Hanna say anything about where she was going?"

Javier thought for a moment. "Not really. I assume she meant Órgiva, or Los Tablones, the local towns, but no, she did not say where."

"Was there anything else? What did she say exactly? Try and remember. Think carefully."

Javier exhaled and scratched his stubble.

"Ah, *si*. Okay, so after the second day of the shutdown, she says she wanted to go on a recce and see what's happening. Check in on some friends. Of course, not a bad idea, but as I said, someone should go with her, but she shook her head." Javier paused. "She said something like, 'Everyone should stay home, I'll go.' But then, I said, 'We discuss later,' as I had so much to do at that time. Then, at dinnertime in the evening, she didn't come. Gone. This was about three hours after we talked. She went without telling anyone, and no one saw her go. After that, I couldn't find Diego either."

Joe stared at Javier, waiting for more, but the man just shrugged. "That's it, Joe. All I know."

"That's it?" Joe asked.

"*Si*, I'm sorry, Joe. I hope she is ok. Do you want to search for her?"

"Yeah, of course, but I'll go by myself. I'll need you to keep working on the power situation and whatever needs doing here. I'll look at some maps and head out as soon as I can, but we'll go over everything before I go. Okay?"

Javier nodded, apparently satisfied.

"By the way, did you update the cypher book recently?"

The only two people who knew about it and used it were Joe

and Javier.

The Spaniard thought for a second. "Not for many months. I leave that to you. Why?"

Joe stared at Javier, trying to read his expression, but it was only one of mild confusion.

"And you've not told anyone?"

Javier. "No, no one. Like you said, I kept it a secret. Why?"

Joe waved his hand dismissively. "No reason. Thanks. Don't worry, thanks, Javier." With that, Joe headed down to the basement to retrieve some bug-out supplies, his mind wandering back to the disturbed floorboard.

Chapter 21

St Mary's Hospital,
London
Day 3

The ground floor foyer of the hospital was bustling with people, surrounding the reception desk, where a few hapless security guards and a nurse tried to calm them down. It was verging on chaos.

Zoe led John around the edge of the crowd before they slipped out of the main doors, leaving the sound of chaos behind them.

They headed south, along Park Lane, skirting Hyde Park. As they came to the affluent area of Belgravia, they encountered two long queues of people, some with large water containers and buckets, waiting to get water and emergency provisions from a food bank that had been established on the ground floor of an old two-storey office building. An army truck was also in the car park, where armed soldiers unloaded boxes, taking them to the food bank for unpacking and distribution.

"Something positive is happening, at least," Zoe said as they passed.

"Do you think we need to try and get anything?" John asked.

"Well, I've got plenty of snacks and a full bottle of water, but then it depends how long it'll take and what's available at the other end." After a slight moment of consideration, he concluded

"There'll be plenty of provisions at the Singh's, trust me. Let's just keep going."

As they crossed the Thames at Vauxhall Bridge, John began to find his stride and moved a bit better now, although compared to Zoe's motion, it was still a shuffle.

The light faded in the bleak, cold afternoon as they reached the Clapham area. Zoe tried to keep them on the main roads, not that it felt any safer. It still felt isolated, with threats ever looming. No street lighting turned the city into a dark concert forest, where the mind plays tricks with the shadows. The low winter sun blocked by building a cloud did little to illuminate the streets and was just enough to navigate by.

As they veered off the exposed main road and headed for Brixton, Zoe's nerves were on edge. Was John really in a fit state to be walking across the capital? Now, she could hardly run off if they ran into trouble, and she couldn't exactly see John being much good in a fistfight now.

As they passed the fire escape for a large office building, a figure stepped out of its shadows and directly into their path. Zoe stopped in her tracks, lifting a hand to John's chest to stop him. She was so focused on the ground he was unaware of the situation they had just walked into. Zoe's heart started beating at double time. She glanced over her shoulder from across the road to see four or five more figures approaching. Before Zoe could begin to respond, they were surrounded. All wearing hoodies, trainers and dark clothes, the standard uniform of street thugs.

"Hand over your bag," a young male with a pockmarked face

demanded casually, just like he was asking for a cigarette.

Here we go again, thought Zoe. Was this going to be a fucking regular thing now? She felt angry, more than she had ever been. All her life, she had been the little sister, quiet and obedient, while her older brothers had dominated her with their loud and outlandish behaviour. That had helped shape a certain inner toughness, too. Sure, she had encountered a lot more overbearing masculinity when at university, then through her career and new life with Ed.

"It's our stuff," she replied defiantly.

"Do you and your dad want to get hurt?" came the reply. The thug stepped toward her threateningly.

John turned to Zoe. They both ignored the 'Dad' comment. Zoe wished her dad really was there. He'd kick their arses into next week.

"Best hand it over," John said.

Zoe thought for a second. It was just basic supplies: crackers, biscuits, a flashlight and her pocket knife.

Shit.

Her meds were in the bag, too.

"I've got my medicine in here. Pills I need."

"Throw it over! We'll look," the pock-faced thug insisted.

She slipped off her backpack and threw it at the guy, causing him to flinch. This annoyed him, and his mask of nonchalance slipped.

"Don't fuck wit' us, bitch." He tossed it to one of the other thugs, who then proceeded to go through the pack, with an increasingly disappointed expression on seeing the contents, until he found the pen-knife which he slipped into his pocket.

"Just snacks, we'll keep them."

He pulled out the medicine bottle with Zoe's buspirone pills.

"This ya' meds?" he called out to her.

"Yeah," Zoe replied with a tone of despondency while half expecting him to pour them onto the floor. He surprised her by throwing them back to her. She managed to grab them and slipped them into her pocket.

"Feeling generous," he said. Then added with a smirk: "Now, give us your coats."

John gave Zoe a sideways glance.

"Hey, it's fucking freezing," Zoe exclaimed, with venom in her voice.

"We're not your size," John interjected.

One of them, a short skinny shaven headed runt, pulled a knife and began to wave it about with an air of menace.

There is no point in arguing with these arseholes, she thought Zoe as she slipped out of her jacket while John took a while longer to remove his long overcoat. They handed them over, then, mercifully, the gang moved away, up the street.

"Hope all your mothers are proud!" Zoe called after them.

A few 'bitch' comments came back before they disappeared around the corner.

"Come on, let's get to this bloody place of yours," said Zoe. Her humour, patience, and any feelings of charity had all but vanished.

"I'm sorry," John said. "I'm slowing you down, and I'm weak. I'm no good at all."

Zoe felt bad and shook her head. "No, no, I'm sorry, John. It's been a shock, the whole bloody mess!" She rubbed her arms. The bitter cold felt close without a jacket. She loved that jacket.

"Fucking bastards!" she said out loud.

There was nothing to do except soldier on. There were

165

crowds of people outside most of the banks they passed, demanding their money be returned to them.

Any shop that was open invariably displayed a 'Cash Only' sign in the window. There was an odd energy to the city, an undercurrent of desperation, like people could sense things balancing on the edge. Without power, a lot of the cafes and takeaways couldn't prepare food, so now the supermarkets and stores had become the focus of people's attention. They overheard a heated rise in tension of voices and turned to see two men fighting each other, the stress finally breaking through.

"Come on," John urged, "there's going to be a heck of a lot more of this."

Zoe patted her belt, grateful that the gang had failed to spot it.

"We're not dead yet. I've got cash hidden in this beauty," she said to herself with a satisfied smile.

They managed to get into one shop and grab a few dwindling supplies of cereal bars, crisps, chocolate and bottles of water. Inflation was rampant now, and according to the man behind the counter, the prices were increasing by the hour as supplies dwindled. "Nearly fifty quid just for a few measly snacks," Zoe exclaimed as she left the shop, shoving the precious items into her jeans pockets.

They headed along the road, slowly but surely moving south.

"If this outage continues," Zoe asked apprehensively as if not really wanting to know, "how bad will it really get?" She could easily guess. Millions of people confined in built-up areas, demanding ever-decreasing resources.

"Well, London and other big cities will be the worst affected," John replied. "Food will run dry really quick; it already has in many places by the looks of it. The whole supply chain will have crashed by now, and any attempts of help by the authorities will be piecemeal at best. They'll never be able to adequately deal with it all. Riots will become widespread, and I expect millions will be leaving the cities for rural areas looking for food and supplies. And, let's face it, it's not getting any warmer." John shivered as if to emphasise the point. "That's why we need to get to a hive," he continued. "We prepped for events like this for years and have some modest means of survival. Unfortunately, though, as we see the actual scale of this event, I am not sure if it's enough."

I was right, Zoe thought. *I really didn't want to hear this.*

They continued walking in silence into the late afternoon. The signs of people carrying bags and shopping trolleys of food away from food stores were everywhere. Those places that remained closed were now getting invaded by gangs of looters circling an abandoned place like vultures before bricks and heavy objects crashed against shutters and through their windows. There had been no further sign of the police or army personnel anywhere. The authorities, it seemed, had melted out of sight, allowing the normal rules of society to crumble.

Avoiding such scenes of disruption and violence, they were making good progress, passing through the areas of Streatham and Croydon just as the light faded.

"I don't want to get stuck out here in the dark," Zoe said with trepidation.

"I know, and we won't," John replied with some confidence, although his face seemed a little paler.

"You okay?" Zoe asked, concern etched in her voice.

John nodded without saying anything at first, then pointed to a bench nearby. "Maybe take five?"

They sat down. Zoe could feel the exhaustion setting in. Not having a coat meant her body was burning the extra calories to keep warm. She glanced over at John. He was clearly suffering. His skin had taken on an ashen hue, even if he didn't want to say. After a few minutes, John stood up. "Let's keep moving."

They moved through the city side streets, avoiding the protests and looting as it ebbed and flowed around them. If they kept their heads down as they walked, people generally ignored them. But what more did they have to offer anyone now anyway.

"I keep thinking about Joe, Zak and my parents. Wondering how they are going to be dealing with this?" Zoe said, seemingly out of nowhere.

"They're good people, strong. They'll be doing fine," John reassured her.

"What about your wife and son?" Zoe asked.

"Anna was with friends in Chile. They're well prepped for this. After our meeting in Chile, Troy went back to New York, which concerns me. If the same thing has hit there, it'll be one of the worst places of all to be. But he's a grown man, no idiot, and we were all briefed on basic precautions and plans."

He stopped walking and rested his hand on a wall.

"My worst fear is I'll never see them again," John said with genuine grief etching his voice.

"I'm sure that's not the case," Zoe reassured him.

They continued on as the light faded, and the temperature seemed to drop with it. Finally, they came off one of the endless roads that brought them into Addington.

"This is it," Zoe said, pointing to the turning to the cul-de-sac where the Singh family and the rest of the city hive were based. They turned the corner into a cul-de-sac and stopped at the sight of a huge crowd of people clutching bowls, plates and bags congregating in the street, queuing up for something ahead.

"Bloody hell," John said with a gasp.

"What the hell's going on?"

They moved down the road, passing alongside the people waiting in line. A few glared at them as they walked by. At the end of the street were lines of trestle tables on which were large bowls and tubs, from which a group of Indian families dishing out hot food. The smell drifted down the street and instantly made Zoe realise just how hungry she was for a decent meal.

As they approached the line of tables, one of the family, a tall, well-built, middle-aged man with a black turban, looked up and broke into a broad smile before saying in a booming voice.

"Well, well, well. John bloody Rhodes!"

Chapter 22

Addington, London
Day 3

For Zoe, the hot meal of rice, vegetable curry and Chapati breads cooked on camping gas stoves tasted like heaven. She scooped up a load of the spicy food onto a plastic fork and savoured every mouthful. John Rhodes was wolfing down his portion while sitting opposite her at a large oak family dining table set in the spacious kitchen area. A few candles and an oil lamp provided the only flickering light that cast continuous moving shadows on the walls. They had just been joined by Raj and his two children, Deepak, a nine-year-old boy and his younger sister, Varsha.

"So good," Zoe mumbled for about the fourth time.

"One of Binta's classics," Raj said, referring to his wife as she walked in.

"Good timing. Were you slagging my food off when I was gone?"

They both laughed.

"Although no one ever mentions it, I can cook as well, you know." Raj said, "You know that, John, right?" He gestured to the old man.

"Yes, I do remember. Although it was a long, long time ago," John replied.

One of the girls volunteered. "I like the Baingan Bharta dish best."

"Ah, that's a great one, too," Raj said, nodding his head in agreement.

They finished up their food, and everyone mucked in, washing all plates and pans as best they could with what little water was available. The large pots used for the food they had been handing out to neighbours and friends earlier were now stacked and cleaned.

Raj invited John and Zoe to the back portion of the house, where they were soon joined by his brother, Harish, a much shorter man who lived next door with his family.

From what Zoe had seen, Raj's family members and friends occupied the whole cul-de-sac, making it, in effect, their own enclave. From the outside, the houses weren't much to look at, but extensive work had been done inside, making it far more spacious through extensions having been made at the rear.

They followed Raj into a conservatory lounge area that looked out onto a small dark garden surrounded by high fences and took seats at a round coffee table.

"Well, this is a pleasant surprise, John, and totally unexpected," Raj said and held up a bottle of beer. He had his long black hair tied into a ponytail, his turban having been put away.

John tipped his head and smiled. "Thank you. Yes, all a bit last minute. It was a matter of helping Zoe here, but it's all a moot point with the blackout."

Raj nodded. "And you're doing okay? With the grumbling appendix, I mean," he added, gesturing to John's general stomach area. John and Zoe relayed, over dinner, their day about getting John from the hospital. "Time will tell, I guess, but for now, I'm okay. How long do you think you can give away your food?" John asked.

"Exactly!" Harish interjected, looking at Raj accusingly. "We need to think of ourselves and our families."

Raj's upbeat demeanour evaporated, replaced by a look of frustration. Clearly, this had been a conflict point between the two brothers before John and Zoe showed up.

"I think you know why," Raj started. "Firstly, we're helping those in need. Our neighbours and friends. Secondly, as the power is down and our generator has so little fuel, all our frozen meats will go bad anyway. So we needed to cook it all. There's way more stored than we can eat before the meals all become spoiled."

"I get that, but if this goes on, we'll regret it," said Harish, his tone low and accusing.

"If this goes on, we'll have bigger problems than giving away surplus food we can't use," Raj replied. "Listen, we'll do another cook-up tomorrow for whoever is in need, then I think we'll ration what we have left and look at our reserves and supplies, what we can preserve."

Harish seemed grudgingly satisfied with that and turned to John, leaning forward.

"This blackout. Do you know anything about it? Is it a minor blip or—" He paused. John sipped on his mug of tea and slowly placed it on the table.

"Well, we know it has to be an EMP or, rather, multiple EMPs that have been released. And there's not much I can say except guess. As this power blackout goes on, my instinct is that it's not going away anytime soon and that things are going to get pretty bad and real fast. That means a lot of displaced people and widespread starvation. It's also getting cold, and where there's no power, there's no heat. Big cities like London are going to become hell holes very soon. Even within just a few days, it's going to be like nothing ever seen in our lifetimes."

Everyone went quiet and stony-faced. It was the reality they feared but hoped wouldn't come to pass.

"There's still a chance, no? It's just a hiccup?" Harish asked with empty hope.

"Well, most vehicles have stopped working. Zoe tells me planes have even crashed from the sky. In an EMP event, most things controlled by electronics are fried beyond repair, and that means no going back to how things were anytime soon, I'm afraid. Brought about by whom? Well, I have my theories."

"Your blueprint was spot on then, John," Raj said.

"What's that?" Zoe asked, turning to John.

"For the past few years, well, decade, actually, we've assessed all the scenarios that the cabal might try to pull off. We've seen an increase in their attempts over the past few years, well, you know the stories. The engineered wars, the droughts, the release of viruses—all contributing to an increasing global instability—" John paused, looking around for the words. "I don't know if they did this, but it was always a high possibility that they might. So, our prep document was a guide for getting prepared. The blueprint gave all our members and hives the instructions as to how to protect ourselves and survive."

"Yes," Raj said, "and we stockpiled for years. All in the basement and a few other locations. Not only food and stuff but also"—he held up a finger—"the Faraday cages to protect some electrical stuff, including the ham radios," he said with a grin.

"Faraday cages?" Zoe asked. That's the protection from any EMP, right?"

"Yes, against any external electromagnetic activity. So, we included info on creating protection for electronic devices. Metal boxes to keep all the gear in," John added. He looked at Raj.

"So, are your radios working?"

Raj shrugged. "I haven't had a chance to look yet. That's something we should do. But I don't know what the backup generator situation is."

"Yes, of course. Be good to check, though. Even for comms within the cul-de-sac. If you have enough walkie-talkies?"

"Yeah, there's a batch down there." Raj stood up. "Let's take a look."

They all followed Raj again, holding an oil lamp, this time through a metal door that he unlocked with a key, and then they descended into a dark basement.

"It's dark down here at the best of times," Raj joked as he lit a few other oil lamps. The resulting glow of light revealed a large, spacious basement with racks of shelves filled with boxes and tubs of supplies. They walked along one of the shelf aisles towards a room at the back.

Raj placed the lamp on a desk, and as it brightened, it illuminated a makeshift office and communications room with several dead computer screens. Reaching under the desk, he hauled out a large metal box. He pulled off the tight lid that had suction padding around the inside rim and revealed a small radio box and other equipment. Then, he grabbed another metal box and opened that one to reveal a portable power station, which he lifted.

"This beauty should be fully charged. Now let's see."

Below the display were USB ports, plug sockets and other ports. He tapped on the display screen, and a backlit light came on.

"Aha, that looks promising," Zoe said, leaning down to study the device.

"Yep. It's on, it's working. We can run it off its lithium battery for about forty hours or so, depending. Enough wattage capacity to power lots of appliances, fridges, TVs, if any of that stuff isn't fried, of course, which it probably is."

"So, you wouldn't be able to keep your freezer going with this?" Zoe asked.

"It's a good point, but the freezer itself wasn't protected in any Faraday shield, so no. The electrical components will all be screwed," Raj replied.

"Yes, that's the problem with an EMP," John explained, joining in, "it can fry everything unless it's protected."

"What about keeping it charged?" Zoe asked.

Raj thought for a moment. "We can use our solar array if we can get that rigged up and working. Big 'if'. The panels themselves don't have electronics in them, but—" He sighed and paused. "No, the inverter and controller will be fried, and I didn't get any spares."

"We can check it out," John said reassuringly and, after looking at the unit, said, "if I am not mistaken, this power station has its own internal inverter and controller. Come on, let's see if we can get this toy lit up."

Everyone watched with growing anticipation as Raj pulled out the High-Frequency (HF) Radio Transceiver and placed it on one of the desks. It took a good ten minutes to get everything set up, but everyone almost cheered when the lights came on, and the radio drew its power from the power station box. Those lights represented so much more than just electrical power. It represented communication and hope.

They drew up plastic chairs and huddled around the radio as Raj scanned through the frequencies.

"Can we listen in on the emergency services?" Zoe asked.

"Maybe once you could, not anymore," Raj replied.

"They most likely protect their frequencies with encryption or are using higher frequencies like UHF," Harish added.

Raj pressed the switch on his microphone.

"Raj001 calling—anyone out there? In London. Anyone? Over."

They listened in silence. Then Raj repeated his message.

After a few moments, the radio crackled into life with the voice of a woman.

"This is Deviant5. Hear you loud and clear. We're over in Whitechapel. What's your location and your situation? Over."

"Holding up okay, thanks, Deviant 5. Sounds like you're central. We're in the Addington area. How's it going out there? Over."

"Not great, Raj001. Lots of looting of department stores, lots of gangs roaming the streets and not many coppers about, which is typical. Over." the woman replied.

"Will you be okay? Are you in danger? Over," Raj responded with clear concern.

"My brothers and I are okay right now; we will do the best we can. We're looking at leaving the city if this situation continues; over."

"That sounds like a sensible choice. Stay safe. Out," concluded Raj.

Raj turned to the others with a grimace on his face.

"Well, it sounds like it's getting as bad as we thought it

might," John said.

"What's the range of that thing?" Zoe asked.

"Good point. Could we reach Suffolk?" John chimed in.

Raj shook his head. "That's too far. Well, there have been cases of these radios reaching that distance," Raj replied.

"But even if we could reach them, we don't know if they have set up their rig yet or if they managed to protect it all," he added.

"What about that Quantum tech set-up? That was the whole network plan for emergency Liberatus comms, wasn't it?" Zoe asked.

John sighed. "We had the boxes sent out but only weeks ago. I know Tennessee, Oregon, Andalucía, and Munich received their package, but I never got confirmation from Suffolk or you, Raj?"

"No. Ours never arrived," Raj said, holding his arms apart. "The supply chain problems really worsened in the last week, like some kind of prelude to all this."

"Zoe and I are going to head to Suffolk soon. I know you're set on staying here, but let me know if anyone wants to come with us." John said.

Raj nodded. "I think we're good here, but yes, I will ask around."

He leaned down and switched off both the radio and the power bank. "Time to sleep, I think."

"Roger that," said Zoe with a yawn.

Chapter 23

Addington, London
Day 4

Early the following morning, Binita and the children began chopping vegetables and prepping spices for another big cook on the gas stoves. John wasn't feeling great but managed to haul himself out of the spare bedroom as the smell of coffee wafted through the house.

After a modest breakfast of wheat biscuits and the last of the oat milk, Raj and Zoe checked the radio again, firstly scanning the emergency frequencies. Raj talked Zoe through what he was doing, just the bare basics of radio operation.

"You never know when it might be useful," he said as he eased one of the knobs through the frequencies. Then, a clear, authoritative voice came through the speaker.

"—stay indoors. We repeat, due to a current power issue, we advise people to stay in their homes, where possible. Food banks and army help points are being set up across the country."

Then, the message began to repeat itself.

"You know, hardly anyone will hear this. They switched to an emergency alert system that sends SMS to phones, but of course, they don't work. Ironic, eh?"

Raj's walkie-talkie crackled into life.

"Raj?" It was his brother, Harish.

"Here. What is it?"

"We've got a problem outside."

"Why, what's happening?"

Then Raj heard the distinct crack of a gunshot outside as well as through the radio speaker.

***

The crowd pouring into the cul-de-sac seemed twice or even three times as large as the previous day. The neighbours and friends were there again, but this time now joined by faces Binita did not recognise.

"Shit," Binita mumbled under her breath as she began to spoon rice and curry onto paper plates.

"Well, once this lot is gone, it's gone," Harish said, perhaps a bit too loudly. Those who overheard him pushed forward, and the crowd seemed to swell and sway like waves pushing against the rocks. Several hands began to reach for the bowls of food as Binita dished it out.

"Please wait your turn!" Harish ordered, but the momentum of the crowd swelled forward, pushing into the trestle tables. There was a commotion further down the line. Angry shouts and jostling, then what looked like some kind of fight erupted at the back.

Harish picked up his walkie-talkie and radioed his brother.

"We've got a problem. Outside—"

Another loud gunshot rang out, followed by screams.

"Shit!"

Harish gestured to Binita. "Get back inside. Go!" She began to argue, and then yet another shot rang out. There were more frantic screams now, and some of the crowd dived for cover. Harish and Binita ducked instinctively.

Several men brandishing handguns moved through the crowd, pushing people out of their way as they approached the trestle tables. There were four of them, all wearing similar baseball caps, tracksuits and trainers. One began helping himself to some rice and curry while another faced the crowd.

"Hmm, check this," he muttered, spooning the food onto one of the paper plates. One of the others, a tall, skinny youth, pointed his weapon directly at Hamish. "Get up. That's your house?" He jerked the gun in the direction of the houses behind them.

"That's my brother's house," Harish replied, observing the youth with hooded eyes. "Listen, we're just tryin' to help people—"

"Shuddup. We're gonna take a look at your house." He turned his head slightly to talk to one of his mates. "Chris, get 'em out of here."

Chris, the man facing the crowd, held up his weapon in the air.

"Food giveaway is over. Go home or get som' of dis!" he shouted. There was a murmur of voices, and the people began to disperse, fear evident in their eyes. These were just ordinary people, either retirees or working people, all now scrambling for food and warmth and completely unused to the blatant lawlessness now creeping into their lives. A few people who knew the Singhs hesitated, frowning at the youths who had gate-crashed the cul-de-sac. Harish gave them a frown and a slight shake of his head to warn them from getting involved.

The other youths scoffed down some of the rice and curry, clearly not having had a hot meal for a while.

"In the house," the thug demanded, waving his gun at Hamish, who was now standing in front of his wife.

"We've got nothing in—"

"Yeah, we'll see about that."

"We have kids in there. You hurt my kids and—"

The thug moved quickly and slapped Harish across the face with the butt of his weapon. Harish grunted with pain and stepped back, holding his mouth. He clenched his fist and made a move to throw a punch back, but the thug now had his pistol with the barrel aimed at Harish's forehead.

"Harish!" His wife almost threw herself at the thug, but Zoe had appeared in the interim and held her back.

"Please stop!" she shouted.

Harish and the thug stared at each other for a few seconds.

"You chill out, hear me?" the thug said, breaking the tension. "We ain't after your kids, see? We want your food an' shit."

He stepped backwards, keeping his pistol still trained on Harish, then turned and marched up to the front door and began banging hard against it with the butt of the gun.

***

The gang went through the house and upturned everything, sending the sound of smashing glass and shouts reverberating through the house.

Raj's family, Harish and his wife, along with Zoe and John, had been shoved into the living room with the door shut behind them. One of the thugs told them to stay put, and he would be outside the door, and anyone coming out would be shot.

In the midst of the chaos, Binita enveloped her children

in a protective embrace on the sofa, her heart racing as she tried to shield them from the terrifying experience going on around them. They clung close to her and sobbed, their faces buried to her chest. Zoe, her own expression, a mix of concern and determination, sat nearby on a chair, her attempts at reassurance drowned out by the aggressive noises and banging echoing from different corners of the house. She reached into her pocket and pulled out her meds, the simple action of taking them helping to calm her nerves.

"Fuck this. Why aren't we fighting them?" Harish hissed through gritted teeth. He was standing with Raj in a corner, away from the kids.

"It's too dangerous with the kids here. They just want food. Let them take it," Raj whispered.

"And then what? We all starve?" said Harish, spitting out his words in undisguised anger

"We'll find a way," Raj insisted.

Harish shook his head but didn't say anything.

After nearly an hour, the gang had moved tubs of the family's stored dry foods up the basement stairs and piled them outside. Harish and Raj watched from the window as they took what they could carry, and one had stacked up the tubs on a wheelbarrow they had stolen from the garden.

When they had disappeared around the end of the cul-de-sac, Raj and Harish walked around the house, inspecting the damage. The kitchen cupboard shelves had been stripped bare, with glasses and plates dropped and smashed over the tiled floor. Zoe joined them.

"We'll get things back together," she offered, but the comforting words seemed lost on the brothers.

"Bunch of bloody wankers!" Harish hissed, slamming his

hand hard down on the countertop.

They headed downstairs to the basement to find glass and debris scattered around the floor. There had been stored glass jars of flour and various beans. Some of them had been dropped to the floor, the contents spilt. The marauding thugs hadn't been able to take it all, but they certainly had given it a good go.

"Fuck!" Raj walked quickly to the back of the room and saw the radio smashed. He held his hand over his face.

"Radio's gone—" he said with despair entering his voice

"What about the generator?" Zoe asked.

"It's still here," he replied.

"That's something, at least," Zoe said before voicing the obvious question in everyone's mind. "Think they'll be back?" she asked, placing an unbroken jar back in place.

Raj shook his head. "Hope not."

"Listen," Harish said, his tone bristling with anger, "we've just got to defend ourselves against this crap. Otherwise, we're done. Anyone can just come in here and take all our shit whenever they please!" He shouted the last part, aiming all his rage at his brother.

"Alright. What was I supposed to do? They had guns, we don't. My kids are here," Raj replied with a resigned shrug.

"You'll need to shore up the defences or leave. I don't think it's going to be very safe here," Zoe said as diplomatically as she could.

"Bloody right, it ain't safe," Harish said, still glaring at Raj.

Zoe tried to break up the tension. "Just to put it out there, as you know, John and I are heading to the Suffolk hive. Maybe that's an idea for all of us. Something to think about," she said calmly. "And that's not to say we're taking off right away. Of course, we'll stick around and help out any way we can."

Harish lifted a hand and felt his cheek, which had swollen up into a nasty purple bruise.

"Those bastards piling into our homes was just the start. Pretty soon, the whole of London will be crawling with more hungry hordes, desperate for food and shelter from this freezin' weather." His tone was laced with frustration at his brother and growing anger at their situation as he paced around the gloomy basement.

"Look at this shit," Harish gestured at the spilt plastic tubs emptied of their food rations, canned foods, sacks of beans and rice that the Singhs had squirrelled away for just such a desperate need as the one they currently faced. Numerous glass jars, once filled with flour, had been smashed onto the hard ground, the contents strewn into mounds of white chalky powder mixed in with shards of glass. The dickheads didn't know what to do with flour, so they just threw them on the ground.

"How long before we get raided again?" Harish asked, continuing his frustrated rant, "And what if it's much worse next time? What if they harmed your wife or one of the kids? What if it was worse than this?" Harish stepped closer to his brother, pointing at his bruise.

The brothers stared each other out until Harish stepped back from his older brother, the muscles around his jaw quivering.

"At least, here is what we know." Raj walked to the narrow oblong window, looking out onto the backyard that was the basement's only source of light, "We say 'our home, our castle', right? If we don't fight for that, what can we fight for? Out there is—well, god knows what waits for us out there."

Raj swung around to face his brother, then looked at Zoe.

"This place in Suffolk, is it safe for all of us?" he asked, a gleam of hope in his eyes.

"If John says it is, then you can bet it should be," Zoe replied.

Chapter 24

Addington, London
Day 6

It had taken less than a day for Raj and Binita to come around to the idea of leaving their home. For Raj, the main concern was the journey to the Suffolk hive and their safety en route. It was inevitable there would be dangers whether they stayed or went, but the important thing was that they stuck together.

Strength in numbers and all that.

When a neighbour and friend called Max, a burly middle-aged builder, offered to come with them and throw in a baseball bat and handgun to help with their security, Raj seemed more assured.

Raj, Harish and Zoe went door to door to speak with other neighbours about joining them. Some were keen and ready, but some weren't convinced and opted to stay.

Soon, they had a small group ready to hit the road. The families had tents, some camping gear, and some supplies the gang hadn't got their hands on.

When the house had been cleaned up and all possible resources that could be carried packed, the group headed off at dawn, Raj and Zoe up front, the families, a small group of neighbours and John Rhodes in the middle, with Harish, Max and John at the rear. That's how wolf packs did it, Zoe had said. The weaker and more vulnerable members being protected by the outlying strongest ones.

A decision had been made collectively to circumnavigate the main city of London that stood between them and the road towards Suffolk. Things were falling apart fast, and they needed to avoid the hordes of people, the millions of people, most of whom were just realising that this 'power cut' was something far worse than they had initially thought. That growing realisation would feed fear, anger and desperation. Not a great scenario to potentially be heading right into.

The long walk would take them to Bromley, onto Sidcup, then Dartford and across the Thames and onward, avoiding the main city and always heading east.

In Bromley, on one of the suburban B roads, they passed a farmhouse with a painted sign offering fresh eggs, potatoes, fruit, and vegetables. However, any hopes of that bounty were quickly dashed when a barricade came into view, blocking the entrance to the neighbouring farm yard. It was at the gates, a hastily constructed affair made from a couple of vehicles pushed into place and the gaps filled with a mesh of barbed wire and scaffold poles.

Heading east along seemingly endless roads was painfully slow, especially with the young ones. Also slowing the pace was John Rhodes, a man usually fit for his age, but following his bout of appendicitis, his pace was much slower than it had been. Their route took them past rows of red brick council houses, ranks of closed shops and looted supermarkets, all of which had nothing to offer them.

"Just don't worry about it, John," Zoe kept repeating as he

continuously apologised for his slowness. "We'll be resting soon. The kids are tired, too."

A large sign propped alongside a line of traffic cones stopped the walking convoy, and a discussion began.

"What is it?" Zoe asked as she walked up. She proceeded to read.

'Food and Shelter provided at Biggin Hill Airport', the sign read.

"That could be well worth a look?" Binita said.

"It's well off our route. Besides, once you're in there, there's no getting out." John said.

Zoe glanced at him.

"Are you sure?"

"Everything we need is in Suffolk," John insisted, "Trust me, we'll be safe and looked after. We just need to get there. The Government, the army will all have their own agenda," he went on. "Yes, they'll give you some food, along with potentially hundreds or thousands of other people. Then, we'll just be given ID numbers and put to work. Any freedom will be—" John stopped suddenly mid-sentence and seemed to hold his stomach.

Raj and Harish seemed to agree.

"Let's keep going," Raj said and started off again.

"Wait." It was one of the neighbours. A couple in their fifties both looking scared. "It sounds like a good option to us. Some food and shelter sound good," the man said.

Raj looked at the couple, nodding in understanding. "Alright, Rob. That's your decision. Good luck!" he said, extending his hand as the couple left for the direction of Biggin Hill Airport.

It was late afternoon, and the bitter cold seemed to intensify as the remaining huddle pack moved in silence through the roads and streets of suburban London.

Eventually, they came to a school where the playground was full of marquee tents, including one with a sign hung up outside reading 'medical help'. Inside the gates, people who looked like they were from the local community milled around.

"Let's see if they'll let us stay here tonight," Zoe said. After speaking to one of the women organisers for a few minutes, they returned to where the group stood around waiting.

"She said we can pitch up in the sports field at the back. I said if we could help them out with anything, then we would."

When their tents were pitched, the camping burners came out of a backpack, along with pre-prepared chilli and rice in a couple of Tupperware boxes.

Raj and Zoe built up a pile of sticks gathered from around trees at the edge of the field and started a fire. It kept everyone's spirits up and almost felt like some kind of camping holiday as they chatted around the dancing flames.

When the kids had gone to bed inside one of the tents, the adults gathered closer around the fire and started planning.

"We should have someone stay awake. Just in case," John suggested.

Everyone agreed. "A couple of shifts? Myself and Raj can take it in turns." Harish said.

Raj nodded. "Alright, wake me at two then."

"We should aim to get going early. Seven at the latest," Zoe suggested.

As the night drew in and people began to disappear into their tents, Raj remained by the embers of the fire, poking it occasionally with a stick.

Zoe appeared and crouched down on an upturned stump.

"I was thinking," she said. "Maybe two is better to keep

guard."

He waved a hand dismissively.

"You don't have to do that. Get some sleep."

She gave him an even look until he caught her eye.

"We're in a dangerous situation. People might attempt anything, including sneaking up and taking you out. Two's better."

Raj was about to argue, then seemed to stop himself.

"Sure. You're right."

There was a distant hacking noise from beyond their camping circle.

Raj and Zoe both looked at each other. Zoe grabbed a flashlight, and they walked towards where the noise had come from. They heard it again. It sounded like someone throwing up. Then, along a line of trees, Zoe caught a glimpse of John Rhodes in her light beam. He was crouched down on his knees, attempting to get back up onto his feet, where a pool of vomit splattered the grass.

"John? Are you alright?" Zoe asked as they approached.

"Yeah, a bit of a rough night," he replied, trying to make light of it.

John waved a hand dismissively, but as the light fell onto his pale face and haggard features, Zoe felt sick with worry.

***

The Following Morning

The group prepped a modest breakfast: tea, fruit, and cereal bars, and then began to dismantle the tents under a stark white sky. Overnight, the temperature had dropped even further, and everyone now wore headwear and winter jackets and coats.

John skipped breakfast and still didn't look very good but seemed to perk up after sipping on tea that Zoe brought him in his tent. She crouched down by the tent entrance flaps.

"Are you sure you're up to this?"

He managed a weak smile.

"I'll dig deep into the reserves and find that grit. Don't worry yourself, Zoe."

She fixed him with a level stare.

"But I am bloody worried. Appendicitis can be serious and might need an operation," she insisted, her face full of concern.

"You think I should have stayed in the hospital?"

She stared down at the remnants of her tea in a mug. Perhaps she should have left him there. Chaotic as it was in the hospital, if they had somehow restored power, at least he would have been in the best place, not trailing along the increasingly dangerous roads.

"Doesn't matter now," she said, instead, "what matters is whether you can actually make it to Suffolk."

"I'll make it. And thank you, Zoe. I know you didn't ask for any of this."

"You and Joe helped me when all that shit kicked off after Ed's death. It was my decision to dig deeper into that, and now it's my call to get you to the hive."

He looked at her, but his eyes seemed distant, as if he was thinking something through. "You'll make a great leader, Zoe. I can see it in you."

She let out a snort of derision and stood up outside the tent. "Not sure I want that honour in this new shit state order. Now, come on. If we're going, let's go."

The group returned to the long suburban road, and after an

hour, Zoe and John began to lag behind at the rear, with the rest of the group drifting further ahead.

John had another bout of abdominal pain, so they stopped to rest on a low wall and sipped water from their bottles. Zoe fished out painkillers from her backpack and offered them to John.

"Take some of these."

"Thanks." He put two in his mouth and swallowed them down with a few gulps of water.

The others had disappeared from sight now.

Zoe just hoped they would notice and wait up before turning north towards Chelmsford, their first destination. The plan was to camp up in a national park that Raj had taken the family to a few times. He had pointed the place out to Zoe on a map, so at least there was a route plan.

Depending on whether everything went to plan, of course.

Zoe was about to suggest they press on when John doubled over, clutching his side and cried out in agony.

"Oh god, John." Zoe stood and gently put a hand on his shoulder.

"Goddamn it," he hissed through clenched teeth.

"Can you breathe through it?" she asked hopefully.

He exhaled and then groaned again.

Zoe was unsure of what to do. In normal times, you would call a doctor or an ambulance. She leaned over him, trying to offer comfort but beginning to feel anxious herself. A feeling she had surprisingly not felt for a few days. That old fear. Her hands started to shake as she felt the waves of anxiety building. She reached for her meds, quickly taking a few to keep the attack at bay.

What the hell was she to do?

She should go run after the others and get them to wait. To come back.

Where the hell were they anyway? Weren't they supposed to be a wolf pack, staying together for safety? That one had been forgotten quickly.

Zoe was so caught up in her thoughts she didn't hear the unfamiliar sound of an engine coming closer. John, through his pain, looked up in surprise. She turned to follow his gaze and saw a large modern military vehicle coming up the road towards them.

It was the first working vehicle she had seen since the power cut. But, of course, the army would have some EMP-proof vehicles, she told herself. And anyone else who had the foresight to keep them in underground protected shelters. Besides the military, that probably meant hardly anyone else would have any.

Zoe felt a wave of relief. This was good. They would help.

The truck pulled up alongside them, and a young soldier looked down at them from the window.

"Everything alright?" he called out.

John waved a hand dismissively. "Yes, we're alright. Thank you!" Zoe looked at John, astonished.

"Er, well, I don't think you are." She lowered her voice and said to John, "for god's sake. This is the help we need. You're ill!"

"Madam?" the soldier said again.

"He's ill!" she called back. "He has appendicitis, but we left the hospital as their power went down."

"That's the case everywhere," the soldier replied. "Look, we have our orders and normally would have to leave you to it, but we can get you to Biggin Hill Airport though. It's

193

been converted into a refugee camp. There might be medical treatment available for your dad."

Zoe didn't bother correcting him and stood up. "Great, thank you," she replied, "John, come on."

The old man looked up at the truck as the soldier peered down at them with mistrust. "Not a good idea," he said to her under his breath.

"You'd rather be dead on the road? Come on," she said, commanding him to move.

"Are there any others?" the soldier asked again.

Zoe looked up to the driver again. "We're with a group of friends. They're ahead, not far. Can we let them know we're going with you?"

The soldier shook his head. "No can do, sorry. We need to move now; we're heading back the other way.

"Right," Zoe said. "It's ok, John. We know where they're going. You're the priority."

John, clearly too weak and ill to argue, shuffled after her to the back of the truck.

After painfully climbing aboard, the truck took off down the road, away from the direction of the hive and their friends. Zoe bit her lip. Was this really their best option? Would John have made it to the hive in his condition? Had she just saved him from a slow, painful death or simply signed away their freedom?

Chapter 25

Day 5
Liberatus Hive
Tennessee, US

As Hugo slowly woke from a deep sleep, he rolled over, slipped an arm around Gianna's waist, and stroked her dark skin. She let out a barely conscious low murmur as he held her closer.

His mind wandered to the few years before when he had met her in that café in Madrid when he was being hunted by that psycho, Jamall. She had helped save his ass from him and got him back to her apartment with all her cool, old retro stuff. There were so many old computers; it looked like a tech museum. All the comics, vinyl records and posters, and all the shit people had swapped for a digital life.

Now, all that was gone overnight. Gianna had brought more than a few boxes of prized possessions over to America. All stacked up in one of the basements. Right now, with all the important things they had to focus on, like survival, there was no time to enjoy it, though. And probably wouldn't be, not for a long time.

He smiled. To think Gianna had left all that to eventually join him in the US to lead the resistance movement here.

Gianna stirred and turned her naked body towards him. "Morning, babe," she mumbled before kissing him with her full lips. Her dreadlocks were draped over the pillow, and they moved quickly to make love before the day began.

There was a quiet desperation to their lovemaking, as if it would be perhaps for the last time. A realisation that things would never be the same again.

When they had finished, Hugo rolled off.

"Well, that warmed me up."

"Glad to be of service," she replied with a hint of sarcasm.

"I was thinking about your pad in Madrid. All the old shit you brought over."

"My cool old shit, you mean."

Hugo grinned. "Yeah, that dopest of the dope shit." He sighed. "I wonder if we'll ever get time to get some of your old records out, read some comics and have a smoke."

"We definitely should. Almost like going through that old man's diary."

Hugo grunted in amusement. "The Ljungborg guy and all that Spanish Flu crap? Jesus, yeah. And where did that get us?"

"Right here, with me," she said, leaning over to peck him on the cheek, then ran her hand over his chest.

That experience had brought them closer together, and when Joe asked Hugo to get involved in the Tennessee hive, Gianna didn't hesitate to join him.

Her fingers trailed over to the bullet wound scars on his right arm, bullets that had been fired at him by Jamall Salazar. The first time was outside the hospital in Madrid, where Hugo had been recovering from the train crash that had started the whole episode of him meeting Gianna, where he had been introduced to Joe Bowen and his whole Libertus group.

The second bullet had been on that farm just before Hugo had sprayed the *puta* with gasoline and lit him up like a Christmas tree. How the fuck had he survived that?

The scars and the occasional gripping pain were constant reminders.

They both had physical scars from that time in Spain. Gianna still had the flesh wound from a bullet across her left leg, fired by Jamall's female accomplice.

"I never told you," Hugo began. "I saw him on the television, with the president, a few weeks ago.

"Saw who?" Gianna asked.

"Salazar... Jamall. The *puta* who did this." Hugo held out his arm to show his scars better.

"He's still alive?" Gianna said in alarm, sitting bolt upright in the bed.

"Yeah. Still alive," Hugo affirmed.

"Fuck. Why didn't you tell me?" Gianna hissed.

"Ah, why waste a breath on that *puta*," he replied, downplaying his comment.

"He was a very dangerous operator, and if he's still alive, more so now!" Gianna said with continuing alarm. "Hugo. I really need to know about this kind of stuff."

"Hey, I don't think there's shit to worry about on that front now, eh? The whole grid is down, the Government's fallin' apart. We got much bigger concerns to worry about, babe."

"Hope you're right," she replied, unconvinced.

"I'm always right," said Hugo as he made a playful grab for her, but she skirted away out of his reach with a giggle.

"No! It's time to make hay, Mr Reese."

She clambered out of the bed, grabbed a dressing gown from behind the closet door, and headed to the bathroom.

"Join me for a cold shower?" she said.

He groaned. "Sounds great."

They dressed quickly in the harsh air, but the shower, although cold, invigorated their bodies. They had both been doing the cold shower routine even before the power went. Gianna led, and Hugo reluctantly followed. It made the body work hard to maintain the core temperature, stimulating increased blood flow and improving the circulatory system, so they both actually felt warmed up.

The gas stoves they had were strictly for evenings only, so the last few mornings had been a struggle to leave the warm confines of the bed. The building heating was kaput, and although the generators could, in theory, run the boilers, Gianna had stated to the community that they should save that option for colder weather. No one complained. Every single person in that base camp knew worse times were those that lay ahead.

They dressed quickly and headed down to the kitchens and dining area. Their house was shared with three other families, who were just stirring.

Hugo and Gianna brewed coffee on one of the portable gas stoves and stirred up a big batch of oatmeal with a mix of soya milk. Hugo sprinkled sugar over his breakfast while Gianna cut up an apple and threw a few segments into his bowl.

"Eat nature's sugar!" she ordered with a smile on her face.

He playfully prodded them with his spoon. "I like bad sugar."

"It'll rot your teeth," she replied, pulling a face.

Hugo gave a mock groan. "Okay, I'll eat the apple."

At the front door, the lock clicked, and there was a sound of the door opening, followed by hurried footsteps on the floorboards. Derek appeared at the kitchen doorway.

"Hey."

"Morning, Derek."

Derek nodded but didn't smile.

"UV bulb's gone out on the water filter."

"Oh shit," Hugo said, leaning back in his chair.

The UV filter disinfected water from the stream. It was a vital part of their water filtration system, which killed off microorganisms like *Gardia* and *Cryptosporidium*, both of which could cause serious health problems.

"What about spares?" Gianna asked.

Derek shook his head. "Nope. Can't find any."

"Can't find any? We didn't have any spares? That's odd." Gianna frowned, looking at Hugo, who shrugged.

"Well, we better get some and fast. That stream is one of our main sources of water. If we get some contaminated water, then everyone gets sick," Hugo said, "I'm happy to go. Just need to know where?" he added.

"There's a water system store just outside of Chattanooga. They would definitely have stock if they're trading?" Derek said.

"Chattanooga? Ain't there no place nearer?"

Derek shook his head. "Used to be a place near Crossville, but it shut last year."

"Alright," Gianna held up her palms. "Let's look at the map. In the meantime, we switch to the water bottles. There's not much, only about 5000 gallons in storage. I'll have to work out a ration, but I can tell you it won't last long for everyone in the hive."

"Okay. I'll go and get it," Hugo said, draining his coffee.

"You're not going alone?" Gianna's expression switched to concern.

"Naw, don't worry, I'll take someone, see who's around."

"And a vehicle. You could take the Audi station wagon, considering it's an emergency?"

Hugo winched slightly. "I'd hate to waste the gas."

"Hugo, we need that water to be purified as a top priority. We can't have people getting sick. Not now."

Hugo held out his hands. "I know, G. I'll take a small team, and we'll be back before you know it. It's what, sixty miles away. I know that's a long walk, but we'll be back in a few days. There's way more than enough in the water bottles. Right?"

Gianna stood up, her chair scraping loudly. She grabbed her own dirty bowl and mug and took them to the sink. "So, we waste our vital supplies of water because you don't want to waste gas, so we can all go on some road trip at some point."

"Hey, I thought we were on the same team about that, G. That was the plan. At some point, we take the fight to them, take the road to Colorado."

"Jesus. That was before the whole grid went down. We've got people, families here to think about. Our own survival."

"Now, you sound like Marty," Hugo retorted.

Gianna shook her head and rolled her eyes.

Derek looked between them, looking awkward, as if he wished to back out of the room and disappear.

"I'm sure we can get more gas, Hugo. When, if we go, there's bound to be options en route."

"Wouldn't count on it," he muttered. Then he sighed and looked over at Gianna, who leaned against the sink, arms crossed, staring back at him.

He had to admit to himself, she had a point. It was vital they had those UV bulbs ASAP, plus it was one helluva long-ass walk.

"Alright." He held up his hands in mock surrender. "I'll take the ride then, first thing tomorrow."

"Kinda makes sense!" Gianna replied, tone laced with sarcasm.

Hugo stood up. "I'll go see who's willing to come with me. Derek, those wheels ready to roll in the morning?"

"Yep, all oiled and gassed." He smiled with relief.

Chapter 26

Day 5
Liberatus Hive
Tennessee, US

Earlier that morning, around three in the morning, under the veil of night, the hive was dormant and bathed in a silvery glow cast by the moon. Marty had slipped out of the barracks and headed through the camp as if he were simply on a patrol run. Even if he was seen, it wouldn't be considered out of the ordinary for him or one of his men to be moving around the camp at all hours. He knew Josh and Dwayne were on shift and walking around the perimeter at that very moment.

Nevertheless, he kept his noise to a minimum as he approached the hill set against the back of the camp and the stream that pooled below it.

Further down the stream, he could just make out the dark shape of the hydroelectric water wheel slowly turning, the water gently slapping along its ridges. Although their main electrical power had ceased, Liberatus had always made building an 'off-grid' structure a priority.

The water treatment system that sterilised them and killed any bacteria, viruses or other microorganisms was a tall metallic cylinder. It was currently powered by their solar panel system and water wheel, but it wasn't a robust set-up. When he reached it, he took a look around, then satisfied he wasn't being watched, he unscrewed the top of the pump housing and slowly pulled out the long UV bulb.

Marty firmly knocked it against a rock on the ground until it cracked, carefully replaced it back inside the cylinder, and re-tightened the lid. It would be difficult to explain how it happened, but none of that would matter. As the water sanitisation was no longer operable, they would have to go get another bulb, and then Marty would miraculously discover the spare ones he had hidden away under the barracks floorboards.

When he returned to the barracks building, he slept, fully dressed until six, then got up, found his binoculars and headed for the window.

He knew the weekly inspection was due that day, and sure enough, as was his routine, bang on 0600 hrs, Derek Smith had left his building next to the garage and was walking along the stream to the water wheel. He checked some settings on the pumping console and then moved on to the water filtration system.

Marty watched him through binoculars from the barracks window. He saw Derek, having inspected the bulb, walk quickly and purposefully back along the track between the row of houses and farm sheds towards Hugo's quarters near the entrance lane.

Marty moved from the window and turned to Dwayne and Josh, who were sitting on their bunks, fully dressed, awaiting his instruction. The others, Diane Yu and Hodge Balfour, were still asleep, along with Kate Copeland and another guy called CJ on patrol, who had just replaced Dwayne and Josh. Since the power went down, Hugo had insisted on a 24/7 watch for intruders in their enclave.

"I'll see you at breakfast," Marty said to them with a knowing smile. "I'm just getting some air." Dwayne and Josh both nodded solemnly as if they were unsure of their part in all this.

Marty walked along the row of houses on the southern track, then he veered off through the farm sheds and crop gardens and further into the woods up to the perimeter fence that circled the hive. He walked along it, back towards the main entrance track to the enclave. He wanted to circle back towards Hugo's house and was trying to think of a reason to stop there. It was essential to know if Hugo would be going to get a replacement bulb and when. A momentary thought made him pause. What if Hugo didn't go? What if Hugo asked him to go and get a replacement bulb? Then, he thought, he'd just have to raise merry hell, really complain and ultimately refuse the order point blank.

Hopefully, he thought with further consideration, it wouldn't come to that. Hugo would go. He was sure of it. Hadn't he already mentioned at the last debrief that he would go on the next recce mission when Marty had returned last time? Then, he'd need to gain access to his goal, the radio room, right in the basement of the main house and to that VH radio. As he rejoined the main track and headed back into the enclave, he saw Hugo coming out of the house.

Great timing.

Hugo saw him. "Marty? You're out on patrol?"

"Yeah. Just checking the perimeter. We've Kate and CJ that have just come on shift."

"Right," Hugo replied, looking unsure for a moment. If he was going to question why Marty was out patrolling when the other two were already doing that, he didn't. Instead, he placed his hands on his hips and breathed out slowly.

"Listen, Marty. We got a cracked UV light, and for some reason, there's no fuckin' spares. I'm gonna have to go out to Chattanooga; it's the only place that might have 'em, so I'm told."

Marty suppressed an inner smile and managed an expression of shock and disappointment. Perfect.

"Aw shit," he said, trying to convey the appropriate degree of concern.

"So, it's a bigger place, with more potential threats. Can I get Josh or Dwayne coming with me?"

Marty felt his stomach sink.

"Ah. Well, Hugo, I'd love to oblige, but I really need them here. Y'know, to keep the place secure." It was a lame response but the only one Marty could summon up in the moment.

Hugo looked at him, his dark eyes searching his features.

"It's kinda like this, Marty. I need experience by my side, and well, it would be good to have one of your guys keeping their eyes on my six, eh, *vato*?"

Then, Marty got it. Hugo didn't trust him, so he was going to take one of his boys. Break up his party.

"What about Kate? Ex-Marine Corp. Pretty solid," Marty offered. He needed Josh to stay with him. For his plan.

Hugo seemed to think about that for a moment, still staring at him, unblinking. Then he suddenly said, "What 'bout Josh? Ex 1st Ranger Battalion, like your good self?"

Marty realised having Josh go with Hugo might be a good idea after all, to make sure he played ball and didn't go off script like deciding to fuck off to some other place instead of Chattanooga.

It was a tough call. It would be dangerous for Josh, and he'd need to play things really smart. How was he going to sell this one to him?

"Look, I highly recommend Kate. She's sharp, but if you're gonna split hairs and make this an issue, Hugo, that's your call. Take both; it's safer, perhaps with more of you. Just let me know where you're headed in case we have to send out a search party."

"We're going to Chattanooga to get a UV lamp, like I said. We need to saddle up and drive out tomorrow first thing."

"You're using a vehicle?"

"Yep. It's an emergency this time. Our supply of clean water is limited, so we need to get there and back pronto. Good idea, by the way, taking Kate and Josh." He smiled malevolently at Marty and walked off.

Little shit.

Still, at least he now knew Hugo was going and where. Now, he just needed to sell Josh the idea of leaving with Hugo and come up with a plan for him. Marty headed back to the barracks, but it was empty. He asked around and eventually found Josh with a few others in the woods, helping chop firewood and arranging it in piles to season.

"You got a minute, Josh?" Marty said, his hands behind his back, standing with his feet wide apart like a Colonel surveying a battlefield.

Josh came over and immediately sensed some bad news coming in the expression of his old army comrade.

Marty gestured with a hand for them to walk away from the other wood gatherers, and they were silent until well out of earshot.

"It's a delicate thing, Josh. I'll cut to the chase. Hugo wants—

you to go on this retrieval mission."

"Uh? But that would mean..."

"You'd be caught up in the plan with the sheriff. Yeah, I know, buddy."

"Can't you delay it? Do it another time, I mean—"

Marty shook his head and grimaced.

"No, no. See, if we delay, there won't be another chance for all we know. Listen, I tried to get you off the hook, but the bastard insisted. Kate's in, too, by the way. But listen, this is how we'll play it. I need you there to make sure Hugo goes into Chattanooga. I'm telling the sheriff he's gonna be going to the store there, so if he tries to divert to some other location, use all your persuasive powers to get him to stick to the planned route. It's important, you understand?"

Josh nodded reluctantly.

"Be ready to bail as soon as you get to Chattanooga. First chance you get, or give him the slip. The sheriff's not after you at all, but if you can avoid being questioned at all, that might be best."

"Sure," Josh said grimly.

Marty slapped him on the back.

"Then, you get your ass back here. Don't let me down, friend."

"No, no, I won't," Josh offered weakly.

"Now, go get packed. You're moving out first thing tomorrow."

Marty stood and watched Josh heading back to the barracks and sighed. He hoped he'd see his buddy again, but if he didn't, it would be a worthy sacrifice.

He checked his watch.

Then, Marty walked quickly towards the main house, knowing it would be pretty much empty now.

He slipped inside the main house with his master key and stood for a few moments, listening carefully. Everyone should be out on their work details by now, but he had to be sure. It would be hard to explain how he was there. If anyone did see him, he'd reel out some BS about looking for the spare UV bulbs. Then, he decided to be more brazen and shouted out.

"Hello?" he called, but no one answered.

He went into some of the rooms. All empty. He went to the bottom of the stairs and shouted again, looking up through the bannisters.

Satisfied there was no one in the house, he descended the steps into the basement rooms where the radios were. The one VH radio with a range that hopefully would reach the sheriff. Marty wasn't sure any of this would work. He realised he had been extremely optimistic about how things might play out. In the small room that was a makeshift radio and comms room, he carefully closed the door and switched on the HF radio. The power of the radio came on, thanks to it having been in a Faraday cage, as well as the solar panel system that was up and running. Marty switched the dial to the frequency the sheriff gave him: Channel 7.

He clicked the push-to-talk (PTT) button and spoke into the microphone.

"Requesting clearance to transmit, over."

"This is the Sheriff's Office. Who is this?"

"This is M7ART, looking to speak to O'Leary. Over."

"This is O'Leary, M7ART. Good to hear from ya. QSK, over," the sheriff replied, indicating in radio code for Marty to go ahead with his message.

"Great, I got some information for you on that guy you're

looking for, over."

"Roger that. Go right ahead. Over."

Chapter 27

Tennessee
Liberatus Hive
Day 6

Hugo grabbed his bug-out bag, containing a personal supply of biscuits, protein bars, MRE packs, dried fruit, a first aid kit, a knife and other essential items. He had put a couple empty gasoline jerry cans in the trunk, optimistically hoping they might salvage some fuel on their trip. He checked his Glock and spare magazine and slipped both into the holster under his jacket. If there was any trouble, they could defend themselves at close quarters, up to a point, but that was it. He threw an AR-15 rifle, along with more ammo, into the trunk of the station wagon as a backup measure.

He zipped up his puffer jacket and pulled a baseball cap over his shaven skull.

"Take care out there," Gianna said before giving him a long hug.

"Will do, mi vida. Keep an eye on Marty," Hugo replied. Gianna nodded. "Sure will."

"Back before you know it," he flashed her a grin, grabbed his bag and headed out to the vehicle.

Derek stood by the Audi 5000 station wagon, a thirty-something-year-old beast that he had somehow kept running ever since he got it in '88. Along with the Ford Econoline, it had, to everyone's surprise, started up without a hitch, unlike all the other modern cars at the camp, now mostly useless hunks of metal on wheels.

Derek tossed the keys to Hugo, who deftly caught them as he approached the vehicle he was going to take.

"Be easy on the old girl," Derek said with genuine concern.

"Oh, I will. Don't you worry, *vato.*"

Josh walked up with his backpack and nodded at Hugo uncertainly. Hugo noted he hadn't looked too happy about being called out to go on the trip. Kate Copeland came soon after and, having placed their respective knapsacks in the trunk, within minutes, they were driving along the track that weaved through the woods and creek that surrounded the well-hidden hive and out onto the narrow public road heading to Pikeville.

Kate was sitting in the front passenger seat, while Josh was in the back studying a paper map.

"Route 127 looks like the most logical way to Chattanooga," Josh said, folding it back up.

"Yeah, I've driven there a few times, Josh. Just keep your eyes out for any problems."

"Sure."

They blazed through Pikeville and turned south onto 127 while a few locals watched. A few days ago, no one would have paid them any attention; now, a working car was a spectacle. One older man, well dressed, waved frantically, but Hugo simply waved back as he sped by. Part of him wanted to stop and help, but there were too many people. What could they do? They cruised past the wintering woodland, a picturesque explosion of autumn colours. On the grassy embankment, a group of around eight people, including younger children with backpacks and bags, strung out in a column, all walking in the same direction. Some turned their heads to watch; others just kept walking, heads down. The dismal reality of their circumstances being visible in their body language.

At one point, they were milling over the road so much that Hugo beeped and made the group disperse, making way for them.

"Resources must be running low in Pikeville or wherever they came from," Kate said.

They passed numerous storefronts, their shutters down and protecting what little resources they had within. A commotion further along, as they passed, a group of people gathered around one store. In the midst of this group was a burly man, his muscles straining as he crouched beside the closed shutters of a store. He wrestled with a tool of some kind, like a wrench, attempting to pry open the unyielding barrier that denied access to the possible goods beyond. His strained grunts and forceful tugs painted a picture of determination mingled with a sense of desperation. What would people do when each of the stores had offered up the last of their meagre supplies?

"Jesus, it's starting," Kate said.

The road opened up to become a four-lane highway, with more abandoned vehicles scattered across their path. At a main intersection, more groups of people were walking along the side of the road, some veering off, making a beeline towards a group of market stores and an abandoned garage.

As they passed through Dunlap, with more stores, restaurants, banks and garages, things were busier with more people milling around, but nowhere was open, and there were signs of forced entry on more than a few of them. Small signs of society breaking down. People trying to flag them off the road. Signs of looting became more frequent.

"Looking a lot worse than when we last went out," Josh said.

"And there's going to be a lot worse to come, no doubt," Kate added.

A mile down the road, they passed a Walmart store set off the main road. Hugo slowed and peered across to the parking lot. There were some vehicles there, most likely useless husks of metal and wisps of a small fire where a small group of people gathered around it.

"Some folks were still waiting for it to open. Are you sure we couldn't have got a UV lamp from somewhere around here?" Hugo asked.

"Nope," Josh said quickly. "I already looked into it. Only place is where we're going."

Hugo shook his head. "Damn, shame. Might be an idea to take a closer look at this place coming back, see what we can pick up."

"We need to head left, stay on 127, should be coming up," Josh said.

They passed a Taco Bell drive-thru with a 'cash only' sign. For a moment, Hugo thought it was still open but then spotted one of the windows had been smashed through.

"Damn, sure coulda murdered one of those right now," Hugo muttered.

"Stop!" Kate said urgently.

Just ahead, a group of armed men were constructing some kind of barricade across the forked split in the road. The road they needed to take.

"Shit."

Hugo pulled the vehicle over and stared at the scene ahead.

They had manoeuvred a line of cars to block the road and were piling all kinds of other junk to build up the barricade.

"Josh, any other way? I don't think we wanna take this crew on," Hugo asked quickly.

Josh was already unfolding the map.

One of the figures at the barricade looked over in their direction. A young guy in fatigues.

"Yeah, we can get around it. Just back up to Taco Bell. There's a back road that'll get us back on track soon enough."

The man unslung his rifle and began to walk in their direction.

"Have we got enough fuel to divert?" Kate asked. She was watching the man and already had her pistol in her hand, resting it on her lap.

"Should be ok, not too much of a detour," Josh reassured them.

Hugo pulled into reverse and did a swift three-point turn. In his rearview, he watched as the man with the rifle stopped walking and then turned back to the barricade.

"Do me a favour, Josh. Mark out that barricade on the map."

They continued to drive in silence as they deviated around a narrow hill road through a very quiet suburban area and, within ten minutes, were back on the main highway, heading into an area with thick woods on either side.

Apart from avoiding a few abandoned vehicles and trucks, it was quiet on that stretch, and they powered on through Signal Mountain. After ten minutes, the road widened into a two-lane highway as they entered the industrial sprawl of the Chattanooga outskirts. At a large intersection, they headed south on the last stretch before the city.

"Do you hear that? Sounds like a chopper," Kate said, her face concentrated into a frown.

Hugo opened his window, letting in a blast of cold air. There was the distinct thrumming of a helicopter carried by the wind, and then it faded.

"Yeah, must be military," Hugo replied with a shrug, and he wound the window back up. "They must have protected some of their transport."

"Yes, I know that for a fact," Kate chimed in. "When I was with the 3rd Battalion at Twentynine Palms Base, I saw some of the Faraday bunkers packed to the hilt with planes, choppers, transport vehicles, and tanks. All could be protected by any EMP."

"Like they were expecting it?" Josh said.

Chapter 28

Tennessee
Day 6

The repetitive whupping sound of the rotor blades vibrated through the hull of the CH-47 Chinook. Through the portholes, there were glimpses of the sun through fast-moving clouds. The flat, colourless fields of Tennessee raced below them, interspersed with flashes of farmhouses and passing industrial buildings.

Captain Kurt Coleman flipped through the deck of cards handed to him by his operations XO and paused on the Ace of Clubs: the grainy photofit of a bulldog-like Mexican who stared back at him in the reddish hue: their latest target: Red Rum. This was a guy Coleman had come face to face with just a few weeks previously in Alaska at the Geo Weather Project facility.

Reese, according to the operation file Coleman had just read, was a commander of a Liberatus base somewhere in Tennessee, although the precise location was unknown. However, a local law enforcement officer had received a tip-off that had been fed up through the chain of command, and so they were now en route for a bag and tag op.

The guy looked like a thug, and Kurt didn't like his face much, but maybe he was being too harsh on the guy. This Mexican had certainly outfoxed his team, and it smarted to think he had gotten out of their grasp.

Colman shifted in his seat and glanced up from his PDA at his two comrades opposite: Lieutenant Harry 'Dubz' Dubicki, chewing gum as always, his bulldog-like head looking even more bulbous in the red light of the cabin and Specialist Aaron 'Fitsch' Fischer, wiry, lean but hard as nails and an excellent marksman to boot. Then there was Master Sergeant Mike Conner, always solid and reliable and as competent a soldier as they come.

Best operatives Coleman had ever worked with. They had only been together for a few years, but after the numerous missions they had been on, it seemed like they had been a team for decades.

Alongside them were the Privates Geinham and Joyce, rookies to his squad. Fresh fodder for the machine.

They were donned in all-black military attire, their profiles inflated with the additional gear strapped to themselves, their M4 Carbines held facing upwards. The grey horned goat skull motifs sewn onto their jacket pocket lapels looked satanic in the red cabin light. Coleman summarised that they may as well be in hell. With all that was going on, they were probably racing to the gates to dance with the devil.

Dubz nodded at Coleman, who checked his watch. Fifteen miles until the LZ.

It was bad enough before, but now? Their world had turned FUBAR, at least in the States, although Kurt had heard the whole of Europe had been hit, too. From the briefing, a massive terrorist attack had been cited as the culprit: maybe by forces allied with China, Russia or Iran; even North Korea was never ruled out.

Take ya pick.

And our commander-in-chief, along with this VP, was dead, apparently?

Goddamn.

But they hadn't been told how. No details given to anyone.

Emergency broadcasts were due. Maybe they'd explain some more detail.

And that goddamn EMP had fried everything. Except the military gear, stashed in Faraday bunkers, like the chopper they were riding on, wheeled out from the darkness. Yet despite all this, they were still running ops like nothing had happened. Mopping up the code blues'; subversives, activists, terrorists, insurgents, whatever you wanted to call them. They were being detained and recorded into the database, processed for the work camps, or, in the case of the more dangerous ones, had their faces stamped on the playing cards and thrown into a hole after extensive interrogations.

The mop-up had to be done before the Federal Emergency rolled out when the National Guard was going to start herding up the civvies into areas prepared for them.

At the back of the hull, sitting away from his team, was their new intelligence special agent attachment, Officer Salazar, who had been pretty aloof with them all since their intro and brief back at Denver. Coleman didn't trust the fucker. But then he didn't have time for any of these dicks that greased the pole, sliding down from on high.

Salazar's obvious ice-cold indifference to scenes of dis-tressed groups of people and that hint of inhumanity brought Coleman unwanted memories of someone else.

The memory of Colonel Stark. That's who this fucking guy reminded him of.

Stark.

The psychopathic killer who had run his team ragged while on covert ops in Iran. His calculated insanity had pushed them right to the edge, and he had killed, no, he actually murdered one of his team, Corporal Wellman.

That betrayal had forced Coleman to take extreme measures.

Even though Stark was no longer alive, Coleman squeezed his eyes shut, trying to rid his brain of the whole scenario.

Coleman wondered how many more False Flag ops he could stomach.

Zip it, Soldier. You've got a job to do right here, right now.

He checked his watch. Three miles. They were flying over Chattanooga now. A few plumes of smoke rose up to greet them. Groups of civvies clustered themselves around a few stores, looting them of everything, no doubt.

Coleman could picture what was playing out. Hospitals would be overwhelmed by a clamour of desperate citizens, suffering either from the cold or hunger. If you got ill, you were fucked. Then there were the people who couldn't get their prescriptions filled; people who consequently could be losing their minds, go cold turkey and turn to firebombing pharmacies and hospitals when it had become apparent there would never be any more meds—and these would just be the legal addicts.

With the supply chain dead, stores would be looted and empty by the end of the week. The worst was yet to come.

It had been a surreal week, seeing the world change so quickly and knowing there was no way back to the way it had been, not for a long time. And yet Coleman felt like it was always going to happen. The preparation, exercises and training had always been moving towards this point in time—part of him sensed the powers above already knew this would happen. He shook his head. Paranoia kicking in again.

Dubz adjusted his weight and slacked his jaw before chewing on his gum again, staring out across the city as the chopper descended down towards a highway.

"On the ground," came the pilot's voice over their comms.

"Ride's over, folks. Debuss!"

The team stood up, all positioning themselves to exit. Conner and Fitsch went to the rear door and, when the Chinook had landed, jumped down onto the tarmac and moved quickly to form an arc guarding position. The others followed, moving away from the helicopter.

The captain checked the deserted highway both ways and the scattering of vehicles as the helicopter took off again and hovered overhead. Using the winch system and rigging equipment, the Chinook began lifting vehicles that were scattered around the highway, moving them into one place designated by Coleman to form a barricade. All the usual safety protocols for such an operation were pretty much out of the window. This was a rush job.

The team in the Chinook and the ground team moved quickly and efficiently for an hour until they had an effective blockade for the main highway route into Chattanooga.

"Connor. Gather some fuel from the vehicles and light this baby up," Coleman instructed.

"Yes, sir."

From the sidelines, Jamall Salazar simply let them get on with it, scanning the city and surrounding areas through binoculars.

Thirty minutes later, as the makeshift barricade of vehicles burned, Coleman signalled the pilot with hand signals, and the Honeywell T55 engines touched down nearby. The soldiers filed up into the rear ramp, and then the Chinook ascended into the overcast sky.

***

Just a few hundred metres shy of the Tennessee River in Chattanooga, the Chinook dropped the team on a wide road and took off immediately again. The 'whupp' of the blades faded as it disappeared across the city to a nearby airport to refuel and await further instructions.

Fanning out into staggered file formation, they walked to the road leading to John Ross Bridge, where the target, according to the intel, was supposed to be heading. When they reached the road, they came to a stop, the squad automatically spreading out in a line. All head weapons were in high port position except for Dubicki, who was hauling a large metallic suitcase.

The few civilians they had come across were told to stay back and return home.

Coleman came alongside Jamall.

"So, anything else you can share about the target? How many friends will he be bringing?" he asked.

"You know what I know. It's all in the report," Jamall replied, who was scanning the bridge and seeing a rising column of smoke beyond the range of his field glasses.

"Right. And the source for this intel was a local sheriff, right? How reliable is that?" Coleman asked.

"He's coming," Jamall simply replied. Then, he pointed

across the bridge. "I suggest a blockade of cars at the other end. Split your crew into two teams, and we can capture him when he comes across."

"Agent Salazar. I'll be the one who directs my men, if you please," Coleman said, affronted by this spook's instructions.

"Of course," Jamall replied, then dropped his binoculars and turned his dark, lifeless eyes to Coleman for the first time. "Just be sure you get him alive."

Coleman stared back into the abyss for just a moment.

"There are other bridges. The hornets should give us enough warning if they divert, but we need to be ready for that."

"I'll position myself on the far side," he said and began walking across.

Coleman turned and gestured to Dubicki.

"Lieutenant. Prepare to get some eyes in the sky. We're looking for an Audio 5000 station wagon, apparently."

Dubicki responded with a salute, then placed his metal box on the tarmac of the road and opened the lid.

"Conner, take Privates Geinham and Joyce to the far end of the bridge, set up a barricade with anything you can find over there and then stay hidden until they come at you." the captain continued. "Remember, to be careful where you are shooting; we need to use potshots to pincer and then capture. Don't kill them. We'll be coming at them from this side, so no rapid firing. We need them to feel cornered and for them to surrender."

"Copy that, Captain."

Conner gathered his team, and they headed across the bridge, just behind Jamall.

Dubicki opened a suitcase that contained a Parrot ANAFI surveillance drone and prepared it for operations. He took the

Skycontroller 3, which had joysticks and buttons for precise flight control, and switched on a screen inside the suitcase lid. The screen flickered to life and displayed a close-up camera view of Dubicki's boots.

When he was satisfied it was all operational, he stood up with the controller, and the drone's four propellers began spinning before the machine lifted into the air.

The lieutenant guided the drone to a higher altitude and then directed it across the city out towards the incoming highways from the north.

Captain Coleman and Specialist Fischer gathered round, watching the screen as it cut across the sprawling landscape of suburban Chattanooga and eerily empty roads devoid of any traffic.

"Has this toy got enough range?" Fischer asked, with just a hint of sarcasm.

"This *toy* shouldn't have a problem in this weather," Dubicki replied, glancing up at the sky. There was barely any wind, just a cold, cloudless expanse. He continued to expertly work the controls, re-focusing on the screen.

"There's the highway barricade," he said.

"Great, any sign of Red Rum?" Coleman asked, referring to Hugo Reece's moniker.

"Nope—just a few hordes on foot and lots of fires." He continued to circle the area.

"Let's hope they took Dayton Turnpike," Coleman said, referring to the alternative route that would bring them right down to the bridge.

Dubicki continued navigating the drone over the intersection and the spaghetti junction of different routes. He followed the Signal Mountain Road that jutted east before a junction abruptly switched the road's direction.

"Hey, I see movement," Coleman said.

"Where?"

Coleman pointed to a moving vehicle, taking it slowly as it took a turn onto Dayton Boulevard. All they could see was its shadow and roof.

"Can you get closer without being seen?"

"A little," Dubicki replied. "That's gotta be it."

And, as the drone zoomed in on the number plate, Coleman smiled and patted Dubicki on the back.

"Yep. That's our boy, well done, Lieutenant."

Chapter 29

Tennessee
Chattanooga
Day 6

The sprawling mesh of abandoned cars and trucks seemed never-ending, and Hugo slowed their vehicle, moving through the gaps cautiously. Ahead of them, a column of rising smoke spiralled lazily up into the sky.

They passed an exit road to their right side, leading to another intersection. Ahead, just on the crest of the hill, the source of the smoke revealed itself. It came from a distant black mesh of smouldering cars and trucks that formed yet another barricade across the entire width of the highway and over on both sides.

"Shit. This one looks hardcore," Hugo said. "What can you see?" Kate lifted her binoculars and scanned the makeshift wall blocking their way.

"Looks pretty damned solid to me. I can't see any way through that, not with the car, anyway," she said after scanning.

"Any sign of people?" Hugo asked.

"Negative. That's a well-built barricade," she added, con-

PALE HORSE

firming all their thoughts.

Hugo turned his head to speak to Josh in the back.

"We got no time for this shit. Josh, what's that map sayin'?"

But as he looked, Josh was just staring at the barricade, his mouth slightly open.

"Josh!" Hugo said sharply.

He snapped out of his frozen state.

"Yeah, sorry." He proceeded to open up the map and study the area.

After a few seconds, Josh jerked his thumb over his shoulder. "We can back up and take the exit road. That'll get us to the John Ross Bridge via Dayton Boulevard."

Hugo glanced at him in the rearview before pulling the gear back into reverse and manoeuvring back to the exit road, then sped down into the intersection.

"Stay alert," Hugo said.

The boulevard took them through the endless blocks, warehouses and suburban sprawl in the build-up to the city. More groups of people loitered; some were elderly, and Hugo felt sick seeing it. He thought of his grandma in Spain. What was happening there? He could imagine a similar scenario playing out.

After ten minutes, they turned off the boulevard and finally cruised down the street toward the bridge.

On their left remained the skeletal metal arches of a pedestrian bridge, and to their right, further down the river, was the larger memorial bridge they had planned to cross. Beyond, they could see more rising smoke from fires within the city. No emergency response services meant these large built-up areas were simply a collection of tinderboxes waiting to burn to the ground.

226

The vehicle moved cautiously forward towards the steel truss bascule section that Hugo had seen lift up once to let through larger boats. The flat concrete edge of the counter weight loomed threateningly overhead like a concrete pillbox. They moved under it, and the blue steel girders cast a myriad of shadows, a rare glimpse of the sun that was quickly darkened by clouds.

A large truck was abandoned on one lane, and as they drew closer, they saw another barricade of vehicles, set side by side at an angle to the first.

"Is that another barricade or what?" Hugo asked, slamming on the brakes. He didn't like it, and he felt a foreboding sense as they were heading into an area of increasing confinement. He recalled his previous training in how to create channels in the surroundings to form a Linear or L-shaped ambush.

"Could just be a fender bender," Kate said, raising her binoculars.

"Let's try another way," Hugo said abruptly, his senses on full alert as he jerked the gear hard into reverse.

As he checked his rearview, he caught movement, and his eyes widened as he spotted a figure in dark military fatigues, rifle in hand, moving from one car to another.

Then, he saw another figure, the same attire, walking more casually in their direction, also clearly armed.

"We got company on our six. Militia, Police or something," Hugo rasped. "There's another," he added, "three of 'em."

"They're trying to corner us; I say we break for the barricade." Kate now had her weapon out. "Josh, head down, get your goddamn weapon out," she ordered.

Hugo pushed into drive, slammed his foot on the gas without another word, and headed for the gap at speed.

"What if it's a trap?" Josh blurted.

"Too fuckin' late," Hugo hissed. "Hope you're all buckled up," he added as he drove the station wagon past the truck and at the barricade of three vehicles.

Hugo went for the weakest point, the front fender of a small Hyundai.

They collided with a shocking jolt, and their bodies jerked against their seatbelts. The Japanese car rocked and bounced but remained intact and in place, blocking them in. He reversed and rammed the vehicle at it again. He caved in the fender and seemed to be just wrecking the front of theirs.

"Derek's gonna be mad," he muttered.

Gunfire erupted from behind them, a side window of the blocking cars fracturing into a spider web of cracks under the hail of bullets.

"Down!"

They all ducked down as far as they could. Hugo felt his heart pumping. How could he have been so stupid? Getting them into this.

"We need to get out of here, get over the barricade on foot. Josh, cover as best you can, *vato*. We'll cover for you from the other side of the cars, got it?" Hugo said hoarsely.

Josh nodded from his hunched position in the back seat, but he didn't look up for it.

"You ready?" Hugo almost growled at him.

Josh held up his pistol clutched in both hands and nodded. "Yep." He pushed open the rear door, leaned out, and began to take random pot shots towards the closing figures, slowing their advance as they took cover. Hugo and Kate exited their vehicle from the far side of the Audi and leapt over the hoods of the blocking vehicles onto the other side, then crouched down to offer to cover the fire for Josh.

Kate began firing, then Josh moved, clambering awkwardly over the Hyundai and dropping down onto the other side.

"Alright, we peel back across the bridge. Right?" Hugo said, looking at Kate for confirmation. It was a classic tactic to withdraw from engagement with a larger force in a staggered formation, with each member of the team taking turns to lay suppressing covering fire while the others moved back.

Kate nodded and turned to check the rest of the bridge behind them.

"Maybe not," she said.

Hugo looked and saw another group of figures moving up towards them from behind, blocking their direction of retreat.

"Fuck."

Kate aimed her pistol and fired. It was pointless at that distance. "We need the rifle."

Hugo glanced back at their vehicle but knew that getting the trunk was far too exposed.

Another couple of shots rang out from their enemies, pounding into the vehicles on either side of their position.

"Move to that black sedan," Hugo ordered, jerking a finger at the vehicle behind them that was angled in such a way that it might give them some limited cover on both sides. Josh went first, then Kate and Hugo followed last.

A few shots rang out, whistling over their heads as they all crouched on the nearside of the vehicle. Kate pointed her pistol towards the group behind them, and Josh aimed for the makeshift barricade they had come through.

"What'll we do?" Josh said, his voice quavering. "We should give up!"

Hugo glanced at him, surprised to hear an ex-military man

speaking like that.

"Okay, soldier, get a grip!" he snarled. "Whether they coming for our food or weapons, I don't know, but I do know we didn't come all this way to give up. The hive needs us to return."

"It ain't worth it if we're dead." Josh countered, staring at Hugo.

Another shot rang out, hitting the cars in the barricade.

"Hey!" Kate called out. "Do you notice they're pretty poor shots?" Kate said without turning her head.

"Yeah, they're either poorly trained or, more likely, they ain't tryin' to kill us. Just pin us down."

Through the gaps in the bridge wall, Hugo scanned his eyes across the wide pillar-lined concrete steps leading up from the landing path, where an empty boat was moored. On the far side of the path, the Tennessee Riverpark nestled into the side of a large red brick building with pyramid glass roofs that looked like either some kind of museum or aquarium.

"We jump in the river, make for there." Hugo pointed at the building. "Maybe get behind that boat first."

"Oh shit," Josh muttered.

"As one, right? We all go at once. Now or never, after three," he hissed.

"Okay," Kate and Josh said in unison. Holstering their weapons, they set themselves up for the break towards the water.

"One, two, three..."

They all ran at the low wall and jumped down towards the water below. Hugo heard a shot ring out, and then a rush of the ice-cold water shocked his whole body like a jolt of electricity. As he plummeted, he began frantically pumping his arms and opened his eyes to a dark, inky cloud of bubbles.

But he had lost his bearings. Was he going in the right direction?

What if he was wrong? What if those guys wanted them in the water to pick off like fish in a barrel?

Hugo swam just below the surface of the water towards the distant light of the sky above and finally saw the blurry structure of the bridge, then knew where he was.

He swam underwater for as long as he could, but his breath was running short. Despite this, he continued pumping his arms and kicking his legs like a frog to get as close to the shore as possible.

Then, when the air in his lungs was all but gone, he risked bobbing his head above water and gulped into desperately needed air.

Dark figures on the bridge were running at speed towards his side of the river.

He was close to the boat, so to minimise his disturbance of the water, he swam in a breaststroke away from the bridge and got behind the back of the boat. He checked around and saw Kate's head bob up from the surface a few metres away, then start moving towards him.

He checked the way to the park and saw a curious couple had been watching him from a bench in the park. Another shot rang out from the bridge, and they got up and ran, disappearing into distant trees.

"Can you see Josh?"

"No," she said in between deep breaths.

"Shit. Well, if he's still alive, he knows the plan. Come on, we gotta keep moving."

They cautiously waded out of the water and climbed up onto

the first step, then crouched low to minimise their profile.

Then they sprinted across the park, towards the riverside road, zigzagging as they ran, criss-crossing each other's trajectory and then finally ducked down behind a row of vehicles.

Hugo glanced up at the bridge and saw two militia figures, one scanning the shoreline for them through binoculars; the other was talking on a radio.

"Come on," Hugo urged, and they moved again, up into the gardens of what turned out to be an aquarium, moving parallel to the river, through the grounds and then onto a side street, passing by hotels and restaurants that were all shuttered or had obviously been looted. A group of people were carrying out goods from one of the restaurants.

At the next junction, they switched right and kept running between a movie theatre and a multi-story car park.

Another shot rang out, and they ducked behind a vehicle sucking in gulps of cold air.

Hugo checked down the street. The team pursuing them had come off the main bridge road and were headed in their direction.

Hugo looked up the road and saw a series of steps leading towards a baseball stadium.

"Up there, come on," Hugo urged.

They moved again, sprinting to the bottom of the steps, and ascended in a crouch. The two men in black fatigues were in hot pursuit, running down the street.

At the top of the steps, they reached the stadium pavilion and a metal fence leading to the field.

"Come on," Hugo panted as he ran at the fence, grabbing the top with both hands. He reached up his right boot and hauled himself over. Kate followed, her face strained.

"What the hell are we going to do?" she grunted as she dropped down on the other side. "We are outnumbered and out-equipped."

Hugo only managed to gasp, "C'mon."

He felt his lungs burning now. The recent fitness regimes he had been taking had helped, but his energy was low, and it was just the last of his adrenaline keeping him going.

They headed up into the stands and ran between rows of folded-up seats before jumping down into a concrete stairwell. They both looked at each other, breathing heavily. They heard the sound of the fence rattling and of heavy boots hitting the concrete ground as their pursuers came relentlessly after them.

They moved again along a walkway that led around the pitch to a length of railings with a narrow parking lot on the far side that looked out onto a highway. Without hesitation, they both clambered over and jumped down the short drop onto a path. With a short sprint, they reached a narrow embankment on the highway.

There were shouts from behind. They were still being hotly pursued.

Hugo looked across the multiple lanes of a highway, empty save for one abandoned truck. The direction to the truck was open ground and fairly exposed, but beyond it, there was woodland with dense foliage on the far side.

Perfect cover.

Perhaps they would have a chance to lose them there.

Perhaps.

Hugo looked at Kate, who shrugged.

"What are we gonna do?" she asked.

"Make for the truck. Last one buys the beers."

"Fuck you, Reese." Kate snorted, and she went first, racing across the lanes. Hugo went after her, and as he got closer to the truck, another couple of rifle shots cracked through the air.

Hugo instinctively ducked but kept moving and followed Kate around the side of the vehicle and slid down next to her on the tarmac.

Hugo took a peek back towards the stadium.

"Looks like four or five of them, armed. Looks like they have functioning comms as well."

He looked down at Kate and noticed the blood soaking through her T-shirt and her pale, ashen face.

"Shit, how bad is it?" Hugo gasped in concern.

"It's my shoulder, bullet clean through, but I'm losing too much blood. I'm not going to make the next sprint."

"I'll hold them off here," she continued. "I've still got my piece, but whether it still works after that water is another thing. You make a break for it."

"Fuck that. I'm not leaving you here."

Hugo took another quick look around the front of the truck. Their pursuers had split into two groups and were scrambling down the hill from the stadium car park.

"Come on, on your feet and let's go."

Kate shook her head, "I'm already light-headed. No chance of me outrunning them now."

Hugo hesitated and gritted his teeth.

It was now or never.

To save himself, he needed to run to those trees and leave Kate to these pricks.

He looked again. The figures were headed to either end of the truck to flank them with practised efficiently and were already halfway across the highway lanes.

Hugo slumped back against the wheel arch of the truck, back against the car, a mix of defeat and anger etched across his face.

"*A la chingada!*"

Kate stared at him incredulously. "Fuckin' go already!" she hissed.

"Forget it. I ain't goin' anywhere," Hugo said with finality in his voice.

Shadows appeared on either side of the truck, ninja-like, their weapons trained on Hugo and Kate.

"Do not move! Hands in the air!" came the curt commands.

They both did as ordered.

Hugo looked up at the men circling them with a fierce blaze of defiance in his chest.

"Fuck you all!"

Then, he noticed something familiar about their fatigues. And his eyes focused on the badge on one of the men's chest pockets.

The emblem symbol of the Baphomet belonged to the Ghost 13 military.

"It figures," he whispered almost to himself, dropping his head.

Then, Hugo sensed another figure come around the truck, who stopped right in front of him and stood staring down at him, cracking his knuckles.

Hugo craned his neck to look up at the man with slick black hair, brown skin, and dark eyes that lacked emotion or interest. Half his face was burned, the skin mottled in red and light pink patches and then smooth in places like the surface of some faraway planet. Skin grafts.

"Remember me, Hugo?"

Hugo did remember. How could he forget—Jamall Salazar.

Then, Jamall pointed to his mottled skin and disfiguring scars on his face, his expression impassive, yet his eyes burning with the desire for revenge.

"You have to answer for this, amigo."

Then, Hugo felt his heart sink almost to the pit of his stomach.

Chapter 30

Andalucía
Day 5

Joe took a bottle of bourbon down from a cupboard in his living room and poured a generous amount into a glass, then opened up a local map and spread it on the dining table. He sat down and began studying it.

Hanna probably would have gone to Órgiva first, which was five miles away. It was the nearest town, relatively small, with a population of around twenty thousand. It was the logical choice if she had been looking for information or whatever she had been planning. He looked at the map again and followed the route to the town with his finger. He wondered if she would take the standard road route or cut cross country?

She had been gone for three days now. Joe's mind raced at all the things that could go wrong. Was she injured? Had the army picked her up? Had she been captured by who knows who? Was she dead?

He couldn't lose her.

Joe felt sick thinking about it. Why the hell had she taken off on her own like this? While she had done it before, this was the first time in a very long time. Joe felt scared about what might have happened to her. Although he hadn't been back long, he already felt like he was wasting time and should get back out there as soon as possible.

There was a knock at his door.

"It's Andreas," came a voice from the other side.

"Yeah, come in."

Andreas opened the door and stepped inside the room. His eyes darted to the map on the table and back to Joe.

"Me and Javier were gonna go through all the comms stuff. See what we can salvage."

Joe continued studying his map without looking up.

"Good," he said simply.

"Wanna join us, mate? We could do with your help. Need to see what we've got, make some plans."

"I've been thinking. I might need some help looking for Hanna," Joe said, ignoring Andreas' request. "If we have two teams, say I go to Órgiva and you or Javier head to Los Tablones. Those would be the logical choices. She must have gone to either one of those first. We might be able to find witnesses."

Andreas walked slowly up to the table, causing the floorboards to creak under his footfall.

"Okay, mate. Listen, I know we have to find her, I get it. I really do. But we need to sort this place out. And do we really want to leave this place vulnerable?"

Joe sighed, leaned back in his chair, and looked up at Andreas for the first time.

"What about Pablo and his men? Or those new intakes Javier brought in. Can they fight for their supper?"

"Well, yeah, but we need to have leadership here if anything goes south."

Joe pressed a forefinger against his temple and began to rub it back and forth.

"You look exhausted, mate. Physically and mentally," Andreas said. "Look, we'll work something out. We'll find Hanna and Diego, but we need power and heat, and we need to make sure the defences are sound," he added.

Joe stood up, walked to the terrace doors and stared out across the rugged terrain.

"You know, when I saw this place about ten years ago now, I knew I wanted to make it not just a home but a refuge in bad times. I think we've built something great. It's the hill I'll die on, Andreas. I'll kill anybody I have to in order to defend it."

He turned back to face Andreas, who was looking at him with a confounded expression on his face.

"I don't doubt that, Joe," he said slowly.

Joe nodded, a calmness now behind his voice.

"Good. So, let's go and look at the comms and power situ."

They headed down to the basement of the house. Javier was already down there and had lit the place up with oil lamps. There were three large rooms in the cellar of the house: one for storage, a communications room, a locked armoury and an adjoining small room that contained the Faraday cages.

They gathered in the comms room where a row of monitors stood in the flickering light, dark and asleep—now all dead, never to work again, along with a load of other equipment. They all stood looking down at the generator.

"Hunk of useless junk now, eh," Joe said.

Andreas sighed. "Yeah."

"Okay, let's see what we've got in the cages," Joe said.

They opened the door to the room used for the Faraday cages. There were three, all constructed with wooden frame structures, with every side covered with reflective insulation

239

foil and an access door.

Joe opened one up, got down on all fours and stuck his head inside. He hauled out a plastic box of equipment and pulled out a walkie-talkie from inside. He thumbed a switch, and it fizzed to life.

"Hey, it works," Andreas said.

"I built these things. Why wouldn't they work?" Joe replied. He tossed the radio over at Andreas. Taken by surprise, he nearly dropped it.

"Careful," Joe said with a smirk before he went back inside and began pulling out the other equipment boxes.

One large box contained what looked like standard radio equipment.

"That's that special comms tech, the Quantum thing, that Troy set up," Joe said. "We tested it all before, and it worked, but maybe we'll need to again. Not a priority right now, though." They needed to get their own house in order before trying to communicate with any other hives.

Finally, when everything was out of the cages and strewn across the room and corridor outside it, separated into discrete piles, Joe stood up.

"The main thing we need to do is to get the solar panel system working, as we only have gas generators. We can only use those for a short time. So, let's get these panels online and charge the battery packs. Then, they should be good to run."

"While I'm away, you'll need to go through all this. See if the VH radios work. We might pick up chatter. I'll take one of those walkie-talkies to try to keep in touch with you here, but its range is only six miles or so. I'm going off now to pack my gear."

Joe checked the storage room, briefly scanning the shelving

units. All were still well stocked with tins and boxes containing MRE packs and freeze-dried meals. He filled a bag with enough for three days, then went to get a Glock pistol and extra magazines of ammo from the armoury.

Then, he headed back to his apartment rooms with his new supplies.

Back in his rooms, Joe replenished his backpack with MRA packs, water bottles, and ammo. He folded up the map and added that, too. Then, he tested his walkie-talkie handset with Javier, who was still in the cellar. All good.

"Alright, I'm ready to get going. I'll be checking in every six hours. Let's not waste batteries."

"Best of luck finding her, Joe," Andreas said over the radio.

"Thanks, Joe. Out," he replied.

As Joe shouldered his backpack and headed down the stone steps, footsteps rang out, coming up towards him. It was Pablo.

"Joe! Joe! We have a problem. Big problem."

From one of the watch-out positions, set into a tree behind the walls, Joe scanned the hill road that led up to their home. A crowd of people, mostly on foot, with some horses and carts. There were also two large trucks leading the pack, driving slowly.

Vehicles that Joe recognised. Dark green trucks.

He lowered the field glasses.

"How the fuck?" he said out loud.

Pablo stared up at him from the courtyard below.

"They're coming here?" he asked.

Joe returned the binoculars to his eyes.

"Yeah, they're coming here. Alert the others. Get weapons. Move!"

Joe shook his head. It was the Travellers he had run into a

few days previously.

It was Carlos and his horde slowly ascending the hill directly towards their sanctuary.

This was no coincidence.

But how the hell had they found him?

Chapter 31

London
Day 7

With every bump in the road, John winced with gritted teeth and clutched at his stomach. They were sitting on benches in the back of the army Bedford truck as it sped along the suburban roads.

Zoe heard occasional desperate shouts from people on foot and shuffled over to the rear of the vehicle to peer out through the canvas cover.

There were groups of people moving in both directions, some families with kids and elders, like a grey stream of refugees. Some carried what seemed like all their processions; some had nothing but the clothes on their back.

She returned to John and clutched his hand. He lifted his hand and smiled weakly.

"I'm so bloody sorry, Zoe," he whispered, barely being heard above the rumble of the tires and the whine of the engine.

"Forget it," she said, more bluntly than she meant to.

After another forty minutes, the vehicle slowed, and there was a distant murmur and sound of distant shouts and a megaphone voice, but the actual words were unclear. The noise of a crowd grew louder like a swarm of bees, and then the vehicle pulled up, and the truck shuddered as the engine died.

When the rear canvas was pulled back, the soldier's face appeared, gesturing to them to get out.

"All change, Piccadilly Circus!" he shouted over the background noise, then smirked at them as they climbed down from the truck.

Zoe and John found themselves on the edge of a chaotic scene with groups of people being herded into long queues by soldiers, which passed through a line of fences into an open area in front of a group of buildings. A sign on a nearby fence told them they were at Biggin Hill Airport.

Zoe saw the soldier shouting instructions.

"Stay in line for processing. Food, shelter and water inside. Stay in line. You will need to give your name and address. Stay in line—"

Zoe turned to the soldier who gestured to the end of the queues and milling crowd.

"Processing comes first. Then you should be able to get what you need."

"Will we get medical help, and will we be free to leave after we're inside?" she asked.

He gave her a questioning look and merely repeated, "Processing first," before walking away.

Zoe turned to John, who was resting against the tailgate. Zoe looked around at the milling collection of humanity. This was the last place she wanted to be, with crowds of desperate people all trapped inside a camp. It seemed like the logical thing to do, but something didn't feel quite right about the place.

But what was she supposed to do? What other options did

she have?

"I'm not sure about this," she said to John, giving voice to her misgivings.

John began to speak, but she stopped him and her hand, palm out.

"I know what you're going to say: 'Leave me here, blah, blah, blah.' No, I'm not. Come on. We're here now. Let's get in, and let's get you seen to."

He smiled and nodded weakly.

"Thank you, Zoe."

They edged along with the crowd and found themselves snaking along towards a line of trestle tables where soldiers were checking baggage and belongings and asking questions. Behind them was a group of large marquee tents that acted as a conduit into the basecamp.

After a slow crawl, they got to their turn. They put down their backpacks, and the soldier began to go through their bags, pulling out their belongings.

"This man, my friend, needs to be examined by a doctor. He has appendicitis and was at St Mary's in London when the power cut out—can he get medical attention here?"

The soldier merely glanced at John as he opened Zoe's backpack pockets.

"There are medical checks inside, yes?" she asked, but he didn't answer.

He pulled out Zoe's buspirone pills and examined the bottle closely.

"Those are mine—for anxiety," she said quickly.

"You'll need to declare these to the duty doctor."

He pulled out a camping knife from her bag and eyed her quizzically.

"Protection," she hissed.

"We'll have to keep that, I'm afraid." He put it to one side.

He slipped the rest of the stuff and meds into a clear plastic bag and handed them back to her before jerking his head for them to go through.

They shuffled through into another line that led into another vast marque. Inside, three army medical staff members were examining patients. A row of trolley beds lay half-occupied with still figures, some with bandaged limbs, some just looking like they were at death's door.

A medical officer took John aside and began to examine him while Zoe was ushered out by a soldier.

"I want to stay with my friend," she protested.

"You'll see your friend inside the camp. No patients allowed in the triage area," the soldier grunted.

She walked over and grabbed his pack, "I'll see you inside, John," she said, resting a hand on his arm as he lay back on the trolly bed. He smiled weakly at her, concentrating too much on merely moving to be able to engage with her more.

As she walked back into the open air on the far side, making her way onto the airfield, the reality of their situation started to dawn on her. She looked back at twelve-foot-high fences topped with razor wire and at the circus of marquee tents she had just walked through that had been set up around the main gates and buildings of the airport.

Across the whole airfield, now converted into a camp, there were groups of people huddled around open fires. A shantytown of tents clustered alongside an endless row of porta cabins. It was like a refugee scene from another country, and Zoe shuddered at the sight.

This wasn't where they wanted to be.

The best thing she could do was find somewhere as warm as possible to park up and then find out what they were going to do about John. She stopped another passing army private.

"What's the process for getting shelter here then?"

The soldier shrugged and waved a hand towards the housing blocks and tents. "If you can find anywhere empty, it's yours."

"That's it? What about—" Zoe began to say.

But the soldier was already walking off, leaving her standing and looking at his retreating back.

"Fuck you very much," she muttered and turned towards the clamour and chaos of her new temporary home. There were streams of people coming through behind her, so she moved fast and walked through the sea of tents, all of which were occupied. She didn't want a tent, though. *One of the block buildings will be better*, she thought.

She wandered through into the rows of those housing blocks, looking through windows, knocking on doors. All were occupied. One appeared empty, but as she approached, she saw a man and his young daughter inside, sitting on their beds, unpacking their bags.

"Oh, sorry," she said. The little girl smiled and waved. Zoe waved back and continued looking. After ten minutes, she finally found one with the key still in the lock. She took it out and closed the door behind her, putting down their backpacks.

There were two new-looking bunk beds, a sink and one window. Better than a tent but still very basic.

She sat down and rummaged around for a protein bar in her bag. She still had warm coffee in the flask from the morning and took a swig. After being exposed to the harsh cold for so many hours, even the minimal heat from the dark liquid felt good.

Looking around at the prefab unit, she wondered how this whole place had been put together and organised so quickly. It felt recently constructed, not something that had been here for years, awaiting some other emergency.

She wondered where the rest of the group had got to? Would they wait for them at Chelmsford as agreed? Or would they continue to Suffolk?

The loss of mobile phones and instant communication was still something she was adjusting too. Maybe they should have discussed this, how long they would wait if they lost people on the journey or other places they could rendezvous. She couldn't blame them, whatever they decided. She just hoped the children were okay.

Zoe locked the door of the housing block behind her and then headed back towards the medical tent where she had left John. When she arrived, more people with various ailments seemed to crowd the area. A murmur of voices drifted through the air, punctured by cries or groans of pain. She spotted John lying on a bed and went up to him.

"You okay? What did the doctor say?"

John opened his eyes, his lower lip quivering. He looked worse.

"Well, they can't operate. Not enough—" His voice drifted away, unable to find the words.

"I'll be back," she said, and she went in search of the doctor. She found him crouched over a patient and waited for him to finish.

"Doctor," she said when he turned to leave. "My friend, John. What's the verdict?"

He cast his eyes over her for a moment, checked his clipboard and then nodded. "Ah, Mr Rhodes. Yes, if things were normal, we'd have him booked in to remove his appendix, but we don't have the resources to do the kind of operation he needs. Unfortunately, hospitals are closing due to the power outage, and we are being inundated with people needing medical treatment. I'm sorry. We advised him to rest and hope it settles down. If it helps, the lieutenant did say he was trying to requisition more medical supplies, something to help with the pain, but there's a slim chance they'll arrive anytime soon."

"Jesus," Zoe mumbled, lowering her head.

"Keep him warm and hydrated if you can. Come back here regularly to see if we get that delivery. That's all I can suggest."

"Right," she replied flatly.

"Sorry," the doctor muttered again before moving off.

Zoe took John back to the block and left him wrapped in blankets as he lay in the other bunk bed while she went to check out the food situation. Zoe walked through the huge camp, along isles of tents, with people milling on either side, some in groups huddled around small fires. Some had set pots on top, stewing whatever concoction simmered inside.

A young man told her the score on how to access the camp's resources.

"You need a stamp book. That's the only way you'll get anything here. Everyone is rationed. If you want, you can sign up for work duties for extra rations. Over there." He threw a hand up towards a queue snaking towards a marquee tent with a large handwritten sign outside saying 'ration books'.

Zoe joined the queue and held her arms around herself, stamping her feet to keep warm. The icy air swept around her and everyone in its path, cutting through them with harsh gusts. By the time she got her ration book forty minutes later, her teeth were chattering. She was also given a plate, a mug, a bowl and a set of utensils. The soldier handing them out wouldn't give her anything for John.

"You'll need to bring either him or his ID."

She looked at him with cold indifference but couldn't face arguing and headed straight to the food pick-up. After another half hour queuing, she was given a ladle of soup, a serving of weak black tea, a small bottle of water, and a carrier bag of what looked like a small bread roll, five MREs, a small pack of oats and three cans containing tuna, vegetables and a fruit cocktail.

The stony-faced female soldier stamped her book and brusquely waved her away to make room for the next person in line.

When she got back to the block, John was sitting up and judging by the plastic basin balanced on his lap, he had been vomiting again.

"How're you doing?"

"Marvellous," he said, still clinging onto his sense of humour, even now.

"I got some food anyway. It's a ration book system, but I couldn't get one for you, but if you've some kind of ID, I can go back?"

John grunted.

"You finished?" Zoe gestured to the basin.

"I think so, for now."

She took the bowl, threw it all down the sink and washed it out before placing it back next to John's bed.

"Could you stomach some soup?"

He grimaced.

"Gotta eat." She passed him the bowl and gave it a sniff. "Some kind of broth, it's not too bad. See how you go."

As the daylight faded outside, the distant flicker of fires sent the reflection of dancing orange hues onto their wall. Zoe and John sipped their broth, grateful for the small amount of warmth it brought to their stomachs.

"I don't know how to thank you, Zoe," John said, breaking their silence.

"Forget it," she said,

"You need to find the others. Get out of here. I'll be fine—" his voice trailed into a subdued cough.

"*We'll* find the others when we're ready," Zoe retorted.

"When you're there," John continued, ignoring her, "Make sure you put in place the means to survive before you start to fight back."

He grimaced again, this time in pain. His forehead gleamed with sweat despite the cold air.

"I've got codeine for the night?"

John placed his mug down and nodded through a deep frown. "Sounds good," he managed. "Sounds good." With that, they settled down on the hard beds, wrapping themselves in the thin blankets against the chill of the night.

***

Zoe stirred from her slumber, jolted awake by the bitter chill that clawed at her exposed skin. As she shifted, the frost-kissed window revealed a faint hint of the approaching winter dawn, while the distant hum of the generator coming to life signalled the new day's beginning. Yet, something felt amiss as she lay there watching the clouds of vapour from her breath.

"John?" Her voice trembled, breaking the silence.

A sense of dread propelled her as she sat up and walked over to his bunk.

"John?" she said again with alarm.

Her heart pounded in her chest as she pulled back the blanket from his face. She saw his waxy skin, hard and lifeless. His eyes rested peacefully shut, yet the absence of life was unmistakable.

She reached for his neck, searching for a faint pulse from his carotid artery, only to find stillness. Tears started forming in her eyes, blurring her vision as her hand pressed against his chest, pleading for a response, but there was nothing.

He had slipped away in the silent embrace of the night.

"Oh god," Zoe blurted out and slumped her head into her hands. The realisation hit Zoe with a staggering force, her breath catching in her throat as grief overcame her. A torrent of emotions surged forth, her sorrow pouring out in uncontrollable sobs. Warm tears traced down her cheeks, a stark contrast against the coldness that seemed to permeate the room as she grappled with the truth of the old man's passing.

***

Day 28
Three weeks later.

The distant klaxon alarm drew Zoe into a cloudy state of

consciousness. She turned onto her side and let out a groan in her slumber. As the alarm persisted like waves throughout the camp, Zoe gave in to it and forced herself upright. The air was sharp against her face despite being inside the block hut. It was getting colder. Much colder.

She dressed quickly, rolling on her orange jumpsuit, puffa jacket and wool hat. She sparked a small gas stove into life and placed an aluminium pot of water onto the flames. She had bartered for it, and it had been expensive. The gas bottle wouldn't last too much longer, and she doubted she would be able to get another, but while the weather was so harsh, she determined she was going to use it.

Still cold, she rubbed her hands and opened the door, stepped outside onto the square of concrete that was her 'outside garden' and went into her morning exercise routine. This involved fifty star jumps to get the blood flowing, followed by a sequence of squat thrusts and pushups. This always kicked her metabolism into life, and after finishing these, she began to stretch out her limbs to loosen up. A few neighbours looked at her like she was mad. Another older woman called Kelly, whom Zoe had befriended, gave her a wave as she prepared for the workday.

"I'd try doing that, but I might break a leg!" she called over in her broguish Irish accent.

Zoe let out a chuckle as she finished her routine.

"Keeps me warm for about two minutes," Zoe replied.

"Ah, god, but is it worth it?" The woman waved an arm dismissively. "You going up?"

"Yeah, in about two minutes," Zoe said.

"Okay, I'll see ya up there," Kelly said.

"Okay," Zoe responded and went back inside. She leaned

253

down over the gas stove as the water began to boil and poured it into a flask over a couple of reused dry tea bags inside. She closed up the flask and placed it into her bag, then hid the gas stove under a loose floorboard. She rummaged through a plastic carrier, took a bread roll, wrapped it in a smaller carrier bag, and put it in her canvas bag with the flask. Finally, she took out her old purse, which still had cash, now useless, and a few other of her old bank cards, equally useless. She fished out the passport photo she had kept of her deceased fiancé, Ed Flannigan, and placed it in her pocket.

As she turned the key in the lock, the metallic click echoing in the air, she stepped back outside into the cold and walked towards the pick-up point at the edge of the camp. The rows of block houses, an assemblage of bleak structures, stood in solemn uniformity. The pick-up point, situated at the camp's edge, lay shrouded in an air of both anticipation and desperation, a hub where individuals gathered, seeking the faintest glimmer of normality amid the grim reality.

How long had it been since John had passed? Three, four weeks?

Zoe wasn't sure. The endless grim days had merged into one long, constant fight for survival. The meagre rations didn't go far enough. Even working in the fields, as Zoe had been doing, the extra stamps seemed a scant reward for the effort.

Well, John is out of this hell hole now, she thought. He had done his bit, and some part of her had actually felt relieved when he died. That thought racked her with guilt, but then again, how would he have survived all this?

They had put him into a bodybag, zipped it up, then threw it unceremoniously onto the back of a truck, along with around five other unfortunate souls that had also passed. The driver had indicated to her to join him in the passenger seat and then drove the truck to some fields at the far end of the airfield through a wasteland and a series of ditches, well away from the block houses, tents and citizen zones. Workers in grey jumpsuits were still digging part of a ditch system with shovels. They came over to the truck and began offloading the bodies before placing them in one of the ditches, which Zoe realised was just a part of a big open grave.

"There'll be a lot more going in these, like your friend, before this winter's out," the driver said. No one responded and just shovelled the earth back over the body bags. Zoe helped and whispered, "Goodbye, John. Thank you for looking out for me."

That was all she could muster at the time. No great speech, no wise words. Here was a man who fought against the system, saved countless people over the years, and was thrown into a hole in the ground without a second thought. Who would even know he was dead? The founding father of Liberatus had been laid to rest, but Zoe blanched at the lack of dignity with the whole burial.

She vowed to give him a worthy memorial of some kind if she ever was able to.

The murmur of small talk among the workers drew Zoe out of her thoughts as she approached the pick-up zone. A line of army trucks and their armed drivers stood waiting, and Zoe caught sight of Kelly, then beelined towards her.

They gave each other a hug as they tried to do every day. It was a small gesture, but it meant the world to them both. It was a way of saying, 'You're not alone.' Against the harsh backdrop of a new reality, bonds had to be formed, and Zoe intended to survive.

Kelly gave her a knowing smile, raised an eyebrow and looked downwards. Zoe followed her gaze and saw her hand open with a bar of dark chocolate. Not just crappy kids' chocolate, either. It was a big bar of really smooth Lindt with 70% Cocoa content.

"That'll be dessert, I reckon," Kelly whispered.

"Nice work. How the hell did—"

"Connections," Kelly replied with a wink and tucked the bar into her jacket pocket.

The sharp clatter of wooden batons striking against the sturdy metal of the trucks reverberated through the air, a jarring sound that signalled it was time to embark. Everyone quickly formed queues and surged forward, pulling themselves into the back of the vehicles. Zoe and Kelly managed to scramble into one of the trucks, swiftly taking a place on the narrow-planked seats. Their relief was palpable as they settled in, huddling close together for warmth in the limited space afforded to them. Those coming after them, not lucky enough to get to sit down, were limited to crouching on their knees or stooping in the cramped middle section of the vehicle, which got really uncomfortable after the twenty-minute drive.

The trucks moved off, heading out of the camp. Some veered off to different destinations, as was the daily routine, while theirs continued straight down a narrow road lined with high uncut hedges for a few miles before turning down a bumpy track. After ten minutes, it came to a large gate. The gates slowly opened, and the truck drove in. The gates closed behind them as the truck ground to a halt, the driver killing the engine. The passengers clambered out, jumping down onto the frozen mud and stretching their legs. They were on a sprawling farm alongside endless fields that had to be worked.

This was where Zoe and Kelly had been assigned to vegetable

plantation duty for a few weeks. They knew the routine. There was a large former cow shed where the wardens handed out their work tools to the groups. Zoe took pouches of seeds, a towel and a wheelbarrow. Kelly took the spade. Others did the same, and they spread out, walking to their place as the wardens shouted orders, their voices echoing across the farm.

Zoe came to her place, marked by a stick and a red ribbon tied to it and stooped down to continue her planting. She jabbed the trowel into the hard ground.

They were planting carrots. It was carrots, potatoes, and cabbage. That's all they had been planting since she had started this assignment.

Kelly and some other workers, all in their grey jumpsuits, were around her, spread out across the field. Several wardens, rifles slung over their shoulders, were spread out, walking silently along the perimeters. Zoe focused her attention on one of them, a woman who disliked Zoe, as she trudged along a wooden fence at the edge of the field. Beyond the fence, a grass field rolled up to a distant wood, trees dark and barren shapes that were stark against the overcast sky. And beyond them, she knew, lay the distant husks of London, the outskirts of which could barely be seen. Dead buildings, now mostly lifeless, soulless, she imagined. No one could still be trying to survive there now unless they had supplies like Raj and Hamish had.

But even then, rumours whispered in the camp that the army was rounding up the ablest of citizens for work detail. The hoarding of food or water was now declared to be grounds for arrest and detainment.

It was a stipulation within the State of Emergency Act, which had been ushered in years earlier by the powers that be, but with no mention of it in the mainstream media, only in the news feeds of Liberatus, of course. All resources, food, water, certain property and equipment, including what was now classed as 'human resources', were now under the control of the state to do with, as they wished.

Zoe didn't doubt it was true for a moment. After all, when she had tried to leave the camp following John's death, they had thrown that bullshit reason at her. 'Emergency Powers' that were in place to offer her 'protection' and had forced her to remain.

She was a prisoner. Pure and simple.

She cast a glance once more along the treeline, eyes darting to the patrolling wardens, then towards Kelly, who gave her another knowing look.

That's all they could do now. Survive and plan.

Plan their escape.

Zoe took out the picture of Ed and looked at it one last time. She studied the contours of his face. He was a face from the past now.

Like John, he was in a better place.

He couldn't help her, and clinging to his memory wasn't going to get her anywhere. She pushed the photo down into the earth alongside the seed she was planting and covered it up with her trowel.

Then, she continued planting the seeds, covering them with earth and repeating the process over and over again.

Chapter 32

Station 12, Colorado.
Day 9

"Why should I help you?" Haleema asked.

Zak took a sip of coffee and placed the mug down on the table between himself and Haleema. It was a fair question.

"You want to stay here?" Zak said, looking around the featureless white interview room. "You must be going mad sitting in that cell, day after day. I can get you out. You can see your father. He's not—looking great."

Haleema's dark eyes widened. "You saw him?"

"I went to see him, yes. To let him know you're okay. I noticed these bastards didn't." He gestured towards the metal door and the security guards on the far side of it.

"What did he say? What did you tell him? Is he alright?"

Zak held up the palm of his hand. "Yes, he's okay, just looking worn down, tired. I told him you're good, and I was going to try and help you."

Haleema looked forlorn for a moment and stared down at the dark liquid in her mug.

"Your skills are required, Haleema. Come back to work, see your dad. Help me find out what's going on."

"I already told you. It's almost certainly a huge False Flag op."

"There have been certain similarities with what you were saying. That much is true," Zak conceded. "But I'm not 100% convinced yet."

"I'll help you, Zak Bowen. But only if you allow me to show you something. Something that might convince you that I'm right. Hard evidence."

Zak sighed.

"I can't allow you to be digging around in our secret files, Haleema. That would be breaking the rules," he replied.

"Do you really want the truth? Do you want to know what's really going on, Zak?" she replied adamantly.

Just as Zak considered that to be a very good question, the door to their meeting room swung open.

A small, weasel-faced man dressed in a security uniform stood in the doorway. His fists were clenched, and Zac could see the veins in his neck pulsating as he glared furiously at the two of them.

"What's going on?" he almost spat the words, glaring at Zak. "What authority do you have with *my* prisoner?"

Zak stood up now and, facing the irate little man, lifted his ID badge up from the lanyard around his neck, displaying his credentials.

"I'm Officer Bowen from G13COMM, and we've identified Haleema Sheraz as a valuable asset. We'll be taking it from here," Zak calmly answered.

"And I'm Kacper Fagan, head of IT, and I have authority over this prisoner. She's been interfering with our networks. You can't just take my prisoner!"

"In case you didn't know, our president is dead. There

have also been multiple EMP terrorist attacks against our country and allies. All government Emergency Powers have been enacted. Under Executive Order 14333, both military and intelligence departments of Ghost 13 personnel have total jurisdiction for the use of all assets within and outside of government facilities."

Zak then gestured for Haleema to stand up while he continued staring down Fagan.

"I think you'll find putting in a call with Kate Foster, Director of Ghost 13 intelligence, will put your mind at ease if you still need convincing," Zak added as Fagan continued to splutter with indignation.

As he and Haleema walked towards the door, Fagan stood blocking it, his face reddening, his eyes darting from Zak to Haleema. Then, finally, he stepped aside, and they both walked out. Haleema paused in front of Fagan, lifting a single middle finger up to his face, before walking out.

***

"Where do I sign to release this prisoner?" Zak asked the guard who was sitting at a desk in the entrance hall to the prison block. A young, gaunt face looked up at him, confusion etched across his features. Then, Zak sensed movement behind and turned quickly to see Fagan coming up behind. His face was still tinted scarlet with anger, but he didn't say anything to Zak; instead, he gestured to the guard to get on with it.

The guard produced a tablet and electronic pen, handing it to Zak. "Sign in the box and then scan your thumbprint in the reader at the bottom," he said, pointing to the optical scanner lens.

"I'll be taking this up with my superiors, Bowen," Fagan finally managed to blurt out.

"I'm sure you will be," Zak replied as he ushered Haleema out through the exterior doors. They headed back across the dark marble floor and then walked through the narrow tunnel to the main intersection. Haleema made a beeline for the elevators.

"I want to show you this stuff now. We have to head down a few levels," Haleema said.

Zak was about to protest, but Haleema shot him a look.

"We had a deal," she practically hissed.

"Okay. Will it take long?"

"Does your swipe card access all areas?" she asked, ignoring his question.

"It depends. What areas?"

She simply jerked a thumb downwards, then pressed the button to call the elevator.

Zak, arms on his hips, shook his head.

"Magical mystery tour, huh?"

"This is important," Haleema said. "It could be related to everything that's happening right now," she stated insistently.

The elevator doors slid open, and they both stepped inside. Haleema studied the numbers.

"Where are you looking for?"

"The crypt, but I went there from the direction of my place on the east wing. Let's try this."

She pressed button B4, and their elevator began to sink downwards.

When the doors opened on B4, they stepped into a dark tunnel with smooth concrete walls and were met with a blast of harsh, cold air.

"Jesus," Zak muttered. "They skipped the heating down here."

Emergency lighting, triggered by their motion, flickered to life, illuminating concrete walls and a steel door just metres away at the end of the tunnel.

"What is this?" Zak asked again.

"The crypt, I hope," Haleema walked up to the door and waited for Zak, who was a lot more cautious.

"I don't think we should be here," he muttered.

Zak felt uneasy. If they were truly in a restricted area, would he get into trouble? But at the same time, he was intrigued about what Haleema wanted to show him. If it related to all the attacks that were happening as she claimed it would be, then this had to be worth seeing, worth knowing.

He also realised in that moment that maybe part of the reason he was cutting her so much slack now was her connection to his siblings, especially Zoe. They were good friends, and everything that was happening across the pond was affecting them too. He was worried about her. Joe, well, that was another story.

Zak took the card hanging on a lanyard around his neck, swiped the control reader in the access panel, and the large metal doors in front of them parted with a soft swishing sound.

Beyond the threshold of the doors lay an abyss of darkness, an eerie void that swallowed the surroundings. As they stepped into the room, their motion triggered a mechanism, and the overhead darkness gave way to soft blue lighting. Slowly, the vast expanse unfurled before them, unveiling a large underground chamber. He saw row upon row of towering shelves looming in front of them, each stack burdened with an array of boxes, all meticulously labelled files. The ceiling-high shelving units created a sprawling maze within the dimly lit space.

"This is it," she said.

They both walked into the cool interior, and the doors slid closed behind them.

"What the hell is this?" Zak muttered.

"Storage for a lot of documents, physical ones. My guess is they were brought here from various agencies for safekeeping. A lot of classified stuff shipped over from the vaults in DC. I had to come down here soon after I arrived for a work detail. I sneaked down a few times afterwards and had a little look around before I was arrested by Fagan."

Haleema strolled quickly along the endless aisles of stacked shelving units, forcing Zak to quicken his pace to keep up.

"Right. So, this place contains stuff that is probably highly classified," Zak said with a groan.

Ignoring his question, Haleema said, "It should be over here. Look for row E, okay?" She scanned the ends of the rows as she walked by them.

At one of the rows, Haleema stopped.

"It's here. Look around for a step ladder. There are plenty around."

Zak soon spotted one down an aisle, retrieved it and brought it to where Haleema stood waiting, looking up at the stack of boxes towering over her.

After pulling down a box she had selected onto the floor, she crouched down onto her knees, took off the lid, and began rummaging around, pulling a tube container out of its interior.

Then she tossed him to Zak. He held up his hands and caught it.

"Have a look at that."

He pulled out two rolled-up sheets and laid them on the floor. One was a map of Station 12. All the levels and areas that stretched deep underground.

"Yeah, I already have access to this on my computer," he replied.

"The other sheet," Haleema said.

He opened out the rolled sheet headed with the words: 'SNS: Subterranean Network System' and looked closely.

It was a map that covered the United States as well as the UK and Europe. Superimposed over the top was a schematic map of a system that was connected with nodes and icons in a hexagonal shape. The index on the top corner revealed this was a subterranean system.

Zak realised Station 12 in Colorado was one of many other underground hubs. Of course, Zak knew there were other DUMBs or deep underground bases; the clue was in the name, Station 12, but he never imagined that there were so many stations extended far and wide and that they could all be connected, even across such vast distances.

"This is—massive. This can't already be built? Surely?" said Zak incredulously.

"They have all been built. Yes, they were all put in place over many decades."

Zak pointed at the connecting lines between the bases.

"These lines. Are they what I think they are?" he asked.

"Yes. A railroad system and tunnels connecting them all," she confirmed.

Zak traced his finger across the line that crossed the Atlantic.

"This one? Surely, they haven't built this yet. I thought it was a proposal."

Looking at where he was pointing, she said, "You mean the

265

Maglev line? Yes, they have built it. In fact, I was brought here on it—from Europe. I saw it with my own eyes. They have a flexible floating tunnel tethered to the seabed." Pausing to look at him, she said, "But you must know all about this?"

Zak shook his head.

"No, no. Obviously, I'm not privy to everything. It just doesn't work like that. That sounds like a massive black budget operation."

Zak began re-rolling the schematic sheets and putting them back into the tube.

"Haleema. This is all very fascinating, but I don't think it warranted dragging me—" he said to her as she was rummaging through more boxes.

"Yes! It's still here," Haleema said, pulling out a thick-looking file.

Haleema looked up at Zak, holding the folder for him to take.

"Read this," she demanded.

Zak stared down at the black letters stamped onto the cover: 'Special Projects by order of the Council of 13.'

"The Council of 13?" Zak asked quizzically.

Haleema shrugged, and Zak opened the file and began reading through the documents.

There was a page that outlined a handful of these 'special projects' titled with names like White Horse Project 113, Red Horse Project 114, Black Horse Project 115, Pale Horse Project 116 and Monarch 112.

"Horses of the Apocalypse," Zak whispered under his breath.

The head of all of these projects was apparently led by a 'Doctor Black', a pseudonym used for this particular role that originated right after World War Two with Josef Mengele, the Nazi war criminal who performed diabolical experimentation on prisoners of war but also mind control experiments on the hapless prisoners in Auschwitz. After the war, he apparently disappeared and was assumed to be dead, but according to this document, Mengele had actually been brought over to the US to join the cabal, who were intent on using his knowledge and research.

Mengele was reborn under the pseudonym Doctor Black, then after his natural demise, the codename was re-assigned to others operating in the same field, right up until the current Doctor Black, Klaus Klasfeld.

Zak glanced up at Haleema, who continued to check through the endless stacks of document boxes.

"Mengele?" he said simply.

"Yeah," she replied.

He read on, turning the pages.

'White Horse Project 113.'

The Project was led by David Gertner, known by his alias, Doctor Green.

His project was to re-engineer the genome of the H1N1 flu virus, commonly known as the Spanish Flu, which killed an estimated 50 million after the First World War.

This section outlined how Wes Helms, the grandfather of the new US president, Natan Helms, had been head of the American Secret Service at the end of World War Two. As a young man, Wes Helms had originally helped unleash the flu as a bacteriological warfare weapon at Camp Funston in March 1918, from where it had spread around the world.

No reason or motive for this evil action was written down. Zak had heard of so-called 'depopulation agendas' but never believed them to be actually true before today.

In 1951, a doctor-turned-virologist called Klaus Ljungborg

led a team to Alaska and dug up the frozen remains of victims from the permafrost who had died from the virus in order to learn more.

One of his students, Nicolas Batchman, who just a few years ago was about to present a decade's worth of research on the Spanish Flu virus, which would have led to a possible breakthrough in the complex world of vaccines, had been assassinated. This was achieved on a train in Madrid, with a detonated bomb exploded shortly afterwards to cover his murder.

Batchman's research was needed by the cabal in order to modify the virus to release a new potential plague. Unfortunately, the documents Zak was studying did not reveal any updates on this 'flu research' and what they might be doing with it.

Then, Zak flipped the page to reveal the next project, hoping for some respite from the depressing reading material.

'Red Horse Project 114.'

Major General Dean Wexhall had the cabal pseudonym Doctor Blue and headed this project.

"Wexhall!" Zak spat with contempt. "He's part of this?"

Haleema simply nodded as she turned to check the boxes on the shelves behind them.

Zak swore under his breath and returned to the text.

One part of Operation Paperclip was to grab the Nazi technology. More recently, Wexhall was part of the conspiracy to engineer a power grab of the Cryostone, a military tech corporation, using murder and even hijacking a commercial flight to 'disappear' a group of shareholders within the corporation.

Yes, thought Zak, he remembered that flight disappearance. With a sickening familiarity, Zak then continued to read about the Project's funding and facilitating the United Islamic State with weapons that had caused so much chaos in the Middle East and instigated a war he had been directly involved with.

Another segment of text revealed a dirty bomb that had detonated near Tehran, blamed on Turkey and the UIS, which had actually been a covert Ghost 13 operation.

"Those bastards made this happen?" he muttered to himself, growing ever angrier at the words he was reading. His heart pounded as he gripped the pages hard in his hands.

'Black Horse Project 115.'

This was the HAARP (High-Frequency Active Auroral Research Program) operation for 'weather modification', including the cause of droughts, earthquakes, and tsunamis. Experiments conducted with electromagnetic frequencies to fire pulsed, directed energy beams to alter the energy in the ionosphere. They had a fleet of such ships, more like floating oil platforms, that could target specific countries or areas from anywhere. Officially closed in 2015, it was simply renamed to Geo Weather Project with a new main facility in Alaska near Tok airport.

Zak recognised all this information immediately. He had sent a Ghost 13 team there to intercept a Liberatus crew on the back of intel supplied by an agent under the pseudonym Darklight.

"Wait, could this GWP technology have caused these EMPs?" he asked out loud.

Haleema thought for a moment before answering, "It's possible. Likely, even. I don't honestly know. But that directed energy is a powerful technology that could be used to turn weather into a weapon of war."

Zak shook his head. His emotions were swinging from disbelief, to anger, to outright fear.

He forced himself back to reading the documents.

'Pale Horse Project 116'.

This had Operation Hallows at its heart. A fake drill on a massive scale masked the preparations for a series of Electromagnetic Pulse attacks, knocking societies back into another Stone Age. It would create widespread and absolute chaos, just as he had recently witnessed.

Zak almost gasped out loud. "This is it. This is saying 'Hallows' is a ghost, a fake... a False Flag—" his voice trailed off as the awful realisation dawned on him.

He felt like he was in a nightmare. The darkness that surrounded them, swallowing him up.

"I think I'm going to vomit," Zak muttered, holding his belly.

Haleema turned from the shelves behind them, crouched down next to him, and placed an arm around his shoulder.

"I know it's all hard to take. I'm sorry I have to show you this. But you needed to know the truth, Zak."

She turned the page for him, which displayed the text: 'Project Monarch 112'.

"Read," she once again ordered.

On Monarch, there was a lot more detail. It was headed up by Doctor Red, identified in the document as Otto Bielek. It was an operation, Zak read on with a growing sense of unease, to bring trafficked children into secret locations inside the United States. Here, the members of the cabal, specifically Doctor Red, oversaw the breaking of their minds, a horrific 'de-patterning' of rape, torture and electro-shock therapy until they could be successfully moulded into loyal agents for their masters.

Zak inhaled sharply and felt the bile in his stomach churn.

These kids would eventually become highly trained agents within the Special Forces, the Intelligence Services, the Government and all other offices of power. Those that failed to be so moulded were simply killed.

"My god," he said out loud. "I knew there were programmes in the past. The CIA MKUltra Project, but I thought that was all outlawed in the 1970s—I thought we'd moved on, learned from past mistakes, but nothing like this. This is beyond evil."

"They rebranded that MKUltra thing," Haleema replied. "They learned everything from Mengele. This is what we're fighting against. This cabal has infiltrated the central powers like a vicious cancer. The death of our president and vice president? I've no doubt it was them. This is their end game. Their plan."

"So, these doctors. Black, Red, Green. Where the hell are they? Except I know where Wexhall is, I've met with him."

"I'm not sure, but I think maybe they're right here too, here in Station 12. When I was brought here, I saw Doctor Black when I arrived. I'm pretty certain they all came here before the EMP. Just a guess, though."

Zak nodded.

"I think they're all here."

Zak forced himself to focus back on the words.

So, there was indeed a secret network run by this cabal, originating with Operation Paperclip once again, to bring German scientists and technology back to the US. The network continued to bring in special talent and expertise from scientists and engineers, and not always with their willing consent.

Zak lowered the file and looked up at Haleema, who was

hauling down another box.

"This is me too, right? I am part of this ... thing?" he said, his voice wavering. "Your father, his capture, with his colleagues in Iraq from the United Islamic State. They were simply 'cattle' in this network?"

"That's right, Zak," Haleema said. "All of it sanctioned by your paymasters. You're in deep. You're directly involved," she said with a tone of accusation that penetrated Zak to his very core.

"Well, all I understood was that we were saving them from terrorists," he replied defensively.

"But they couldn't go home. They had to come here because you made them." Her tone hardened.

Haleema pulled out a tube and opened it.

"And you?" Zak asked. "Were you brought here against your will?"

She laughed, a reaction that seemed so out of place it startled Zak.

"Funnily enough, no. I was actually sent here," she paused, seeing the look of astonishment cross Zak's face before she dropped her bombshell.

"Zak, I was sent here by your brother."

Zak stared at her, and then the pieces began to all fall into place. He nodded slowly.

"He sent you here? Into this hell? To spy?" He shook his head. "Bloody hell."

Haleema stared at him defiantly but said nothing, allowing the enormity of what Zak had seen to sink in. After a moment, she said, "So, do you understand why I'm showing you all this?"

Zak stared down at the files.

The drip, drip of inconvenient truths had finally penetrated through the barriers of his mindset.

If they, the cabal, had built such a vast subterranean system, then they had been planning an apocalypse like this for literally many decades. It could even be considered a generational strategy.

And if they were wicked enough to abduct, torture and mind-control thousands of children to become tools and assets of this cabal, as the documents suggested. Then, they were the worst scum of the earth.

If this was true, as Zak was now certain it was, they had also engineered past wars, planned pandemics, and created endless strife with False Flag operations, climaxing with the mother of all False Flags. Then, he understood that he was certainly aligned with the wrong side.

What had once seemed so crazy he would never have believed it seemed so clear now. He recalled all the times he'd argued with his brother, calling him a crackpot conspiracy theorist, yet here before him was the documentation backing it all up. Their blueprint and dark plans for how to take over the world.

He felt he had been totally ensnared in a web of falsehoods and treachery, trapped within the icy heart of their malevolence.

"Yes. Yes, I understand now," he replied.

Epilogue

Andalucía, Spain.
Day 3

Hanna Friedmann had left the community hive alone, against the wishes of Javier and Andreas. In the end, she had slipped away when they had become distracted. It was the only way. She had a backpack filled with water and rations, a Beretta 92 pistol, spare magazines and a small boot knife holstered to her left leg.

She walked down the pebble-strewn hillside road that circled the mountainside before descending to the lower farmlands of the region and in the direction of the main town in the area, Órgiva.

Instead of continuing the route into town, Hanna diverted off the main road and headed along a path through a grove of lemon trees until she came to a ditch of running water, no wider than a metre; the *'acequia'* or aqueduct that came down from the mountains.

Here, the terrain became much more rugged, consisting mainly of rocks and shrubs that ascended steeply. However, Hanna moved up the mountainside expertly, as she had taken this route so many times before. She soon came to a familiar

trail and followed it west for several miles, occasionally stopping to refresh herself with water from the frequent streams
she encountered and also pausing to look across the peaks
of the distant mountain ranges. The views always helped
relax her. It reminded her of a painting from her childhood.
An imposing series of peaks and ridges that stretch across
the landscape like nature's own fortifications, covered with a
white sky. Órgiva could just be seen further down in the valley,
nestled away and sheltered from the worst of the weather.

Eventually, the relentless scrubland finished at the edge of a
mountain road, and Hanna turned north, following it until she
came to a cluster of trees and groves on the right-hand side. At
the centre of the trees stood a stone shepherd's house perched
on the side of a hill. Steps at its base led up to a sheltered
veranda, where a concrete table stood unused.

Hanna fished out a key from under a flat stone next to
the entrance and, with it, unlocked a large padlock on the
front door. Initially, it remained stubbornly shut before she
encouraged it open with a shove of her shoulder. The inside
was basic but clean. The air was damp and musty, and so Hanna
opened the main window slightly to let in some fresh air.

Inside the main living room, there was a simple wood burner
and an old wooden dining table with two chairs. Set at an angle
in front of the stove, a two-seater sofa covered with a dust
blanket. She took off her backpack, set it down on the sofa and
headed into a small kitchen at the rear. A back door led out
into a small garden area with a small stone hut and the rugged
terrain of the mountain beyond.

She checked the bedroom. A simple single bed covered with
a sheet, a bedside table and a wardrobe. Hanging on the wall
was a lone print of a painting depicting the very mountains on

which the old house stood.

All seemed quite undisturbed from her previous visit.

Back in the kitchen, Hanna opened a cupboard and gripped her fingers around the edges of a board at the back, pulling it out and revealing a stash of survival rations: an MRE pack, some dry biscuits and a small bag of tea bags.

She found a saucepan and filled it with just enough water from her own bottle for a mug of tea. The cooker was fuelled by a gas bottle, so there would be no issues there, not until all the bottles ran out. After getting the flames going under the saucepan, Hanna went out the back and entered the small stone hut at the rear that served as a tool and storage shed.

On one side was a stack of gardening and field tools that had come with the rental, and on the other was a stack of plastic crates filled with junk. There were three spare gas bottles and water canisters, all filled and hidden within them. It wasn't the greatest of hiding places, but she hoped the remoteness of the hut itself would prevent most people from snooping around too much.

She shifted a group of tools, a rusty spade and fork, to the side, then loosened one of the stones in the wall, reached into the hole behind it, and pulled out a small key. After replacing the stone, she then headed out onto the hillside, where, behind a group of shrubs a few metres from the house, she found the familiar spot she was looking for. Bending down, she moved a group of more flat rocks to reveal a dug-out hole in the ground. Reaching down into it, she pulled out a large box, around the size of a small suitcase and carried it back to the house.

Once inside the bedroom, she opened the box with the key, pulled out a small military SATCOM radio, and put it on the bed next to her. It had been stored in the Faraday box and had long-range satellite data transmission capability.

Assuming the satellite and the receiving station were intact, which she reasoned they still should be, any of her messages should get through. Also inside the metal box was a battery pack, which she hooked up to the radio. She flicked a switch and watched with relief as the lights and displays lit up.

She needed the notes.

Hanna walked to the living room door to retrieve her backpack and froze. She heard a noise through the open window, the sound of someone coming up the steps at the front.

It was possible that it could be a passing farmer or even the house owner. But they had never come by unannounced; Hanna had insisted on that. But then, this major power outage had occurred, so anything was possible.

She stepped back behind the doorway to remain unseen.

Through the main window, she saw the head of a man looking around.

A glimpse of a familiar face.

It was Javier's brother, Diego.

He must have followed her here.

**

Two years earlier.
Seville, Spain.

Angelika Balmer casually walked around the fountain set in the grand grounds of the Plaza de España as she had been instructed. The fountain, a centrepiece of artistry, cast dancing reflections in the morning sunlight, its crystal clear waters offering a serene contrast to the bustling activity nearby. As she strolled along the circumference of the fountain, her gaze was drawn to the Instituto Geográfico Nacional, its magnificent structure forming an elegant arc along the plaza. Despite the early hour, the Plaza de España was already coming to life. The first trickle of tourists, eager to explore the marvels of the Instituto Geográfico Nacional, wandered through its grand arches, their footsteps echoing against the cobbled pathways.

To one side was a line of horse-drawn carriages; their handlers stood around chatting and smoking, waiting for the main throng of tourists to arrive.

As she leaned on one of the railings on one of the many bridges taking in the scene, she spotted a woman dressed in a navy business suit with a shoulder bag approaching. As their eyes met, she made a beeline for her. They greeted each other with a hug, like old friends and continued to walk towards the edge of the Plaza and a line of trees.

"Everything is arranged for your transfer, Ms Balmer. The papers are all in order." The woman, known to Balmer only as 'Cellach', said.

"So, keep using your current legend documents and passport."

"As Hanna Friedmann?"

"Yes, develop a relationship, get close to Bowen and his organisation. The more information we have on the whole set-up, the better. Of course, instructions may change, but send through what you can find out regularly."

"Of course," Balmer replied.

She was glad that she had no need to stay with Carlos and his travelling group of anarchists. Her previous employers, the

German Federal Intelligence Service (BND) or Bundesnachric
htendienst, had sent her there as a field agent to investigate
the group. Their leader, Carlos Sagan, originally from Berlin,
had been associated with several on BND's persons of interest
list. The service was compelled to keep tabs on him.

When Balmer had reported a chance meeting with Joe Bowen
at one of their parties, it turned out he belonged to a 'group of
interest', Liberatus. She was offered a transfer from the BND
to G13COMM. The re-organisation of the Western Intelligence
Services was now in full swing. Now, she would be a sleeper
agent, following instructions from her new handler.

They reached the columned wall by the trees and stopped,
leaning against it.

"When you're established with the target, find a suitable
place nearby to rent, a safe house. Not too big, somewhere
isolated. We'll need to work on a cover story, giving you
reasons for you to go away from time to time. You'll get the
usual references for any rentals or jobs and any funds you need
to cover this."

Cellach handed Balmer a mobile phone. "You can use this
to start with: it's safe with all the usual secure boot processes
and encrypted storage. But as soon as you can switch it up,
use disposable SIMs as necessary, and we may get you more
equipment depending on how it develops.

"There won't be many opportunities for face-to-face re-
porting, but just keep sending through the intelligence as you
are able.

"Remember, once you're integrated within Liberatus, report
on who comes and goes and what supplies and weapons they
have. What is the nature of their comms and find out what
capabilities they have to launch any kind of operations."

The woman turned to look directly at Balmer.

"Are you ready for this? It might be a long-haul assignment."

Balmer nodded, pocketing the phone. "Yes, I'm ready."

Cellach nodded, stood up from the wall, and then walked away.

Balmer put the phone into her backpack, headed straight back to where she had parked her car and drove back to Andalucía to cultivate her relationship with Joe Bowen.

***

Andalucia, Spain.
Day 3

Hanna, real name Angelika Balmer, always thought Diego was suspicious of her. She had seen it through his body language. It was subtle, but she could read him. She had ignored it, though, hoping in time his suspicions would ease. Perhaps that was a mistake?

She must have been sloppy, as he obviously had followed her. But who else knew he was here?

Balmer moved around the side of the house with a pitchfork in hand. Then, changing her mind, she placed it against the stone wall of the house and casually walked out the front. She acted shocked as she found Diego looking through the window at the front.

"Diego?" she said. He turned to her, unsmiling. He was unshaven, his blond hair tied back into a bunch. He looked nothing like his brother, Javier.

"Hanna."

"What are you doing here?" she asked, moving closer.

"I might ask you the same," he said in a hard-toned voice.

Balmer gestured to the house. "My friend Annabella stays here. I came by to see if she was ok. Is that alright with you?" she said sharply, the lie coming easily.

She followed up with her own challenge by asking, "Why are you here? Have you followed me? Are you checking to make sure I'm not cheating on Joe or something?"

Diego looked around.

"This is the first I heard of her. You said you were heading to town to check on things. When I saw you take the mountain road, I got worried. Is your friend—is she okay?"

Balmer pulled an expression of concern.

"No, she was not here. The door was open, but—I'm worried. Very worried. So, you followed me?"

Diego went to open the front door, then hesitated and looked at her.

"Mind if I come in?"

Balmer sighed. She would have to work quickly.

"Of course," she said, forcing a smile.

He went inside, and when he was out of sight, Balmer felt the knife in its holster in her boot. Her pistol was still in her backpack on the sofa in the living room.

She walked in behind him as he looked around the small space.

"So, did you follow me here or something?" she said again.

"*Si.* It doesn't look like anyone has been living here for a while. When did you last speak to your 'friend'? I don't know what you're doing, Hanna, but something is not adding up."

He had his back to her, looking back into the kitchen. Then, he turned to her, his face turning from suspicion to something else, and his eyes furtively scanned up and down her body.

"Perhaps we do a deal," he said, almost in a whisper.

Balmer realised he didn't perceive her as a threat, not a physical one. She also now knew for sure that he hadn't told anyone else at the hive that he was following her.

There was another agenda at work here. A sexual one.

He stepped into the small hallway and stared into the bedroom. He seemed to freeze before his head switched to stare at her in shock. He had seen the radio equipment and began reaching for something at his belt.

Balmer had already drawn her knife and threw it with immense force and accuracy.

An action she had practised thousands of times.

The blade plummeted straight into his throat.

Diego staggered backwards, hitting the doorframe, his hands reaching for the blade, eyes wide with astonishment.

He tried to scream, but only a deep gargle left his lips, along with torrents of spurting blood.

Balmer walked towards him, stomp-kicking through his knee to bring him down to the floor. She knelt over him and pulled the knife free with one swift movement. Diego clutched his throat as blood continued to gush through his fingers.

His eyes locked onto hers, wide with horror as his face went ashen and pale. Balmer watched as his breathing slowed, and then, finally, his eyes glazed over in death.

She locked the front door, returned to the kitchen, and switched off the gas stove. The water had almost boiled away, and she washed her hands and knife in the sink.

Then, she opened the rear door and walked out to the small hut.

Inside, she rooted around in the boxes and found some plastic sheeting as she thought through her options.

What could she do? There was no choice but for her to eliminate Diego. Her cover would have been blown. There was no alternative, she repeated to herself as she rolled the body onto the sheeting and arduously dragged it up the hill behind the garden.

It seemed to take an age to bury Diego on the hillside and then to clean up the mess. When she was finished, Balmer gulped down some water, retrieved her bag and notepad, and then began coding a series of messages.

First, she detailed the cache locations and supply details that she had decoded from Joe's handbook.

She glanced out towards the rear garden and the steep hill, then added to the message: 'Near comprise. Threat eliminated. No further threat. Awaiting instructions.'

Then, Angelika Balmer sent the coded message to her handler, signing off as Darklight.

Free Thriller

Exclusive offer. To grab your FREE Novella eBook, head to:
www.jaytinsiano.com/secret-access/

PLUS, you'll get access to the VIP Jay Tinsiano reading group for:
Free Books and stories
Previews and Sneak Peeks
Exclusive material

Also Available

White Horse (Dark Paradigm #1)

ISBN: 978-1-9162397-4-6

Half a world away in Spain and running from his past, a Los Angeles gangster unwittingly takes a train that's headed straight into a terrorist attack. He survives only to face an even deadlier threat.

On that same train: a virologist with clues to a deadly epidemic. Did his secrets die with him in the strike?

Raging in the aftermath, a foul-tempered police chief with a daughter caught in the attack thirsts for revenge. But against whom?

An orphan child without a name disappears down a dark, illegal CIA mind-control programme. Now trained in the ways of death, he prepares to do his master's twisted bidding.

From its first pages, the relentless techno-thriller White Horse drops you with a thunderclap in the middle of these colliding worlds. This tale of a global conspiracy that threatens humanity itself will keep you guessing whether anyone can survive.

Red Horse (Dark Paradigm #2)

ISBN: 978-1-9162397-5-3

A hacker's mission to find her missing father leads her into a deadly game of political intrigue and danger in this electrifying techno-thriller.

Haleema Sheraz, a skilled cyber hacker for the Iranian government, receives devastating news: her father has disappeared without a trace. With the authorities dragging their feet, she takes matters into her own hands and uncovers a shocking conspiracy dating back to Operation Paperclip during World War II.

Meanwhile, her brothers have joined an ISIS-inspired uprising, plunging Iran into chaos and leaving Haleema no choice but to risk everything to save her family.

As the conflict escalates and the stakes grow higher, Haleema calls in old allies Joe Bowen and Hugo Reese to help in the desperate struggle for survival.

Red Horse is a pulse-pounding, action-packed thriller that is a must-read for fans of high-tech espionage and gripping suspense.

Black Horse (Dark Paradigm #3)

ISBN: 978-1-9162397-6-0

As the clock ticks down to a devastating world event, Zoe Bowen's investigation into her partner's apparent suicide takes her down a dark, dangerous path.

Zoe Bowen, part of the banking elite in London, is thrown into a conspiracy when her partner throws himself off his Canary Wharf balcony.

But nothing points to suicide apart from the official verdict. As the clock ticks down to the cabal's devastating endgame, Zoe and her allies race against time to stop them before it's too late.

False Flag by Jay Tinsiano. (Frank Bowen #1)

ISBN: 978-1-9997232-2-4

1991: A plan to destabilise Hong Kong is emerging; the key players are being put into place, the wheels are in motion, and innocent people will die.

Frank Bowen is a Londoner on holiday in tropical Thailand. Half drunk and strapped for cash, he's the perfect bait for a political plot that will leave him running for his life with nowhere to turn.

Pandora Red by Jay Tinsiano. (Frank Bowen #2)

ISBN: 978-1-9997232-3-1

Frank Bowen's mission is to find a GCHQ whistleblower, but in doing so unwittingly risks everything, including his own family's safety.

As part of a covert team assigned to dangerous missions, Bowen believes he knows what he's up against until a team of Russian mercenaries are thrown into the mix, leaving everyone and everything hanging in the balance.

It's a race against the clock to save all that he holds dear and uncover the dark truths behind his mission.

Ghost Order by Jay Tinsiano. (Frank Bowen #3)

ISBN: 978-1-9162397-0-8

Frank Bowen attempts to piece together a fractured life at home but finds himself pulled back into the dark state once again.

Only, this time, he's playing both sides.

This is the third fast-paced thriller in the Frank Bowen series by Jay Tinsiano.

Blood Tide by Jay Tinsiano.

ISBN: 978-1-9997232-6-2

Detective Douglas Brown transferred to Hong Kong to forget his past and the dark memory that still haunts him—Richard Blythe.

Blythe, an explosives expert gone rogue, had terrorised London and outwitted Brown, leading to the deaths of countless innocents.

Now the detective's worst fear has come true. Blythe is free from prison to wreak havoc and lead Brown on a deadly cat and mouse game in the city of Hong Kong.

Blood Tide is a gripping terrorism thriller from Jay Tinsiano.

Blood Cull by Jay Tinsiano & Jay Newton

ISBN: 978-1-9162397-2-2

A series of ritualistic killings.

A retired detective inspector desperate to save his wife.

A horrifying secret.

Detective Inspector Doug Brown has retired to Scotland, but when his wife falls ill, there is no choice but to take on a private contract offered by an old acquaintance.

Soon he finds himself on a dark path, tracking down a ritualist killer of affluent men who has so far eluded the police.

But as the merciless killings continue, Doug is unknowingly getting closer to unveiling a sickening conspiracy.

About the Authors

Jay Tinsiano

Jay was born in Ireland but grew up on the flat plains of Lincolnshire surrounded by cows and haystacks before moving to the city of Bristol, where he has lived, apart from far-flung nomadic excursions, ever since.

He is the author of the Frank Bowen thriller series and, in collaboration with Jay Newton, the Dark Paradigm Apocalyptic thriller series, Doug Brown and the shorter Dark Ops stories.

Jay is an avid reader, specifically of crime, sci-fi and thrillers, with occasional non-fiction thrown in. He can be occasionally found in a Waterstones bookshop café or perhaps a quiet pub, furiously scribbling notes and whispering to himself.

Jay Newton

Jay Newton practices and teaches martial arts, is a keen cyclist, manages a band and is an avid fiction reader.

He is currently working on the Dark Paradigm and Dark Ops series with Jay Tinsiano and lives in Bristol, UK, with his family.

Printed in Great Britain
by Amazon

36589022R00169